THE MANSFIELD PARK MURDERS

A Mystery Set in the Estate of Jane Austen's Mansfield Park

To Susanne

TABLE OF CONTENTS

CAST OF CHARACTERS

Baddeley: butler at Mansfield Park

Mr. Edmund Bertram: second son of Sir Thomas and Lady Bertram, married to Fanny Price, vicar of Thornton Lacey

Mrs. Frances (Fanny Price) Bertram: wife to Mr. Edmund Bertram

Lady (Maria Ward) Bertram: wife to Sir Thomas, sister to Mrs. Norris and Mrs. Price, and mother of Mr. Tom Bertram, Mr. Edmund Bertram, Mrs. Maria Rushworth and Mrs. Julia Yates

Mr. Thomas (Tom) Bertram: first son and heir to Sir Thomas, elder brother to Edmund Bertram, Maria Rushworth and Julia Yates

Sir Thomas Bertram: baronet of Mansfield Park, husband to Lady Bertram, father of Mr. Tom Bertram, Mr. Edmund Bertram, Mrs. Maria Rushworth and Mrs. Julia Yates

Chapman: personal maid to Lady Bertram

Cooper: groom in Mansfield Park stables

Mr. Henry Crawford: brother of Miss Mary Crawford, half-brother of Mrs. Grant, former suitor of Miss Fanny Price, former lover of Mrs. Maria Rushworth

Miss Mary Crawford: sister of Mr. Henry Crawford and half-sister of Mrs. Grant

Baron of Dexthorpe, also known as Lord Dexthorpe: father of Mr. George Yates and Mr. John Yates

Elissa: natural daughter of Tom Bertram and Hetty

Dr. Grant: the official vicar of Mansfield, currently at a residence in London, husband to Mrs. Grant

Mrs. Grant: wife of Dr. Grant, and half-sister of Mr. Henry Crawford and Miss Mary Crawford

Hetty: slave woman in Antigua

Mr. Hawk: vicar taking over the duties for Dr. Grant

Stephen Jackson: groom in Mansfield Park stables

Ann Jones: young housemaid at Mansfield Park

Mr. Charles Maddox: neighbor in Mansfield

Mrs. Charles Maddox: new wife of Mr. Charles Maddox

Mrs. (Ward) Norris: sister to Lady Bertram, widow of Reverend Norris, former vicar of Mansfield

Mrs. Oliver: a friend of Lady Bertram's

Mrs. Otway: a friend of Lady Bertram's; Edmund is a friend of her son's

Mr. Price: retired lieutenant, married to Mrs. Price, father to William, Fanny, Susan and others

Mrs. Frances (Ward) Price: sister to Mrs. Norris and Lady Bertram; mother to William, Fanny, Susan and others

Miss Susan Price: sister to William Price and to Mrs. Fanny Bertram (and others), niece to Lady Bertram and to Mrs. Norris

Lieutenant William Price: brother to Fanny Bertram, Susan Price (and others), nephew to Lady Bertram and Mrs. Norris

Pug: Lady Bertram's lapdog

Mr. James Rushworth: proprietor of Sotherton and ex-husband of Maria Rushworth

Mrs. Maria (Bertram) Rushworth: eldest daughter of Sir Thomas and Lady Bertram, ex-wife of Mr. James Rushworth, sister to Mr. Thomas Bertram, Mr. Edmund Bertram and Mrs. Julia Yates

Mr. Walter Rushworth: cousin to Mr. James Rushworth

Mrs. Rushworth (1): mother to Mr. James Rushworth

Mrs. Rushworth (2): wife of Mr. Walter Rushworth

Wilcox: coachman at Mansfield Park

Mr. George Yates: elder son of the Baron of Dexthorpe, brother to Mr. John Yates

Mr. John Yates: second son of the Baron of Dexthorpe, husband to Mrs. Julia Yates, brother of Mr. George Yates

Mrs. Julia (Bertram) Yates: married to Mr. John Yates, youngest child of Sir Thomas and Lady Bertram, sister to Mr. Thomas Bertram, Mr. Edmund Bertram, and Mrs. Maria (Bertram) Rushworth

CHAPTER ONE

The wedding was a family affair, for the bride was the first cousin of the groom. Miss Frances Price, called Fanny by her friends and relatives, was marrying Mr. Edmund Bertram.

A marriage between cousins might be considered a marriage between equals, but in this case, it was not so. Mr. Edmund Bertram was the second son of a baronet, Sir Thomas Bertram, who was rich, respectable and highly regarded. Miss Price was the daughter of a navy lieutenant compelled to retire early due to injury, and who had the further shame of being poor and drinking too much. Over-fondness for spirits can be found in the rich as well as the poor, but in the poor the tendency is much less respectable.

Although their wives were sisters, the baronet and the retired lieutenant had never met. Sir Thomas resided in Mansfield Park, on his estate in Northamptonshire, making occasional visits to London and to his sugar plantation in the West Indies, while Lieutenant Price dwelled in Portsmouth. Still, after an appeal from Mrs. Price, who had produced nine living children, Sir Thomas had done what he could to help his wife's nephews and nieces. This charity had extended to Sir Thomas and Lady Bertram's relieving the Prices entirely of the responsibility for their eldest daughter and raising her with their own children.

Despite the difference in the positions in society of Mr. Edmund Bertram and Miss Frances Price, Sir Thomas and Lady Bertram were pleased with the match. When Fanny had first entered Mansfield Park, their greatest fear had been that she would marry one of their two sons, but now, more than a decade later, they were rejoicing in the union that was about to take place, for during the years they had come to love Fanny like a daughter. Indeed, some would say that they loved Fanny *more* than their two daughters. Both Sir Thomas and Lady Bertram would have denied this, but certainly they esteemed Fanny far more, for the Bertram daughters had made extremely unwise choices that could be expected to affect the rest of their lives. Julia, now Mrs. Yates, had eloped with the Honorable John Yates, fixing her situation with the second son of a lord with only modest expectations. Maria had done far worse; the divorced Mrs. Rushworth was considered a disgrace.

Fanny, on the other hand, had always been steady, if a little reserved, and her attentions to Lady Bertram over the years – playing games with her, reading to her, assisting her with her carpet work – had made her invaluable to her aunt. Lady Bertram, therefore, would have been seriously distressed at the prospect of Fanny's marriage, as that meant

Fanny would move seven miles away in order to live with her husband – except for the presence of Susan, Fanny's younger sister. A little more than two years ago, Susan Price had joined them at Mansfield Park and had quickly become Lady Bertram's chief comfort.

At the moment Susan was assisting her sister in her preparations for her wedding.

"You look very pretty," said the bridesmaid, Miss Susan Price.

"So do you, Susan," said Fanny.

Susan was pleased with her own appearance, for to mark this great occasion, her uncle had given her a new gown. "I will miss you," said Susan.

"I will not be so very far away," said Fanny. "Only seven miles. Still, you are right, seven miles will make a difference, although we can always correspond. I have confidence in you, Susan; you will manage better than I ever did."

Susan, because of her less timid nature, was better suited than Fanny to dealing with the more unpleasant aspects of Mansfield Park.

Their mutual reassurances were interrupted by a knock at the door. Lady Bertram's maid, who had previously assisted Fanny with her hair before returning to her mistress to attend to Lady Bertram's finishing touches, had come back to inform them that Mr. Edmund Bertram had departed for the church, accompanied by his elder brother, Mr. Tom Bertram, and his brother-in-law, Mr. John Yates. Miss Price and Miss Susan Price were at liberty to emerge from concealment, as Mr. Edmund would not see Miss Price until the young ladies, too, reached the church.

Susan asked Fanny if she was ready – Fanny took a long look at the room where she had spent so many years, had both shed desperate tears and indulged in dreams so sweet she dared not recount them – then took a deep breath and affirmed that she was.

Susan, although she kept her feelings to herself, was impatient to be downstairs. She was grateful to her uncle and her aunt, and she adored Mansfield Park, but if Mansfield Park had a fault, it was that its inmates were a little too quiet. Today, however, the house would be full, for the elder son and the two daughters had arrived for the occasion. Susan was especially curious to meet the disgraced Mrs. Rushworth, as this would be Maria's first time to be admitted to Mansfield Park since her betrayal of her husband and her subsequent divorce. Ever since that wretched event, Mrs. Rushworth had been living abroad with Mrs. Norris, elder sister to Lady Bertram and Mrs. Price. Mrs. Norris was also in the house, a fact of which Susan was well aware, for although Susan had not yet seen her, she had *heard* her; Mrs. Norris had a voice that carried. Susan was not particularly curious about Aunt Norris as they had met when Susan first arrived at Mansfield Park. Susan only wondered if the banishment Mrs.

Norris shared with Mrs. Rushworth had improved or soured Mrs. Norris's temper; it had never been good.

So many people! Susan hoped she could remember all their names. As she helped Fanny through the door and down the stairs, she wondered aloud if Mrs. Rushworth was as beautiful as everyone said.

"You will soon see for yourself," said Fanny.

Susan, perceiving her sister's heart too full for conversation, spoke no more as they continued down the stairs. They reached the empty vestibule where they were to await the return of the carriage. The Mansfield Park carriage was to make three trips to and from the church before the ceremony to convey the estate's important personages (most of the servants had already departed on foot). The first had contained the three young men; the second was to contain the three matrons – Lady Bertram, Mrs. Norris, and Mrs. Yates – and the last was to bring Sir Thomas and the two Miss Prices.

"Has the carriage already fetched our aunts, do you suppose?" inquired Fanny.

"I do not think so," said Susan. As they had descended the stairs, her sharp ears had detected Mrs. Norris's tones. Susan lowered her own voice, and gestured at a shut door, behind which lay Sir Thomas's rooms, his study and a library: "Is Mrs. Rushworth within, do you think?"

They could both hear Sir Thomas's deep voice – like so many older men, unaware that others' hearing was better than their own, he spoke loudly – and he was answered by a voice belonging to a woman. Her words, however, were impossible to discern.

"Possibly, although my uncle could be speaking with Julia. Julia and Maria sound very much alike."

"What made Sir Thomas decide to let Mrs. Rushworth come today?" inquired Susan.

"Mrs. Norris wished to come to the wedding, and Mrs. Rushworth petitioned to be allowed to attend as well. Edmund decided it would be inappropriate for Mrs. Rushworth to be at the marriage service itself, but that he would be happy to meet his sister afterwards."

As a clergyman, Mr. Edmund Bertram had to balance the requirements of stern Christian morality with gentle Christian forgiveness.

"Were you very unhappy when she eloped?" inquired Susan.

"I was shocked by Maria's behavior – I had not thought her capable of such an act – and anxious for her, and for my uncle. I was not unhappy for myself, because I never felt any affection for Mr. Crawford."

"Maria cannot be as pretty as you, Fanny, or Mr. Crawford would not have left her," said Susan. Mr. Henry Crawford was the name of the gentleman – the word has to be used, no matter how ill the fit – for whom Maria Rushworth had deserted her husband. At the time, Mr. Crawford had been trying to persuade *Fanny* to accept his proposal of marriage. Fanny, who had never trusted Mr. Crawford, had refused him with a persistence and a perspicacity that had bewildered and infuriated her wealthy relations, especially Sir Thomas. Mr. Crawford's subsequent behavior had altered their opinion, and the baronet consequently admired her good judgment and sterling character.

Fanny repeated that Susan would soon see Mrs. Rushworth for herself, and then cautioned Susan not to mention Mr. Crawford before Mrs. Rushworth. "*I* am too happy to be disturbed by anything today, but Mrs. Rushworth's spirits may not be as good."

Fanny, on the threshold of marriage with her dear Edmund, whom she had loved for years, easily turned her thoughts away from the memory of Mr. Crawford's elopement with Mrs. Rushworth. Susan, although she agreed not to *speak* of the matter, could not stop thinking about it – and nor did she want to stop thinking about it. Susan was deeply interested in the *appearance* of propriety, and her kind heart would never allow her to do anyone harm or to wish anyone ill – but Susan was not as concerned as Fanny was with restraining her thoughts and feelings. Besides, the story of Mrs. Rushworth was too fascinating not to reflect upon, especially as Mrs. Rushworth was, to her knowledge, actually in the house!

Mrs. Rushworth was the eldest daughter of Sir Thomas and Lady Bertram. A few years before, Maria Bertram had, at twenty-one, married Mr. James Rushworth. Mr. Rushworth was the owner of Sotherton, a great estate only ten miles away from Mansfield Park, with an income to be much admired, of 12,000£ per annum. What could one do with so much money! wondered Susan, who had spent most of her first fifteen years in extremely crowded conditions in Portsmouth with her parents and her many brothers and sisters.

Mr. Rushworth's personality, unfortunately, had not matched his purse; in fact, he had been a dull, stupid fellow. Miss Bertram – who had been in love with Mr. Crawford at the time, but disappointed because the gentleman had not made her an offer – had married Mr. Rushworth to prove her independence from Mr. Crawford and her father. Sir Thomas, although aware of Mr. Rushworth's shortcomings, had tamped down his misgivings and given his daughter away.

After Maria's marriage to Mr. Rushworth, Mr. Crawford had decided that he was in love with Miss Fanny Price. Fanny, already secretly in love with her cousin Edmund, had not returned Mr. Crawford's affections. In fact, aware of his treatment of her female cousins – Mr. Crawford had likewise trifled with Julia Bertram – Fanny had disliked and distrusted him. Still, Mr. Crawford might have conquered Fanny's heart, for she was beginning to find him agreeable, when Mr. Crawford encountered Mrs. Rushworth at a party and the two of them had resumed their flirtation and had eloped.

Susan, who knew most of this and suspected the rest, thought Fanny owed Mr. Crawford a great deal. His pursuit of Fanny made her seem attractive to all – had earned her the respect of their wealthy relatives – for without the confirmation of Mr. Crawford's admiration Fanny might never have been considered beautiful. Mr. Crawford's offer had made her a worthy object to her cousin, Edmund, who had never noticed her that way before. Edmund, whom Susan loved as her cousin, and who had all the superiority associated with a clergyman and an Oxford education – even dear Edmund was subject to human frailty and had not perceived Fanny as a potential wife until after Mr. Crawford paid his addresses. For who does not want what others desire?

Susan had actually met Mr. Crawford, who had once ventured to Portsmouth in pursuit of Fanny. Susan had never seen Mrs. Rushworth, however, and was almost as interested in meeting her disgraced cousin as she was in her sister's wedding.

Susan was aware that it was not supposed to be her place to judge, and she was extremely conscious of her dependent position. Yet she was not her sister; she dared to have opinions, even if she was cautious in uttering them.

"I am glad you are so happy," Susan said to Fanny, choosing a subject to which her sister could make no objection.

"I am. My chief regret is leaving you, Susan. Will you be lonely?"

"I do not think so," said Susan. "All my cousins are here; Mansfield Park will be livelier than it has been in years."

"One can feel alone in a house full of many people." Fanny spoke from experience, for when she had first come to Mansfield Park she had been both lonely and homesick.

"Do not worry about me, Fanny." In truth Susan was concerned about Fanny: how would her shy sister manage as the wife of a clergyman in her new parish? But Susan did not share this anxiety with Fanny; if it had not occurred to her, why mention it? "Here come my aunts," Susan added, for Lady Bertram and Mrs. Norris were indeed descending the staircase. Both women were elegantly attired, Lady Bertram especially so, while Mrs. Norris's gown, though fine, was rather heavy for the warm day. Lady Bertram clutched a handkerchief that she expected to use for her tears when she watched her younger son marry her eldest niece.

Mrs. Norris glanced around the vestibule, glaring briefly at Susan, and then called out loudly. "Where is dear Edmund? I hope he has not changed his mind," she said, but with a sniff that implied that she hoped, very much, that he *was* changing his mind and would not marry Miss Price.

Susan was accustomed to the unpleasant comments of her Aunt Norris, and especially how so many of them were directed towards her sister Fanny. She had wondered if two years' absence would soften Mrs. Norris's antagonism; obviously this was not the case.

"Certainly, it must be better to change one's mind beforehand rather than to marry the wrong person and change one's mind afterwards," said Susan, speaking so that Fanny did not have to. Susan seemed to be agreeing with Mrs. Norris, but she intended for her statement to serve as a reminder that Mrs. Norris had been instrumental in forwarding the disastrous match between Maria Bertram and Mr. Rushworth, information that had been given to her by Fanny.

Lady Bertram ignored the implication and the insult; probably she did not even notice them. "Of course, it is unfortunate to marry the wrong person, but Edmund and Fanny have known each other all their lives, so how could they be making a mistake?" she remarked, and then continued, "Fanny, you look very pretty, very pretty indeed. Chapman did excellent work; I am glad I sent her to you. And I am sure that you will make Edmund very happy." After uttering these kind words, Lady Bertram yawned. "What is taking the carriage so long? I am so anxious, that I cannot bear to wait longer."

"Perhaps you would like to sit while you wait," Susan said to her favorite aunt, and guided her towards a stiff chair in the vestibule. Lady Bertram accepted her suggestion and her assistance, while Mrs. Norris appeared angry that she had not thought of this herself. Mrs. Norris said she could supply her sister with a restorative; she had learned many new receipts while in Ireland and had been of great help to the local populace. Lady Bertram said that was not necessary, and then spent her time admiring several items on a shelf, remarking that she hardly ever looked at these curios.

Sir Thomas came from his rooms; as the door opened, Susan caught a glimpse of a woman who strongly resembled Julia – the woman had to be Maria – then the door closed again. Sir Thomas's expression did not look pleased – what had he and his daughter been discussing? – changed to a smile as he greeted the other feminine members of his family. He asked about the carriage and Mrs. Norris reported that she could see it returning, and that they should make haste, so as not to keep the poor vicar waiting. As the widow of a clergyman herself, she spoke with authority on the matter.

Sir Thomas glanced around the vestibule and discerned that his younger daughter was missing. "Where is Julia? Susan, would you be so good as to fetch her?"

"Of course, Uncle." Hoping that the presence of Sir Thomas would forestall Mrs. Norris from directing unpleasant remarks to Fanny, Susan hastened up the stairs and went along a corridor to the rooms shared by Julia and her husband.

Susan knocked on the door and a voice invited her to enter. Julia, seated on a chair near an open window, glanced up at Susan. "Is it time to go?"

"Yes, the carriage is returning."

"Then let us go," she said, rising slowly and following Susan. Julia placed a hand on the banister as she made her way down the stairs. "Do you know if my sister is here?"

"I understand she is in Sir Thomas's study. You must be anxious to see her."

"Yes, I suppose I am," replied Julia, but with such little enthusiasm that Susan wondered if Julia actually did *not* want to be with Maria. Perhaps the sisters had quarreled? But when? Maria had been banished to Ireland, while Julia and her husband, as far as Susan knew, had never made the journey to that country. Yet these were assumptions. Julia *could* have traveled to Ireland; for that matter, Maria *could* have traveled back to England to see her sister. Their incomes were not supposed to be equal to extra voyages, but people often spent money they could ill afford. Or they could have had a dispute by letter, with some careless phrase causing a rift.

Julia and her husband had arrived three days ago, but so far Julia and Susan had barely spoken. However, Julia had spoken very little to the rest of her family, either, so Susan could not take particular offense. She wondered if something troubled Mrs. Yates. Or was Julia just perpetually exhausted, the way her mother, Lady Bertram, was so often exhausted? At least Aunt Bertram compensated for her fatigue by her general good humor; Julia's expression was as sour as if someone had poured vinegar into her tea.

There were possible other problems, thought Susan, as they reached the vestibule and Sir Thomas then escorted his wife, sister-in-law and married daughter outside to assist them into the carriage. Financial difficulties – marital discord – perhaps Mr. John Yates was starting to drink! Growing up in Portsmouth, Susan had witnessed such aggravations in many families.

She could not utter any of this speculation aloud, thought Susan, but would have to hold her tongue, watching as the carriage door was shut and the coachman started the slow drive with the three women to the church. Susan glanced at Fanny, who controlled her thoughts as well as her words. Maybe she should learn that from her sister.

Sir Thomas turned and was making his way towards the outside steps as the study door entered. A fair, very pretty woman with a well-formed figure paused on the threshold.

"Oh! I am sorry. I thought you had all departed," said Mrs. Rushworth, for Mrs. Rushworth it had to be.

"No, my aunts and Mrs. Yates have just left for the church," said Fanny. "The rest of us will go once the carriage returns."

"Then pardon my intrusion," Maria apologized, but she did not retreat into Sir Thomas's rooms. "Dear Fanny, I wish you all the happiness in the world."

"Thank you, Maria," said Fanny.

Susan said nothing, but studied her cousin who was tall, about her own height, very similar to Julia in appearance, and attired in a blue muslin dress.

"You must be Susan," said Maria, as Fanny went towards the door to speak to Sir Thomas.

"I am," said Susan quietly.

"After Fanny marries, will you be remaining at Mansfield Park? Or will you be returning to your home in Portsmouth?"

The questions startled Susan. She had stopped thinking of Portsmouth as home for a while now, and found it strange to hear someone refer to it that way for her.

Before Susan could respond to Maria's questions, or judge if they had any ill intent, Sir Thomas was back in the vestibule. "Maria!" he said, and his voice was full of disapproval. Susan was certain that Maria had been warned to remain out of sight until the ceremony was over.

"I am sorry, Father. I heard the carriage, and I thought you had departed and I could venture out of your room. Besides, I wanted to congratulate my new sister – and you, too, sir, on acquiring such an agreeable daughter."

Sir Thomas was mollified. "I suppose this meeting will do no harm," he said.

"I will remove myself from your sight. Congratulations, Fanny – a pleasure to meet you, Cousin Susan."

And before anyone could protest or object, Mrs. Rushworth stepped back into her father's study and closed the door behind her.

Sir Thomas apologized to Fanny, but while the bride-to-be assured her uncle and future father-in-law that she was not in the least disturbed by Maria's presence, no one seemed to notice that Susan was ill at ease.

"Maria wishes to return to Mansfield Park," he explained to Fanny. "She is sorry for what she did. But I do not see how I can allow her to live here again."

So, thought Susan, Maria hoped to take *her* place. If *she* were to return to Portsmouth, a vacancy next to Lady Bertram, reading to her, writing her letters, assisting her with her carpet work, might be considered available.

Sir Thomas continued, speaking so loudly that Susan was certain that the words penetrated the door. "Maria is not happy in Ireland, but reflecting, I do not believe she was ever content here, either. I believe she would be happiest living with Julia, if Julia and her husband would accept her. But they have other concerns."

Susan speculated what those concerns might be. Julia's husband, Mr. John Yates, was only the second son, and hence dependent on the whims of his father, the Baron of Dexthorpe, for an income. The baron might not be willing to give money to a son who gave room to Mrs. Rushworth. Sir Thomas's words could explain Julia's reserve, her unwillingness to converse or even to sit with the rest of them. If Julia were experiencing pressure from finances or her sister or both, and was not certain what to do, she might choose to avoid them, and she would certainly not confide in a cousin with whom she was barely acquainted.

"I have not yet decided what to do," continued Sir Thomas, "but for now I will let Maria stay a few weeks. She will not attend the service but will join us for dinner afterwards, as Edmund suggested."

The curiosity Susan had felt regarding Maria shifted to anxiety; she expected that her cousin would use those few weeks to do her best to regain her parents' good opinion. Yet why should she feel anxious? Mansfield Park could easily house them both.

Sir Thomas added: "I should not be spoiling your day with this, Fanny."

In her quiet voice, Fanny assured her uncle that nothing could spoil her day, and Sir Thomas began telling Fanny how happy he was to have her marry Edmund. "I believe you are exactly the wife he needs. You will make him happy."

"I hope so, Uncle," said Fanny.

Sir Thomas continued to speak of his great joy at the match – words that surely were overheard by Mrs. Rushworth, and probably caused her pain, for her own match had failed. As they were not addressed to her, and as they were sentiments that Sir Thomas had uttered before, Susan did not attend closely. She moved towards the door, watching for the return of the carriage, and alerted her uncle and her sister when it approached.

CHAPTER TWO

Sir Thomas handed his nieces into the carriage, then entered himself, and the horses pulled them in the direction of the church. During the short journey the baronet said how much he would miss Fanny, how grateful he was for all that Fanny had done for them over the years – an unusual statement because in the regular course of things most people would have assumed that he had done much for Fanny – then concluded with a smile: "And you have supplied us with a replacement. We are grateful to you, Susan."

These words, so satisfactory, reassured Susan that her uncle had no particular plan to exile her in favor of his wayward daughter.

They reached the church and the ceremony began, the wedding as simple and straightforward as suited the cousins. Lady Bertram wiped a few tears of joy from her face as the vicar pronounced them to be man and wife; Sir Thomas's voice broke afterwards when he congratulated Edmund. Fanny smiled sweetly, and took her new husband's arm.

The rest of the party did not experience such unalloyed delight. Tom was pleased for his brother but wondered if he would ever find such satisfaction. Julia, who had eloped with her husband, regretted the fact that she had not had a wedding herself, even one this plain, while her husband, Mr. John Yates, was distracted by a letter he had received that morning. Susan, despite her earlier protestations, wondered what life would be like at Mansfield Park without dear Fanny at hand for all her questions and confidences. And Mrs. Norris found fault with the reading of the service, as the current inmate of the Parsonage, a Mr. Hawk, did not match the late Reverend Norris for volume and pronunciation.

"Even Dr. Grant did better," opined Mrs. Norris to Sir Thomas.

As Susan, having listened to Dr. Grant a few times in the pulpit, detected little difference between him and Mr. Hawk, she wondered if Mrs. Norris were having trouble with her hearing.

"My apologies," said Mr. Hawk.

Mrs. Norris, who had not realized that the vicar was so close, blushed an unbecoming red, and Susan wondered if her aunt's vision were declining as well.

"I did not notice any problem," said Sir Thomas, "and what matters is that Edmund and Fanny are married."

Mr. Hawk congratulated the new father-in-law, and then explained that he had another point to discuss. He himself had postponed a journey to his ailing mother in another county, but now that this service was done, he wished to visit her. Mr. Hawk needed to be gone some time, for several weeks at least, but he had arranged for a replacement – the very Dr. Grant whom Mrs. Norris had just praised.

"Dr. Grant?" inquired Sir Thomas.

Dr. Grant's wife, Mrs. Grant, was the sister of Mr. Crawford, the man who had eloped with Maria when she was still married to Mr. Rushworth. Mrs. Grant also had a sister, Miss Mary Crawford, who, before the scandal, had been an object of Edmund's affections.

Susan, aware of these relationships, listened to Mr. Hawk with greater attention than ever before.

Mr. Hawk was aware of the awkwardness associated with that family and so was ready with his explanation. "Yes, Dr. Grant has business himself in the area, and now that Miss Price has become Mrs. Bertram, he and Mrs. Grant thought they could venture here for a few weeks without disrupting the peace of the parish."

"Were you aware that my daughter, Mrs. Rushworth, is currently visiting Mansfield Park?"

At this the vicar colored. "No, Sir Thomas, I was not aware of your daughter's visit."

"I suppose you could not be. We have been trying to keep it quiet, and apparently, we succeeded. I assume there is no chance that Mr. Crawford will venture to the neighborhood?" Sir Thomas's tones made his displeasure known.

"I doubt it very much."

"Then I believe we will survive a few weeks of Dr. Grant, who has every right to come to the Parsonage, as the living is technically his. Please, Mr. Hawk, go to your mother for however long she needs you."

Mr. Hawk expressed his gratitude and his apologies, added that Dr. Grant was expected to arrive that afternoon, and departed.

The wedding party returned to Mansfield Park, where the new couple would spend their wedding night; the following morning, Edmund and Fanny would borrow Sir Thomas's carriage to make the journey to Thornton Lacey, where Edmund had his living. As the information about the impending arrival of the Grants could not be kept from anyone, Susan asked her sister if the news affected her.

"For myself, I am not touched," Fanny assured her. If this had happened a year ago, I might have been concerned for Edmund, but now we are married, and I have complete confidence in him and his happiness. Besides, we leave early tomorrow. I am more concerned about the others, especially Maria. Do you know if the Crawfords are coming too?"

Susan explained that Mr. Crawford was not expected; as for Miss Crawford, she did not know.

At dinner that day, toasts were made to celebrate the happy couple, and then the party inevitably discussed the arrival of the Grants. Lady Bertram said she would be pleased to receive Mrs. Grant, whom she had always found pleasant, while Mrs. Norris, who had disliked her husband's successor as a matter of principle, and had been especially affronted by his dinners and his wines, as his style of living contradicted all the economies she had practiced while she resided in the Parsonage, muttered something unpleasant about Dr. Grant. Mrs. Rushworth, permitted to sit with her family at dinner, turned pink but declared she was perfectly indifferent. Edmund Bertram and Julia Yates, who had each suffered from the capriciousness of Miss Crawford and Mr. Crawford, said nothing. Both Edmund and Julia were married, and each had the sense to know that displaying any regret on either part would not improve conjugal felicity.

Sir Thomas assured those at the table that he would not object to meeting with either Dr. or Mrs. Grant, although with so many at Mansfield

Park, they did not lack for company and could certainly amuse themselves. He suggested they find a different topic. Fashion was attempted, but no one had much to say; Fanny and Edmund's living arrangements were mentioned, but that had been discussed at length before. Tom Bertram was the only hunter, and it was not the hunting season, and Mr. Yates knew better than to talk about the theatre in his father-in-law's house.

Urged by Julia, Mr. John Yates was about to speak when Sir Thomas recalled that he had received a letter that morning and that some of its contents concerned Fanny. "From your brother, William," he said. William Price, a year older than Fanny, was a lieutenant in His Majesty's navy, and a credit to his uncle who had done what he could to create opportunities for his nephew. "He has been looking into some business of mine in Antigua and wrote to me about it, but he included a note for his dear sister on her wedding day."

Sir Thomas had the letter fetched from his study; the note was passed to Fanny, who could not help wiping away a few tears as she read the words from her favorite brother.

"How long will William be in Antigua, Uncle?" inquired Susan, who sometimes assisted Sir Thomas with his correspondence regarding his estate in the West Indies.

Sir Thomas explained that it was possible that Lieutenant Price's ship was already sailing back towards England.

"Is everything all right, Father?" asked Tom, who had spent some time with his father at the West Indies family estate several years ago, nominally to learn what mattered in running a sugar plantation, but also to remove himself from the temptation of bad habits and bad connections at home.

"I hope so," said Sir Thomas gravely, and added, "we shall see."

That topic finished, Edmund and Fanny excused themselves to go upstairs; the ladies left the dinner table for the drawing-room, and the other gentlemen remained to drink some of Sir Thomas's finest on this great occasion. Lady Bertram took her place on her sofa and pulled her pug beside her, and spent the time telling her sister and daughters about the most recent litter, and which of her friends had been so fortunate as to receive a pup. "I also gave one to Fanny," said Lady Bertram, "as a present on her marriage."

Maria feigned interest in the pug, offering to brush her. Mrs. Norris sniffed, and Julia looked as if she wanted to take a nap on a sofa of her own. Susan, of course, was already informed about the distribution of the litter, and was able to prompt Lady Bertram when her ladyship could not recall exactly which pup she had given to Mrs. Oliver. Then the gentlemen appeared, putting an end to this topic. Mr. Yates sat beside his wife, and Sir Thomas sat in the chair by Lady Bertram and repeated how happy he was with the events of the day.

After a few congratulations from others, Mrs. Norris said, "Sir Thomas, I hope you are not planning a similar alliance for Tom."

"What are you talking about?" asked Lady Bertram. "Susan, what does she mean?"

Susan, horrified, was unequal to giving an explanation, but everyone else in the room was quicker in understanding than Lady Bertram, and Maria Rushworth spoke. "My aunt Norris hopes that although Edmund has lowered himself to marry Fanny, Tom will not make a similar match with Susan."

Susan, aghast, stared at the floor, so she could not see the expressions on her relatives' faces, but she could not turn her ears away and so she heard their reactions.

"Tom and Susan! Impossible," said Lady Bertram, bewildered and dismissive. "Dear Susan is only seventeen."

"Mother, I was only explaining my aunt's meaning," said Maria.

"Please, Aunt Norris, no matchmaking," Tom called from across the room.

"I think it is too soon to be planning other matches in the family," said Sir Thomas.

Mrs. Norris agreed, and said, in a less insulting manner, that all she had done was express her hope that no match was being planned. Sir Thomas urged another change of subject; Julia touched her husband's arm and Mr. Yates cleared his throat. "Sir Thomas, I do have something to ask you."

Mr. John Yates had received a letter from his elder brother, the Honorable George Yates, just that morning. Mr. George Yates would be traveling near them, and wished to stop and to visit Mansfield Park for a few days. Mr. John Yates had not mentioned it earlier because he did not wish to disturb anyone before the wedding, but he was obliged to do so now because he realized his brother could arrive as early as the morrow.

The new subject gave Susan the courage to look up and to study the expressions of those in the room. Several seemed troubled by the previous topic. On the faces of Maria and Mrs. Norris, she saw irritation; on the face of her cousin Tom, Susan detected frowning embarrassment. Sir Thomas seemed grave, but he was often grave, while the lovely Lady Bertram appeared as placid as ever. Mr. and Mrs. Yates, naturally, were more interested in the matter they had introduced.

"Surely that will be no trouble, will it, Sir Thomas?" asked Lady Bertram. Very little troubled Lady Bertram; first, because her disposition was so serene, and second, because her family and her friends conspired to keep all difficulties from her.

Sir Thomas glanced around the room. "I do not think so. And an additional guest will distract us from the departure of Edmund and Fanny."

Susan knew her uncle would prefer to have just his own family near him, and he certainly would have preferred more warning than had been given, but Mr. John Yates's brother had a claim, even if Sir Thomas had never met the man.

"Is he planning to stay long?" inquired Sir Thomas.

Mr. John Yates assured his father-in-law that his brother would not stay long, that his brother never stayed anywhere long. "Three or four days at most, depending on his horse and on the weather."

Lady Bertram asked languidly if she had ever met this Mr. George Yates and her family assured her that she had not. Through her aunt's questions Susan discovered that Mr. George Yates would someday be Lord Dexthorpe, that he was a little more than thirty, and that he was still unmarried.

"He sounds like a fine catch for some young lady," remarked Lady Bertram.

"I think, Mama, we agreed not to engage in further matchmaking," said Julia. Susan, the only eligible young lady in the room – for the divorced, disgraced Mrs. Rushworth would not be accepted by most families – wondered if Julia were ashamed of her poor relation.

"You are right, we did," agreed Lady Bertram. "Besides, weddings are so exhausting." Then she announced that, regarding the arrival of Mr. George Yates, Susan would take care of the details.

Susan felt the glare of Mrs. Norris, who expressed her doubt in her young niece being equal to such responsibility, and the suspicious gaze of Mrs. Rushworth, who observed that Susan seemed to be kept very busy.

Susan could not read her Cousin Maria's attitude. Was Maria jealous, because she thought Susan had too much influence at Mansfield Park? Or did Maria look down on Susan, who performed duties that might be better left to the housekeeper? "I try to help," said Susan quietly. And she then spoke with Mr. John Yates and Julia to determine when Mr. Yates was most likely to arrive, how he was traveling, and what his preferences were, in order to recommend the best room for him and a menu for the following day. Mr. John Yates assured her that his brother, although he liked the best, would certainly be pleased with everything he encountered at Mansfield Park.

"I should think so!" exclaimed Mrs. Norris. "Few places are more perfect than Mansfield Park."

"It is lovely here," said Julia, who then excused herself. Her husband escorted her upstairs.

"Mrs. Rushworth, are you at all acquainted with Mr. Yates?" Susan asked Maria.

Maria appeared not to hear, then, when Susan repeated her question, Maria deigned to respond. "Only a little," she said.

"How could Mrs. Rushworth or I be well acquainted with anyone, banished as we are?" said Mrs. Norris.

Maria added: "Tom knows Mr. Yates better than I do."

Tom, hearing his name, said that he did know Mr. John Yates's elder brother, but that they were not close. As Tom Bertram formed friendships easily, his denial of being intimate with anyone was unusual.

"Tom, didn't you and this Mr. Yates?" – Sir Thomas began, then stopped, in what for him was a rare instance of delicacy.

"Yes, sir, but that was a long time ago."

"Remember your promise, Tom," said Sir Thomas.

Even though the subject of Tom's promise was not mentioned, Susan was certain she understood the meaning. Mr. Bertram had, several years ago, lost a great deal of money gambling; it sounded as if this Mr. Yates had been involved.

Deciding that they had had enough of uncomfortable topics and doubting that the conversation would improve, Susan asked Mrs. Rushworth, whom she knew was musical, if she would be so kind as to play the pianoforte. Maria obliged; during her performance, Susan slipped away to warn Baddeley and the housekeeper about the probable arrival of Mr. George Yates. The servants received the information calmly; with the house so full, one more would make little difference. Mrs. Rushworth was still at the instrument when Susan returned to the drawing-room.

"How nice it is to hear that again," said Lady Bertram, for Maria had performed one of her mother's favorite songs.

"Maria is looking forward to performing some duets with Julia. A pity that Julia has already retired!" said Mrs. Norris, as Mrs. Rushworth left the pianoforte.

"Perhaps Susan will play something," said Lady Bertram.

Susan rose and obligingly went to the instrument; she perceived the astonishment on the faces of Mrs. Rushworth and Mrs. Norris. "That girl plays the pianoforte?" remarked Mrs. Norris.

Susan, feeling all eyes and ears, some very critical, directed her way, chose a piece that was not too taxing. That finished, after the polite applause, she heard Maria say: "Fanny never even wanted to learn."

"Susan is not Fanny," remarked Sir Thomas.

"But they are both dear nieces," said Lady Bertram.

CHAPTER THREE

Susan was not Fanny. She adored music; she always had; its beauty had provided a respite from her family's dingy surroundings in Portsmouth. When she was little, a neighbor with an instrument had taught her the rudiments. The Prices had moved, but Susan still occasionally found the opportunity to practice. When she arrived at Mansfield Park with Fanny, the family was completely discomposed, what with the elopement of Julia, the illness of Tom, the adultery of Mrs. Rushworth and the apparent destruction of all romantic hopes for Edmund. Susan had assisted where and how she could, sitting with Lady Bertram when Fanny could not and running errands for everyone – but during those first few weeks, she had had many hours to herself. Susan discovered an instrument in the servants' quarters and asked if anyone could assist her; one of the servants, a young maid named Ann Jones, obliged, and in these better circumstances Susan made rapid progress. Her secret did not remain secret long; Chapman, Lady Bertram's maid, reported the information to her ladyship, and her ladyship asked Susan to play. Sir Thomas, discovering his niece had talent and inclination and was willing to make the effort to improve herself, arranged for instruction, and was rewarded for his generosity by having a niece who could entertain them on rainy evenings.

Susan was not Fanny. She had similar features, rather like Lady Bertram's, but she was taller, stronger, and not nearly as fearful. Still, the following day, even brave Susan was apprehensive at the departure of the sister who had done so much for her. "I will miss you," she said, as Fanny and Edmund prepared to step into the carriage that would take them to Thornton Lacey.

"And I you. I will miss all of you," said Fanny, with tears in her eyes as she went to each of her relatives in turn, her embraces somewhat hindered by the basket she carried, a basket containing a son of Lady Bertram's darling pug.

Susan wished she could take her sister aside to ask Fanny's advice about the accusation made by Mrs. Norris, of Susan scheming to marry Tom Bertram. Although Susan had been able to affect her normal composure shortly after Mrs. Norris's angry words, the memory of them had returned to haunt her during the night, depriving her of several hours of sleep. Fanny had been suspected of wishing to marry Edmund – a suspicion that proved true – and so might be able to provide useful counsel, but this was not the moment. They were surrounded by others. Besides, Fanny was busy, her heart full, her head concerned with her new life and new duties, and Susan did not wish to trouble her.

"I will write, Aunt," Fanny promised, embracing Lady Bertram; the latter was much affected.

They all watched as Mr. and Mrs. Edmund Bertram climbed into the carriage.

"Susan, you must take care of me now," said Lady Bertram.

"Of course, Aunt," said Susan, and although the others did not hear the quiet exchange, they all observed how Lady Bertram leaned on her niece's arm as they ascended the stairs. Tom and Maria then went for a stroll on the grounds; Sir Thomas retired to his study, and Mr. and Mrs. Yates went up to their rooms. Mrs. Norris, jealous of her sister's reliance on Susan, followed Lady Bertram and Susan to the drawing-room. After Lady Bertram had been helped back to her sofa, had exchanged one shawl for another and had retrieved her pug, Mrs. Norris insinuated herself.

Susan, seeing that her favorite aunt was cared for, and not wanting to spend any time with Mrs. Norris if she could help it, offered to pick some roses. In truth she longed to go back outside, for the weather was fine, and the fresh air revived her when she was fatigued from lack of sleep.

Lady Bertram said that would be lovely, and Mrs. Norris, eager to have her sister to herself, encouraged Susan to depart as well, only hoping that Susan would not do any harm to the precious rosebushes.

Susan quickly fetched her supplies: a bonnet to protect her face, gloves for her hands, and a basket for the flowers. Cutting flowers was a luxury she had never known in Portsmouth, and she rejoiced in the gardens of Mansfield Park. When she had picked a dozen, she decided to linger a few more minutes outside and sat down on a bench in the shade, recessed among the shrubbery. She was still distressed by the memory of Mrs. Norris's unpleasant hints. She tried to convince herself that Mrs. Norris was just being Mrs. Norris: an unhappy woman wishing unhappiness on others. Surely her ideas held no weight with her uncle and her aunt or her cousin Tom. But the words still vexed Susan, and she preferred to stay where she was, instead of joining Lady Bertram and Mrs. Norris in the drawing-room.

However, Susan was not the only one taking advantage of the fine weather; the sound of footsteps informed her that others were drawing nigh. Before Susan could make known her presence, Maria's voice reached her: "So, Tom, is Susan in love with you? Are you planning to make another Miss Price a permanent fixture in our family?"

Susan, her heart trembling, became very still. This was certainly a conversation not meant for her ears, and the delicate thing to do would be to slip away. But she could not escape; the shrubbery grew so thick around her so as to present impenetrable walls on three sides; the only passage would put her just before the speakers. She held her breath, and could not help listening, for she was extremely curious as to how the conversation would continue.

"I have no plans for matrimony at present, Maria."

A sound on the gravel indicated that Maria had stopped walking; she said, all too loudly: "*That* is your problem, Tom. You have no plans. And because of that, you will find yourself marrying Susan from convenience – or to please Mother."

"I assure you, Maria, that when and if I choose a wife, I will choose carefully. I am aware how important the decision is, and I assure you, *I* will not act in haste. I have a large acquaintance, so my choice is not restricted to a poor cousin."

Tom's speech was aimed at reminding his sister that *her* matrimonial selection had been particularly unfortunate, but the words that stung Susan, which pierced her heart, were those dismissing her as a poor cousin. And they were uttered, not by Mrs. Norris, who was unkind to everyone, or by Maria, who was bitter from her own experiences and who did not really know her – but by Tom, with whom she had shared many laughs. Was this the sort of humiliation that Fanny had experienced during her earlier years at Mansfield Park? Fanny had always been reserved about those days, only giving Susan advice as to each inmate's temper, and hinting at past events, but not describing particulars.

Susan's cousins continued along the path and had the decency to blush upon seeing her and realizing that their conversation must have been overheard, as Susan herself appeared aghast. Maria struggled briefly with various emotions – superiority versus sympathy – and then hastily departed, explaining she could find her way to the house by herself. Tom, although he appeared uncomfortable, paused to speak with his young cousin.

"You heard that, did you not? I am sorry."

"Why should you apologize? What you said is true; I *am* a poor cousin." Susan did not wish to spend time alone with him; she was too mortified. Picking up the basket, she abandoned the bench and started towards the house. "I should take these roses inside to my aunt."

He stepped beside her, and his longer stride made it impossible for her to get away. "But *you* are an invited guest, welcomed by my parents, while Maria has been banished by them. That makes her cross. That and the fact that we just saw the Grants and Miss Crawford arriving at the Parsonage – they are painful reminders to Maria."

"Did you speak with them?"

"No, we only saw them from a distance. I might have gone down the path to say hello, but I could not with Maria; understandably she was unwilling. Sue, there is something else I wish to mention. The words of Aunt Norris and even Maria – you should ignore them. You are too young to marry anyone, let alone someone like me."

Unable to keep silent on the matter for the moment – she would have to be silent on it when inside – Susan voiced her frustration. "Why is anyone discussing this? My sister married your brother. That has nothing to do with either of us, except that I will miss Fanny."

Tom hesitated, and then said, "You are right, that has nothing to do with us. Let us enter the house; your roses need water."

The easy way he spoke almost disappointed Susan, then she chided herself for being so unreasonable. Tom was only repeating her own words! She searched for another subject, and remembered her brother William's letter from the day before. "You were with Sir Thomas in Antigua, were you not?"

"Yes."

"What was it like?"

Tom stared into the distance, in the approximate direction of that island. "Warm."

"You left several months before my uncle did, is that correct?"

"Yes," he answered, with uncustomary shortness.

He clearly did not want to talk about Antigua, thought Susan, although she could not fathom why. They were nearing the door; in a few minutes she would probably be the target of Mrs. Norris's unkind remarks again – and possibly her cousin Maria's as well. Even if they held their tongues, she would expect them to speak cuttingly to her, and the anticipation would be almost as bad as anything they could say.

But Tom did not turn towards the entrance; instead he stopped and gestured towards the long drive. "Yates – George Yates!"

"Oh!" said Susan. A man, presumably the Honorable George Yates, was arriving on horseback. And then she thought that Tom's concise responses might have had nothing to do with Antigua – or with her – but the fact that someone was coming. She turned towards the entrance. "I should let the others know."

"A moment, Sue – I need your help. Over the next few days; I need your help."

Susan inquired how she could be of assistance.

"I do not wish to be lured into a game. I lost money to him before, and that may be why he has decided to visit. If his funds have run short – and George Yates likes to live well – he may wish to tempt me into a game. I have promised my father not to play, but temptation is easier to withstand when it is simply not there."

"Then we should make sure, Mr. Bertram, that you are engaged in other activities," said Susan, suggesting that Tom plan on riding or walking or arranging some game that involved all of them. If desperate, he could plead a headache or indisposition – the idea made him frown because he did not wish to appear frail, especially after having been so ill before – or hide in his father's library – another unpalatable counsel. After several suggestions were repulsed, Susan said, "Fanny would tell you simply to tell him the truth, that you have made a promise to your father not to play and that you intend to keep it, especially when you are under his roof."

With a smile, Tom protested that Fanny would never say such a thing – she might very well *think* it, but that she would never *say* it. Edmund might, however, give him the same advice and the more Tom thought about Susan's last suggestion, the more he liked it, and that the counsel was easier to hear from his young cousin than from his clerical brother.

"You will have to choose your method of resistance soon," said Susan, for Mr. George Yates and his horse were approaching quickly.

"Yes, I will," said her cousin. "What a fine animal! Come, Sue, let us greet its rider."

The horse was a handsome black stallion; the rider was a well-dressed man. The man called out to Tom; Tom called back, and then the stranger descended from his horse. Susan stayed back a few paces, until Tom introduced her, presenting her as his cousin, Miss Price.

"Your cousin! That explains it. I thought I had miscounted your sisters, for I did not recognize her, and yet I see a resemblance. And what a vision she presents! There is nothing lovelier than a young lady carrying roses!"

Although Mr. Yates's observations were complimentary, Susan was a little embarrassed by the pointedness of his remarks.

Tom relieved her by talking about the horse, observing that it was fine and large, and would do honor to the Mansfield Park stables. The change of subject gave Susan the chance to observe the new arrival. Mr. George Yates, the elder son of Lord Dexthorpe, was taller and handsomer than his younger brother, but also heavier.

"It is; it is! That is why I am in the area. A friend, not too far from here, was ready to dispose of him, and so I had to come this way to collect him. I left most of my things in a room at F—, so that I could travel light. I count on you and John for necessaries, should I be wanting. My brother is here, is he not?"

Tom assured Mr. Yates that Mr. John Yates was at Mansfield Park and that the former would be well taken care of during his visit.

"Your horse must be thirsty," remarked Susan.

"Yes, as are we all, including your roses. Jackson!" Tom called to Stephen Jackson, one of the grooms, who had been observing the new arrival, and who hurried over to take the reins, while a footman appeared and removed the burdens from the horse and its owner.

Susan lingered long enough to see the horse being led to the stables, and Mr. John Yates coming out the front door to greet his brother. Both Tom Bertram and Mr. John Yates were friendly and hospitable – but both had reason to resent the new arrival. Tom had lost money to Mr.

Yates in cards, so much that he had asked Susan for her assistance in avoiding temptation to gamble, while Mr. John Yates was a second son whose expectations were nothing compared to his brother's. But could those things really be blamed on Mr. Yates? Presumably Tom could have refused to play, and no one could do anything about whether one was born first or second.

A good-looking man, almost as fine as her cousins, Mr. Yates would certainly be the center of attention this evening. Susan went inside to arrange the roses and to inform the other inmates of Mansfield Park that the eldest son of the Baron of Dexthorpe had arrived.

CHAPTER FOUR

The arrival of someone new, unknown to many, will inspire people to their best behavior or at least to caution in their choice of conversation, especially when that someone is a handsome man and the eldest son of a lord. Whether or not Tom might marry Susan, how Edmund and Fanny were doing now that they were at Thornton Lacey, or even if they should take notice of the Grants at the Parsonage – these topics were all forgotten, or at least set aside, for the moment, in favor of Mr. George Yates.

Mr. Yates was welcomed by his brother, his erstwhile friend Tom Bertram, and even Mrs. Rushworth uttered several pleasant remarks, but Julia Yates greeted the new arrival with such brief sentences and such coolness that Susan's curiosity was provoked. Yesterday Susan had wondered if Julia were becoming a likeness of her mother, Lady Bertram, fated to spend most of her life upon a sofa; now her speculation shifted to wondering if Julia was somehow turning into the image of Mrs. Norris, with Mrs. Norris's general hostility towards some of her nearest relatives. Mrs. Norris, herself, did not seem pleased to see Mr. Yates, and stared at him angrily, an attitude that was unintelligible to Susan, as Mrs. Norris generally valued men of rank and wealth. Could Mrs. Norris be concerned for Tom? Or did she just resent the intrusion of a stranger during this time, on this rare visit to her family? Those sentiments could be certainly imputed to Sir Thomas, who addressed Mr. Yates with guarded gravity. Sir Thomas had to be concerned for his eldest son, although Tom's problems were from long ago and his behavior in the intervening years had been without reproach. Lady Bertram, unaware that Mr. George Yates had been responsible for her eldest son's gambling losses – losses that had cost Edmund an important living, and part of his income for years – was perhaps the sincerest in her friendliness towards her son-in-law's elder brother, except that her position on the sofa and her soft, placid inquiries kept her from attracting much notice.

The servants, unlike the family, had fewer scruples with respect to the new arrival: the eldest son of the Baron of Dexthorpe, later to be Lord Dexthorpe himself! Despite Sir Thomas's rank and respectability, few people visited Mansfield Park, and so they were determined to make the most of it, and discussed his horse, his appearance, and his traveling clothes.

Sir Thomas, unaware that Susan had already been introduced by Tom, brought her forward: "Mr. Yates, this is my niece, Miss Price."

Susan curtsied, while the Honorable George Yates said it was a pleasure to meet any of Sir Thomas's relations. Possibly unaware that he was unwelcome to so many of Mansfield Park's inhabitants, or perhaps indifferent to their opinions, he spoke at length when others would not. He thanked Sir Thomas for the opportunity to make a stop during his journey, as it was always more pleasant to stay at an estate with friends instead of some inn with strangers, and that he was especially grateful for the sake of his horse. The animal was a new acquisition, and he needed to move it from its previous stables to its new home. When pressed, Mr. Yates agreed that he could have entrusted this task to a groom, but that he wished to spend some time with the new horse. Besides, he liked to travel, and he had always wanted to see this area of the country.

Mr. John Yates remarked, "I did not know you had any intention to purchase a new horse."

"It seems rather extravagant," added Julia.

Horses, especially those of high quality, were expensive to maintain. Susan, who sometimes reviewed the estate accounts, had been shocked when she discovered that the allowance for the Mansfield Park stables was far greater than the incomes of many families in Portsmouth.

"I assure you, John, my purse is no lighter for this acquisition," said the elder Mr. Yates.

"Did you win him in some game?" pressed Mr. John Yates.

Mr. George Yates attempted to appear ashamed, but the corners of his lips twitched, pride lurking beneath the counterfeit contrition. He admitted the stallion was the prize of a wager, and that he had won him – "from a fellow who lives about ten miles from here, on an estate called Sotherton."

At this everyone gasped, for the proprietor of Sotherton was Mr. Rushworth, Maria's former husband.

Although she blushed, Maria said nothing, but Mrs. Norris sniffed and said, "So Mr. Rushworth has taken to losing at cards, has he?"

No one else seemed disposed to discuss the unfortunate Mr. Rushworth, and after a long moment of uncomfortable silence, Sir Thomas spoke gravely. "I hope, Mr. Yates, that as long as you are visiting my home, you will not engage anyone in wagers. I do not approve of gaming."

Mr. Yates recast his features into a serious mode, and replied earnestly. "No, Sir Thomas, I would never think of doing such a thing!" Then he added with levity, "*Your* stables are safe from me."

"I hope so," said Sir Thomas, not smiling.

"Of course, I will respect my host's wishes," said Mr. Yates, bowing slightly, but a few minutes later, when the others were occupied by the arrival of the tea urn and Mrs. Norris's insistence on presiding over the procedure, Mr. Yates said to Tom, "So I suppose there will be no cards while I am here?"

Susan was appalled that someone could make a promise, and then attempt to break it such a short while later. Did those with the expectations of riches and rank imagine that they were above qualities such as keeping faith and trust or even honoring their hosts?

"You heard my father."

"Not even for trifling sums? Just enough to make it interesting?" wheedled Mr. Yates.

Tom hesitated, then seemed to realize that Susan was listening, for he glanced in her direction, and then said: "Let us talk of something else," and inquired about the ride from Sotherton.

Susan felt a rush of pride in Tom, for resisting temptation, and then experienced a strange sensation. Although Mr. Yates was fairly young, apparently healthy and most would deem him handsome, she suddenly imagined how he would appear after several additional decades of life: stooped, bloated and cruel.

The image in her head was so peculiar that she continued to stare at the original, and he perceived her attention. Mr. Yates's expression was first puzzled, then his lips twitched, as if he interpreted her interest as admiration. Embarrassed, and unsettled by what she had imagined, Susan averted her gaze. For a moment she lost the thread of the conversation. When she could listen again, she heard Mr. Yates say that he wished to go to the stables to review the situation of his new horse.

"Certainly," agreed Tom, saying that he, too, would like another opportunity to admire the animal.

The summer day was long, with several hours of sunshine remaining, and many expressed an interest in the stallion, and so nearly every member of their party walked out. The only exception was Lady Bertram, who said she preferred to treat herself to a little doze, but everyone else – including Julia, who hesitated but was persuaded by her husband that a little fresh air and movement would do her good – rose and quitted the drawing-room. Maria, having recovered from her previous embarrassment, wondered aloud if she actually knew the animal, while Sir

Thomas was rather grave about the idea that it had been taken, through some trick, from his former son-in-law.

The distance usually required less than five minutes to cover, but with so many, the little walk took nearly ten, extended by their leaving the house through the front door instead of a side door which was much closer to their goal. Susan rarely visited the stables; when she rode, the mare was brought to the front, but like every corner of Mansfield Park, the area was well maintained, everything in its proper place (such a relief after Portsmouth, with its dirt and noise).

Her uncle and her eldest cousin took great interest in the stallion, which Stephen Jackson brought forward. Maria claimed she was familiar with the horse, and was delighted to see it again, stroking its nose, and told Mr. Yates that she trusted he would treat it well.

"I hope you would not suspect me of anything else," said Mr. Yates.

Susan approached her cousin Julia, who, unlike the others, hung back, frowning as if something about the horse displeased her. "Is not a horse like this expensive?" asked Susan. "I understand that your brother-in-law acquired it for nothing, but its maintenance will be dear."

"Yes," said Julia. "*We* could not afford to keep such an animal."

Susan wondered if the income of the elder brother was much greater than the income of the younger Mr. Yates. That was certainly possible; elder sons, expected to inherit, were often awarded greater stipends by their families. On the other hand, Mr. and Mrs. John Yates also had the interest from Julia's dowry.

Perhaps Mr. Yates had a substantial fortune. Perhaps he did not, and was horribly in debt. Perhaps he intended to sell the animal. Her mind came up with a half dozen possibilities.

The elder Mr. Yates seemed to sense her interest in him, for he turned and asked, "What is your opinion, Miss Price? Do you ride?"

Susan was surprised by his addressing her directly, but she answered calmly: "A little." Just as she had with respect to playing the pianoforte, Susan had determined to take advantage of her improved situation and had learned to ride; she enjoyed the exercise a great deal.

"You should try him. I believe he is gentle enough to carry a young lady."

Susan rather doubted that – the stallion was large and spirited – but she simply demurred and said that she expected the horse, after its walk from Sotherton, had already had sufficient exercise for the day.

"Miss Price has another mount at her disposal," said Sir Thomas.

Maria and Mrs. Norris stroked the nose of the animal, while Tom and the elder Mr. Yates discussed the condition of one of the stallion's shoes with a groom. Sir Thomas approached Mr. and Mrs. John Yates. "The horse is very fine," he pronounced, "but I would like to know in exactly what circumstances your brother acquired it from Mr. Rushworth. John, I trust you to find out."

Mr. John Yates solemnly said he would do what he could to learn more.

The baronet added that whatever had happened was certainly not the fault of the horse and that while the animal was in the Mansfield Park stables it would receive the best treatment.

The men gave instructions to the grooms, and then the whole party turned in order to walk back to the house. On their way, to Susan's surprise, Julia aligned her steps to match hers. "Susan, let me advise you: do not flirt with my brother-in-law, George Yates."

Susan, embarrassed and angry, said, "I assure you, Julia, I have no such intention; I have no intention to flirt with anyone." And she quickened her steps so that she was no longer beside Julia.

As she climbed the stairs into the house, Susan wondered at the words. Both her female cousins seemed determined against her making a good marriage. Firstly, she did not know why they would suspect her of any matrimonial ambitions; she did not believe she had flirted with anyone. Secondly, her cousins seemed against any elevation on her part. Why? Did they dislike her so much? She did not see how that was possible, given how little time they had spent with her. She had only met Maria two days ago, and her acquaintance with Julia was not much greater. Did they object to her situation and want someone better for Tom Bertram and George Yates? Yet Maria and Julia had accepted Fanny's marriage with Edmund. Or perhaps, Susan reflected, they only *appeared* to have done so, and possibly the alliance with one poor cousin was reason enough to do whatever they could to prevent another; certainly, that was Mrs. Norris's attitude.

On the other hand, a match with either Mr. Bertram or Mr. Yates would be far superior – at least in the world's eyes – than the one Fanny had made with Edmund, who was only a clergyman. Both Tom Bertram and George Yates were eldest sons, with titles in their futures; Susan could understand if her relations' sensibilities were offended at the prospect of such an elevation. She, herself, was almost giddy at either idea. But why even imagine it? Tom was friendly towards her, but not particularly so; of course, she knew him well as they were both inmates of Mansfield Park. But why would Julia caution her with respect to Mr. George Yates, with whom she had only exchanged a few sentences?

Perhaps their interferences were kindly meant. Susan had known Tom for two years, but Maria was his sister, and undoubtedly understood her brother's character better than she did – or at least Maria had reason to *believe* she understood Tom's character better – and even Tom himself had claimed to be unworthy of Susan's affection. As for Mr. George Yates, Susan did not know him at all, so Julia's warning deserved attention.

Still, the fact that she was receiving so much of this sort of advice was vexing, for she did not understand what in her behavior had provoked it. When they returned to the house, Susan hung back, devoting herself to Lady Bertram, assisting her with her carpet work, and even, at Mrs. Norris's suggestion, turning to the poor basket. Susan *listened* to the others and their conversation – much about the horse, whose value seemed to increase with every mention – but only spoke when spoken to, except to Lady Bertram or to Sir Thomas.

The evening passed agreeably. The men lingered over some of Sir Thomas's claret after dinner, but eventually joined the ladies. Susan was relieved to see that cards were not suggested – Tom was not being led into temptation – instead, Maria and Julia entertained them with several duets. Susan, when asked, declined to play, and her remaining in a corner with the poor basket prevented her from being the target of any of Mrs. Norris's ill-natured remarks. When she retired, she was able to sleep, reflecting that the first day after Fanny's departure had been a little uncomfortable but had passed well enough.

CHAPTER FIVE

The next day was spent riding; that is, the young men decided to ride to Thornton Lacey to see how Edmund and Fanny were doing; Maria accompanied them, using the mare generally ridden by Susan. Susan remained at home, as did Julia. Susan hoped for the opportunity to speak with Julia alone, but Mrs. Yates returned to her room.

Susan, observing that Lady Bertram was attended to by Mrs. Norris, decided to take advantage of the hour to practice on the pianoforte, but before she could reach the instrument on which she learned new songs, Sir Thomas asked her to join him in his study.

"I have a delicate matter to discuss with you."

Anxiety flooded through her; had she caused offense? Or, despite his promise, had Tom lost money during the night? As her uncle continued to hesitate her alarm grew, but she tried to keep her voice steady. "How can I be of assistance, Uncle?"

"There may be a situation. Normally, someone in Lady Bertram's position would address the matter, but my dear wife is not, I believe, up to this particular task. And although you are young, you are the only other woman of the house who lives here now."

Sir Thomas explained that Chapman reported that one of the young housemaids, Ann Jones, had been extremely upset that morning, in hysterics, but that she would not confide in anyone. She would not even speak to Stephen Jackson, the groom in the stables with whom she had an understanding; in fact, when that had been suggested, her weeping had grown even more violent. "I wish for you to speak with her. You are young; you are tactful; she will not feel threatened if you question her. Do your best to determine what is distressing her."

Susan experienced a moment of selfish relief to learn that she was not the center of the current crisis, and then composed her features. "Certainly, Uncle, I can speak with Ann Jones. We have more people at Mansfield Park than usual. Perhaps she has had difficulty with one of the guests."

"I fear that is possible. That is why I have not asked Mrs. Norris, who used to manage these situations, to make any inquiries."

Susan obeyed, first finding Ann Jones and then sitting down with her. Susan knew the housemaid from the music lessons the latter had offered when Susan first arrived at Mansfield Park. Ann was only a little older than Susan, about her height, and usually very pretty, but today her features were marred by copious weeping.

"Ann, what has happened? What is troubling you?"

The housemaid seemed unable to speak.

"You were in good spirits yesterday, were you not?" And Susan hazarded a number of possibilities that could be causing the housemaid's distress. Was she ill? Had she received terrible news? Had someone been unkind to her? Then Susan posed the most difficult question: was she - was she with child?

The last question brought on the tears again. Susan was relieved to have made some progress in determining the cause of Ann Jones's distress, but at the same time her heart sank, for she was not sure the indiscretion would be tolerated at Mansfield Park. Her uncle had not forgiven his daughter; how would he treat a housemaid? But before any action could be taken, it was important to determine the truth.

"So, are you with child?" Susan inquired gently. "Is Stephen Jackson the father?"

The situation was not ideal but not that uncommon. If the two married, and if she could persuade her uncle to overlook the lapse in morality, then all would be well, and the problem solved.

But Ann Jones finally found the strength to speak. No, she was not with child, and she could assure Miss Price that Stephen had never touched her.

Susan tried another approach. Had something happened with one of the guests?

Ann Jones colored and hung her head.

"Did Mrs. Norris say something?" inquired Susan.

"Mrs. Norris?" Ann Jones asked with such bewilderment that it was apparent that Mrs. Norris was not responsible for the housemaid's distress. "Please do not ask me anything more, Miss Price; I just want to be alone. Let me do my work by myself, away from everyone. I promise I will be able to attend to my duties now. I would like to do some dusting and polishing. As for Stephen Jackson – please, please, do not involve him. He has had nothing to do with my distress, and I do not wish to perturb him. Promise me that you will not speak to him."

Still mystified as to why the young housemaid was so troubled, Susan agreed that Ann Jones could return to her duties. She then reported to her uncle on her less than complete understanding of the situation but that, as far as she could discern, Mrs. Norris had had nothing to do with Ann Jones's agitation.

"That is one relief, at least," said Sir Thomas, for he had hoped that a visit from his wife's sister would cause no problems. He expressed the position that if the cause of Ann Jones's vexation were important, they would discover it in time, and if it were not, it did not matter. The baronet was also especially pleased to hear that Stephen Jackson had nothing to do with the housemaid's distress. Mansfield Park could easily find another housemaid – the county was full of young women eager for such a place – but Sir Thomas was hoping for Stephen Jackson to take over the position of coachman; Wilcox had rheumatism and would not be able to continue his duties much longer. A young man with such talent for horses was not easy to find.

"Yes, Uncle. She made me promise not to speak to him of it."

"Very well, *I* will speak to Jackson."

Susan frowned.

"My dear niece, I understand your discomfort. But everyone at Mansfield Park will learn that she is distressed anyway. One cannot keep a secret here; Stephen Jackson is surely aware already of the young woman's unhappiness. If *I* question him, *you* are not breaking your word, and we will have a better idea if anything is truly the matter or if this is just some storm in a teacup."

Susan submitted to her uncle's reasoning. She hoped his actions would not harm her friendship with Ann Jones, who had been so kind to Susan upon her arrival, but Sir Thomas was master at Mansfield Park.

Sir Thomas interviewed Stephen Jackson, who also claimed ignorance of the situation, and who asked to speak with Ann Jones during an hour when their duties were light. Ann Jones refused at first, but finally relented. Stephen Jackson *seemed* angry afterwards, and could be seen pounding a horseshoe with far more force than necessary, but he denied that anything was the matter.

What had happened? Everyone was as ignorant as before, but as secrets could not be kept long at Mansfield Park, the story about Ann Jones and Stephen Jackson found its way into the drawing-room at a time when most of the ladies of the family were present. It was disagreeable to have agitated servants, Julia opined, but Lady Bertram said she was sure they would all be tranquil again, and that Chapman and Baddeley and dear Susan would certainly manage everything, and that those involved were very young and could not be expected to have the steadiness of their elders. Mrs. Norris thought that the passions of the lower classes were responsible for all the trouble. "You will have to let one of them go," said Mrs. Norris, expressing her disgust with the morals of the current staff. "Nothing like this would ever happen when *I* had influence," she pronounced, and then added that she had had an unfavorable opinion of Ann Jones ever since seeing her, and then asked for a description of the maid to make sure that she *had* seen her. As for Stephen Jackson, she had a low opinion of all the Jacksons, despite their many years of employment at Mansfield Park, so she was certain that he was guilty somehow, even though when pressed she did not know what crime he could have committed. Mrs. Norris concluded by saying that Jackson and Jones were very inconsiderate, disturbing the peace of their betters.

Lady Bertram said that she was sure all the tempers would be restored soon, and the subject, which had been discussed to the point of repetition, was closed by the return of the young men and Mrs. Rushworth from their ride. They brought a note from Fanny for Lady Bertram, described how the newlyweds were faring, including a humorous story concerning a pair of noisy geese, and generally dominated the conversation, talking of horses and saddles, jumps and views, and how Mr. George Yates was still concerned about one of the shoes of his new steed. Mrs. Norris attempted to revive her complaints about Ann Jones and Stephen Jackson, but her irritable remarks were drowned out by the good humor of the rest of the party. The conversation only finished when they dispersed to dress for dinner.

Susan quickly arranged her simple attire and decided to seek Ann Jones again to see if she could persuade the housemaid to confide in her, and slipped quietly to the servants' quarters. But as she approached the housemaid's room she overheard voices and realized that Ann Jones had another visitor: Maria Rushworth! Susan paused in the dim corridor.

"Ann, please tell me what is bothering you," said Maria.

"Mrs. Rushworth, I cannot talk about it."

So, Maria had learned about Ann Jones's troubles, probably from Mrs. Norris. Susan was a little surprised that Maria was acquainted with Ann, but then realized that Jones had begun work as an under housemaid before Maria's marriage.

"Have you done something wrong? If so, *I* will not judge." Maria's voice was gentle and encouraging. Susan was surprised to discover that

Maria could demonstrate such warmth to a servant when she was so cold to a cousin.

"No, I assure you *I* have not. Nor has Stephen. You must believe me."

"Then why was he so angry?"

Ann Jones's response was so soft that Susan did not catch it. Susan instinctively moved towards the door so that she could hear better – then realized she was trying to listen to a private conversation. She moved silently away, and just in time, for someone else was walking in the corridor. Leaving the servants' area and descending the stairs, Susan wondered if Maria would ascertain what troubled the housemaid. Susan hoped that Ann Jones would confide in someone, for that would ease her distress, but it was vexing to think that Jones might prefer confiding in Maria to confiding in her. Susan tried to persuade herself not to be so silly. First, there were many reasons that Ann Jones could prefer Mrs. Rushworth as a confidante. Maria must have known Jones when she was first at Mansfield Park; perhaps they had formed a friendship then. Perhaps Jones's difficulty involved something indiscreet, and lowering her reserve with the guilty Mrs. Rushworth could prove easier than with the innocent and inexperienced Miss Price. Perhaps the fact that Mrs. Rushworth did not reside at Mansfield Park made Jones's sharing of her troubles easier, rather than telling someone whom she could expect to see every day. Or perhaps Maria had simply come across Ann Jones at a propitious moment, when the housemaid's heart was so overburdened that she was ready to talk.

Or, as Susan had not actually heard what the housemaid said, it was possible that she had *not* confided in Maria, but had rebuffed her. As the bell rang for dinner, Susan reminded herself of her uncle's words: no secret could be kept for long at Mansfield Park. Susan's curiosity would be satisfied eventually, even if not in the manner she preferred. In the meantime, she should spend what time she could with the visitors; the estate rarely had so much company.

She went to the drawing-room where the family were assembling, and, as the place next to Lady Bertram was occupied, she chose a position near Mr. John Yates. "Is my cousin Julia feeling well?" she inquired, because Mrs. Yates was not in the room. Her honorable cousin-in-law started at the question, and then said he thought she was, and that she would join them momentarily. He rose, and departed from the room, leaving Susan alone near the fireplace. Mr. John Yates returned shortly afterwards with his wife, and everyone went in to dinner.

Susan was correct that Mansfield Park would be less crowded soon. Mr. George Yates announced that, if the weather allowed, he planned to depart the next day. Tom Bertram expressed disappointment, but Susan knew her cousin well enough to comprehend that his regret was perfunctory; Tom uttered only one sentence pressing Mr. Yates to stay longer. In fact, even though Mr. Yates was the elder son of a baron, no one at Mansfield Park seemed to want him to remain. Sir Thomas was eager to have him gone, partly because he disapproved of gaming, but also because he preferred to have his family party to himself. Lady Bertram sensed her husband's wishes and followed his lead; besides, Mr. Yates was too loud and too animated for the placid mistress of Mansfield Park. Mrs. Norris seemed to believe that Mr. Yates was about to succumb to Susan's charms – based on what evidence, Susan could not comprehend – and as Mrs. Norris could not tolerate the elevation of another indigent niece, glowered at him. Mrs. Rushworth was polite, but seemed unhappy with Mr. Yates about something; Susan wondered if some unpleasant exchange had happened during their ride that morning. Julia Yates said nothing, but stared with hostility at the partridge leg on her plate. As for Mr. John Yates, even he did not encourage his brother to stay, but made inquiries about his impending travel. "Will you visit our father?" asked Mr. John Yates.

"I do not plan to," said Mr. Yates. "I do not think he would see me."

Susan wondered at this; what sort of father would refuse to see his son? Not that her own father was known for his paternal affection, but at least Mr. Price was proud of his children, especially of his sons who were making their careers in the Navy.

Her reaction, however, was confined to herself. Mr. John Yates seemed to be the only other person who heard his brother's comment, and apparently the remark did not surprise him.

The ladies' part of the dinner ended, and they withdrew to the drawing-room. Sir Thomas kept the young men longer than usual over wine; Susan suspected that her uncle wished to forestall any card games. The gentlemen entered the drawing-room at last, but only briefly: Tom and the brothers planned to play at billiards. Mrs. Norris and Mrs. Rushworth crowded around Lady Bertram, relating anecdotes about Ireland, while Susan conversed with Sir Thomas about how he wished her to help him inventory a collection of curiosities. Julia occasionally spoke to her mother.

Julia, yawning, retired; Maria excused herself as well. Sir Thomas said he wished to review some papers, and Susan found herself alone with Lady Bertram and Mrs. Norris. Susan had spent many pleasant evenings with Lady Bertram, either playing a quiet game or working together, but with Mrs. Norris in the room, their usual activities needed to be put aside. Susan picked up the poor basket, seated herself near a window, and began to sew.

"Sister, I am glad to have the chance to speak with you alone," began Mrs. Norris.

Susan, across the room, raised her eyebrows at this. Did Mrs. Norris consider her to be little more than the furniture?

"Maria misses you terribly. She wishes to come home to stay."

Lady Bertram remarked that, given the amusing tales Maria had related, it appeared as if she were enjoying her time in Ireland.

Mrs. Norris used that opening to praise her eldest niece, how she tried to be optimistic and cheerful, and that no one had a better nature than Maria, but nothing could supersede home in one's heart, especially if that home were Mansfield Park. "I, too, miss Mansfield Park," added Mrs. Norris. "And most of all I miss you, dear sister."

Susan reflected that Mrs. Norris had not seen her other sister, Susan's own mother, in more than twenty years, but did not seem to miss Mrs. Price. Not that she wished for Mrs. Norris to inflict herself on her poor mother!

Lady Bertram reminded Mrs. Norris that Sir Thomas was still unhappy with what Maria had done, but that he might relent – not to let Maria resume a permanent residence at Mansfield Park, but perhaps he could find her another situation, in England instead of another country.

"I suppose that is an improvement. But I find it strange that Sir Thomas can banish a daughter only to welcome a niece." And Mrs. Norris glanced in Susan's direction and proved that she was aware of her. "Susan, I wish to speak with my sister in private. You can take your work somewhere else."

At Mrs. Norris's words, Susan colored. "Aunt Bertram, do you wish for me to depart?"

Lady Bertram seemed at a loss at being appealed to this way. Mrs. Norris answered for her sister. "I assure you, Susan, my sister and I will do very well together."

Summarily dismissed, Susan took the basket and left the drawing-room. So much for an amusing evening! So many people in the house, and yet there seemed to be no one who wanted to speak with her. On the other hand, the others did not seem to be having a pleasant evening either. What was wrong? Why was everyone cross and dispirited? Had the quarrel between Ann Jones and Stephen Jackson, the maid and the groom, somehow affected the entire household? Yet that did not ring true. Ann Jones had been in tears *before* her conversation with Jackson. Or perhaps people were uncomfortable because of Mrs. Norris, whose sharp tongue made few happy? Then she heard male laughter emanating from the billiards-room; at least some people were enjoying themselves.

Susan went to her uncle's study, and asked him if he needed anything, but he said he did not, that he wished to be alone, so she went to a staircase and climbed towards her chamber.

She reminded herself that she was young, a poor relation, without the ties that went back many years. Mr. Yates and Mr. John Yates were brothers, and Tom Bertram their brother-in-law. Lady Bertram and Mrs. Norris were sisters, as were Maria and Julia. Compared to everyone else, she was an intruder with few claims.

Susan wished she could speak with her own sister. Dear Fanny! Even though Susan had always valued and loved Fanny, now that Fanny was no longer at Mansfield Park, Susan felt that her appreciation these last two years had been insufficient. Was *that* her problem, her reason for feeling so unsettled – that she missed Fanny? And how was the new Mrs. Bertram finding married life? Was she as happy as she had hoped? The reports from the others had been pleasant, but Susan was not confident that the party on horseback had keenly observed everything.

Susan went to her room with the poor basket, but instead of applying herself to seams and hems, she put the basket on a stool and went to her little writing desk to compose a letter to her sister in this last hour of summer sunlight. During the last two years she had occasionally assisted both her uncle and her aunt with their correspondence, and because of that her own composition had improved. *Dear Mrs. Bertram*, she began, and then followed with a sentence explaining how much she missed her.

The evening that Susan had expected to be dull was spent in pouring out her thoughts and ideas to her sister and was more absorbing than she could have ever anticipated. When the sun was setting, and her own words were becoming difficult to read, she paused to light a candle, mended her pen with her penknife, and then continued, telling her sister about Mr. George Yates and Mr. Rushworth's horse, how tired and unfriendly Julia was, how a disturbance among the servants was troubling Mansfield Park, and the awkwardness of dealing with Maria Rushworth, when so many subjects could not be broached because they were indelicate.

Speaking of indelicate subjects, Mrs. Norris has accused me of being interested, in a romantic way, in my cousin Tom, and has advised my uncle and my aunt to do whatever they can to prevent our engagement! Tom was annoyed as well, and he later told me that he was not worth having. I do not know where these suspicions are coming from, and now I am rather uncomfortable, when before our friendship was so pleasant. Can you advise me, Fanny, how I should behave?

That was the awkward paragraph, the one that was difficult to write, and so embarrassing that Susan was not sure she could even send the letter. What if someone else read it? She blushed to imagine even dear Edmund reading it, yet was that not likely? Did not husbands and wives, especially those so recently married, strive to tell each other everything? Yet this was the one matter on which Susan desperately desired counsel. How unfortunate that Fanny was seven miles distant! It was as if she were impossibly remote, like William, on some ship in the Atlantic. Susan sorely missed her sister, and decided she should be more charitable towards Maria and Julia, or even Mrs. Norris and Lady Bertram, and encourage those pairs to profit from their sisters' companionship while they could.

Susan finished the letter with words of gratitude and good wishes, and signed it – but she was still not sure if she would send it. She could not send it this evening, anyway, so she could reconsider in the morning. She folded the letter and hid it under a book.

CHAPTER SIX

Susan glanced out the window. The days were at their longest, and the sky was not completely dark. She had no wish to sleep, and still had a desire for company. Her gaze fell on the neglected poor basket. If she returned it to the drawing-room she might find someone willing to partake in conversation. She picked up the poor basket and started downstairs, passing Mr. John Yates, who was heading in the other direction.

"You are finished with billiards?" Susan inquired.

"I beg your pardon?" responded her cousin's husband, as if his thoughts were elsewhere, and then he seemed to understand. "Ah, Miss Price, no more billiards for me, at least not at present. I – I wish to see how Julia is faring," he concluded, and then his expression appeared so guilty that Susan was confused. "Pardon me," he said, and hastened up the stairs.

Susan hoped that her encounter with Mr. John Yates meant that all the men had stopped playing billiards and that Tom Bertram and Mr. Yates had returned to the drawing-room. Even if she had been warned against making a match with either of them, Tom's good humor made him her favorite cousin, and Mr. Yates's conversation at least offered novelty. She did not need to speak much; she would be content simply to listen. But the sounds from the billiards room promised disappointment in the drawing-room.

Nevertheless, Susan continued to the drawing-room, prepared to amuse Lady Bertram, to listen to Sir Thomas on any subject he chose, or even to endure the unkind remarks of Mrs. Norris. Perhaps she could ask Mrs. Norris about maintaining a household in Ireland. Mrs. Norris was an economist, dedicated to spending as little of her own income as she could; perhaps Susan could divert her remarks.

Yet Susan's good intentions were for naught; except for the fire, the drawing-room was empty and dark. Neither aunt was to be found, which meant that Lady Bertram must have gone upstairs, possibly to spend time with her daughters or probably to her own room. Susan returned the poor basket to its usual position; at least she was spared Mrs. Norris's inquiries regarding how much, or rather how little, sewing Susan had accomplished. She took a seat, hoping that one of her relations would appear, but no one seemed to be around, which was peculiar for a house so full of people. The only person who entered the room was the butler, asking if she wished for the fire to be built up. Noticing that Baddeley seemed fatigued, Susan told him that no fire was necessary on her account. To put him at ease, she left the drawing-room.

Susan could reach her room either by the front stairs, generally used by the family, or by the back stairs, generally used by the servants. Doubting she would see any of her family, she decided to use the stairs in the back. Perhaps she could exchange a word with Ann Jones, and finally discover what had so distressed the housemaid. Yet none of the servants seemed to be around either, although she did hear laughter from down a corridor. Susan slowly climbed the stairs, resigned to retiring; perhaps tomorrow would be more interesting. But as she ascended, she did encounter someone: by the light of a candle, Mr. George Yates appeared to be examining something in his hand.

As she approached he started, and stared, and then smiled as he closed his fist. "Is that you, Miss Price? The helpful niece and poor cousin?"

"Yes," she replied. She did not particularly like his representation of her, but she would not quarrel with it.

"You are very like your cousins," he remarked. "At first I thought you were Mrs. Rushworth or my fair sister-in-law herself."

"I suppose," said Susan. She had longed for a bit of conversation, but speaking to Mr. Yates – and on the back stairs – was not what she had had in mind. With the advantage of the steps he seemed especially tall, and although she did not understand it, his presence made her uneasy. Yet, why should they not converse?

He slipped the hand with the object into his pocket. "Apparently my watch needs repair. But as I will be leaving you tomorrow, I will get it to a man soon enough."

"Then you are definitely leaving tomorrow?" she asked. If Mr. George Yates wished to make an early start, and avoid riding in the heat of the day, retiring early would be sensible for him. She wondered what he was doing on the back stairs.

"That is the plan – unless someone gives me a reason to remain."

"Then I wish you a good evening." Susan attempted to continue up the stairs.

"You are very pretty, Miss Price." He did not move out of her way.

Her heart pounded. "Thank you, Mr. Yates. If you will let me pass..."

He did not let her pass but remained on the stairs. "It must be a dull and dreary life for you here. Oh, not this week – not with your cousins all visiting, and a fine fellow like myself – but most of the time, cooped up with your serious uncle and your silly aunt."

"Mr. Yates, I am very grateful to my uncle and my aunt."

"Yes, you seem capable of gratitude. But you, such an attractive young lady – you are wasting your life here. You should be enjoying yourself. Would you not prefer to be in London – to go to the theatre – to be with people?"

"I have never been to London."

"I could take you there."

His offer – was he making her an offer? – was so unexpected that she was confused. "What? *You* take me to London?"

"Yes, to London, to Ireland, to any place you would like to see. What place would you like to see, Miss Price?"

And then she comprehended that his offer was *not* a marriage proposal, but something far less honorable. She felt her cheeks redden as she said, "You are talking nonsense, Mr. Yates. Please, let me pass."

"Are you sure? You will soon be as pretty as your cousin – Maria, I mean, not my dear sister-in-law. We could have fun. I could show you the world, Miss Price – Susan."

He reached for her hand. His was warm and strong. Susan attempted to pull hers back, but he did not release it.

"*Please* let me pass, Mr. Yates."

"You could leave with me in the morning; my horse could easily carry us both. Your uncle is only your uncle; he will not stop you."

He was making her extremely uncomfortable, even nervous. He was much stronger than she was. Surely he would not accost her here on the stairs? Should she run back down and then return up the other staircase? Or should she even call out for assistance? But to do that – to raise an alarm – would cause even greater consternation than had already been caused.

She was spared from having to summon help when a door creaked, and footsteps announced the approach of another person. The bustle soon revealed Mrs. Norris. "I thought I heard something! I was afraid some thief was coming up from the servants' quarters. I do not like the look of the new kitchen maid! Susan, what are you still doing up? You should be in bed, not inflicting your company on Mr. Yates."

It was not especially late, but Susan did not object. "I am going to my room now, Aunt," she said. With the presence of Mrs. Norris, Mr. Yates finally let go of Susan's hand and permitted her to pass him on the stairs.

"I would hardly call Miss Price an infliction," Mr. Yates called after her, and laughed.

Susan tried to walk with dignity, but as soon as she judged that she was out of their sight, she hurried her steps. To think that she should be so importuned! And in her uncle's house! How could he believe her so susceptible? Of course, Mrs. Rushworth's reputation was blemished, and Susan was merely the niece, and not the daughter, of a baronet. Still, what made Mr. Yates believe she would acquiesce to such an immoral proposal?

Even though he had released her hand, Susan still seemed to feel his pressure on it. What if Mr. Yates followed her up here and attempted to enter? And then attempted something far worse than an improper conversation? The door could not be locked, but never before had she had a need to lock her door. Susan owned few valuable items, only keepsakes that mattered to her but that would be of little worth to anyone else. The one exception was a silver knife that had been given to her by a now-deceased sister.

Susan could not lock her door, but she could barricade it. She dragged a chair and a small table in front of the door, and piled on books and even a pair of shoes. She did not believe that the items were heavy enough to truly stop Mr. Yates if he were very determined, but the noise that would be made by pushing against the pile of objects would give her the time to act, if action were necessary. Susan changed into her night clothes, armed herself with the silver knife – not the most powerful of weapons, but it was all she had – and climbed into bed and tried to sleep.

Slumber did not come easily, however; her mind was too busy. Why did some men assume that their attentions were welcome when they were not? She recalled how Mr. Henry Crawford had persisted in wooing her sister Fanny, despite Fanny's repeated refusals. Mr. Crawford's behavior towards Fanny had at least appeared honorable. Mr. Yates's behavior was inexplicable; Susan did not think she had given him any encouragement. Perhaps the eldest son of a baron believed he needed none.

Susan decided to avoid Mr. Yates as much as possible during the following day. He was supposed to depart, which would make it easy, but if for some reason he did not, she would stay close to Lady Bertram, retreat to the shrubbery, or even do errands in the village.

That resolution made, and the silence of the house convincing her that no one was approaching, Susan finally found repose. Her disturbed night caused her to sleep past her usual hour, and she only woke when a maid exclaimed at her inability to open the door. Susan hurried out of bed and pushed aside the furniture, so that the servant could enter.

The sunbeams streaming through the window gave Susan courage; what seemed threatening in the dark of night became nothing in the light of day. She would make sure she was not alone with Mr. George Yates today, but surely she could dare to partake of breakfast. She dressed hastily and ventured to the stairs. He might already have departed, but if he had not, she could speak to her uncle. She had longed for company, for visitors, and the entertainment they might bring, but Mr. Yates was not amusing, not amusing at all. She now understood her uncle's reluctance to let strangers disturb the tranquility of Mansfield Park.

CHAPTER SEVEN

Sometimes resolutions are easier to keep than expected; when Susan arrived downstairs, Mr. Yates was not in the breakfast parlor. In fact, the room had only one occupant, Sir Thomas; although they were joined moments later by Mrs. Norris and Mrs. Rushworth. Mr. John Yates entered and said good morning; Julia and Lady Bertram, the married ladies, would take breakfast in their rooms.

Susan was still apprehensive, every footstep outside the room made her worry that the man she did not wish to see was about to enter. Mr. Yates did not arrive, however; nearly all footfalls were followed by the appearance of a servant bringing either coffee, bread or boiled eggs. Near the end of the meal, Tom sauntered into the room, yawning, then sitting down heavily and calling for a cup of tea. "Late night. Think it will rain, can see clouds on the horizon. Not a good day to travel, but might take a short ride before the storm strikes. Yates, where is your brother?"

Mr. John Yates said that he did not know. "I tapped on his door this morning, but he did not answer," and then added that his brother was probably sleeping late.

Sir Thomas, frowning, agreed that the weather would be inclement and that he recommended no one ride. "I suppose that Mr. Yates will be obliged to remain with us at least one more day."

This information seemed to please no one at the table, from Sir Thomas, who shook his head at the prospect of this continued intrusion into their family party, to his son Tom, who glanced briefly with an apologetic look at Susan. Susan wondered if Tom had failed to keep his promise and had engaged in a wager with Mr. Yates – or could her cousin be aware of how Mr. Yates had importuned her on the stairs? Mrs. Norris might have said something, with hints and allusions to make Susan appear culpable.

"I am concerned that Mr. Yates has not joined us yet," said Sir Thomas. "Perhaps he is unwell."

Tom remarked that Mr. George Yates had appeared to be in good health the evening before.

Sir Thomas, master of Mansfield Park, would not be derelict in his duty, even to a guest he did not much like. The baronet told a footman to go to Mr. Yates's room and to determine if he required anything. While the rest of them waited for information about the heir to the Baron of Dexthorpe, they discussed possible plans for the day at Mansfield Park.

"I should so like to take a little excursion," said Mrs. Rushworth. "I have not seen Mansfield Common in years!"

Sir Thomas repeated that he believed it would rain. "You will be wet through and through."

Poor Mrs. Norris had to choose whether to support her dear Maria or to flatter Sir Thomas; her decision was assisted by the appearance of several drops on the window pane. "Sir Thomas is right; Maria, you will have to postpone your ride until another day."

"If the rain clears, we could go to Mansfield Common in the afternoon," said Tom. "Sue, do you like that ride?"

Mrs. Norris bristled at Susan's being asked for her opinion and especially at the implication that Susan could be a member of any riding party. Susan hesitated because she did not want to do anything with Mr. Yates, who would surely accompany them, and although the excursion sounded amusing, and this was the first time for Tom to invite her, Mrs. Norris's speculation about them becoming a pair increased her uneasiness.

"The ride is very pretty. I do not know that I could go today, especially not if Cousin Maria wishes to use the mare," said Susan. "Besides, Lady Bertram may need me."

"*I* will attend to Lady Bertram, Susan," said Mrs. Norris. "You had better attend to the poor basket. I examined it this morning, and I cannot tell that you accomplished anything. What were you about last night?" She turned towards the baronet, and continued: "I can tell you what Susan was about last night, Sir Thomas – she was speaking to Mr. George Yates on the back staircase."

Susan was startled by the warmth of her aunt's attack, but she did not protest because she had *not* done any sewing and she *had* spoken to Mr. Yates on the stairs. Nor did she explain that she had spent the time writing a letter to Fanny, because she had still not decided if she wished to send it or burn it.

"*And* Mr. Yates and Susan were holding hands."

This last remark of Mrs. Norris caused all eyes in the room to turn towards Susan; Sir Thomas's expression was most grave. "Is this true?" he asked.

Susan colored deeply, but she was ready to defend herself. "Mr. Yates *took* my hand, Uncle; I did not offer it to him. Only when my aunt appeared did he release it."

Her words provoked changes on the countenances of her listeners. Mr. John Yates appeared concerned; Tom and Mrs. Norris seemed angry, and Mrs. Rushworth frowned. But before anyone could speak, Sir Thomas terminated the topic. "I think this is a matter better discussed privately," he said firmly.

Susan was grateful for his statement. She did not exactly look forward to having a tête-à-tête with her uncle about the incident, but that had to be an improvement to the embarrassment she was experiencing at the breakfast table.

The subject of Mr. George Yates was not finished, however. The footman returned to explain that Mr. Yates was not in his room, and that it appeared that he had not slept in his bed.

"So, has he departed?" inquired Tom Bertram.

The footman did not believe so, for Mr. Yates's traveling bag was still in his room. Sir Thomas frowned and dispatched the footman in the direction of the stables to determine if Mr. Yates's horse were still in the stables. In the meantime, those at the breakfast table plied Mr. John Yates with respect to his brother's habits. Was it like him to depart without saying good-bye? Mr. John Yates said he did not think so, but he could not be sure. Could he be out wandering the grounds? That was more likely; Mr. Yates liked late hours and occasionally stayed up the entire night. Last night the moon, though not quite full, had given enough light for those determined to be outside.

"I know we are brothers," said Mr. John Yates with a sigh, "but we have not lived together for years and we are not similar in our tastes and habits."

"Could he be asleep somewhere else?" asked Mrs. Rushworth.

"Susan was the last person to see him," said Mrs. Norris, returning to this topic despite Sir Thomas's prohibition. "As I say, they were holding hands."

Susan flushed, for the implication was that she had admitted him into her room. "Aunt Norris, I assure you I am completely unaware of Mr. Yates's whereabouts." Then, rallying with logic she continued: "When all three of us were on the back staircase, you saw me leave him. Which means *you* were the last person to see him, not I."

Susan was shocked by her own outburst – Fanny would have never spoken so! – and Mrs. Norris also turned red. "I have never heard anything like"—she began, but then Tom Bertram interrupted to suggest that perhaps Mr. Yates had simply not gone to sleep at all – perhaps he was injured somewhere on the premises.

Susan was grateful to Tom for the speculation. Certainly, it was wrong of her to hope that any guest at Mansfield Park could be lying somewhere unconscious, but she appreciated her cousin's diverting the conversation.

Before anyone could conjecture further, the footman returned and informed them that Mr. Yates's horse was not in the stables, and everyone exclaimed with astonishment.

"He departed without telling anyone?" said Mrs. Norris, full of indignation. "Not even Sir Thomas?"

"Yates did say he was planning to depart today," said Tom. "Perhaps he wished to go several miles before the rain started."

At least she was no longer suspected of hiding him in her chamber, thought Susan, and then aloud asked what they should do with the bag Mr. Yates had left behind.

"Perhaps he will send for it later," said Mr. John Yates. "Or – he may return for the bag himself. Perhaps he only intends to ride a short while, and he just meant to exercise the new horse."

Sir Thomas said that he was certain Mr. Yates could take care of himself. Whether he chose to return or not, they would certainly learn about it soon. The baronet had letters to write that day and could not concern himself with a visitor who departed without informing anyone.

For Sir Thomas, the words were quite harsh, thought Susan, but Mr. Yates had never been an invited guest, only someone who had imposed himself on those residing at Mansfield Park.

The baronet looked out the window; the rain was falling heavily. "Mr. Yates will have a wet ride," he pronounced.

CHAPTER EIGHT

When breakfast was finished, Tom Bertram and Maria Rushworth went into the drawing-room; Mr. John Yates went up to his wife and Mrs. Norris sought the company of her sister. Poor Lady Bertram, assailed by Mrs. Norris, thought Susan. But Mrs. Norris respected Lady Bertram more than she did most – a beauty in her day, and still handsome, with a rich, influential husband – and Lady Bertram's general serenity was a challenge for even Mrs. Norris to ruffle.

Susan asked her uncle if she could join him in his study. Informing Sir Thomas of what had happened on the staircase was painful and awkward, but postponing the conversation would only increase her agitation with unpleasant anticipation.

To Susan's great relief, Sir Thomas listened without comment and, when she was done, assured her that he believed her; that he knew and trusted her, unlike Mr. George Yates, who did not have the best reputation. "Perhaps we are fortunate that he is gone. If he *is* gone," continued the baronet, glancing out the window, where the rain had been joined by wind and thunder. "Given the weather, he may turn back."

Sir Thomas picked up a letter as if he planned to read it, but Susan was not finished; another idea had occurred to her. "Could this – could Mr. Yates be the reason for Ann Jones's distress, Uncle?"

Sir Thomas put the letter back down and sighed. He said he had also wondered about this. If Mr. Yates's horse were not gone as well, he would suspect the eldest son of a baron of being in a room with a maidservant – or worse.

Susan shivered at the "or worse," and what it implied. Even though dragging furniture before her door had seemed excessively cautious at the time, now she was glad that she had done it. Then she thought of Cousin Maria, or even more terrible, Cousin Julia!

"Perhaps one of the servants knows something," said Susan. "And perhaps someone – I suggest Mr. John Yates – should inspect what Mr. Yates left behind, to see if that yields any clues."

Sir Thomas authorized Susan to speak with the servants, especially Ann Jones, in case one had received a message from Mr. Yates and had failed to deliver it. He would send someone to talk to the men who worked in the stables; surely one of them had noticed something – unless Mr. Yates had saddled his own horse in the dark, unlikely albeit not impossible. However, the baronet was not ready, at this point, to search Mr. Yates's things, or even send his brother into Mr. Yates's room to do so.

"I will respect his privacy as long as I can," said Sir Thomas. "After all, he may appear at any moment."

Tom entered, prepared to review the Antigua accounts with his father. Sir Thomas protested that his eldest son only showed up when it rained; Tom retorted that the reproach was not just, yesterday they had had a guest and he had been occupied with his position as host. Susan smiled at the exchange, but as she was still embarrassed to be around her cousin, she left hastily.

Susan spoke to Baddeley, Chapman and Jones, but all of them claimed to know nothing about what had happened to Mr. Yates. Ann Jones colored at the mention of his name, but denied having had anything to do with him.

Not completely satisfied, but not knowing what else she could do, Susan went to the drawing-room and applied herself to the poor basket that she had neglected so thoroughly the night before. The other ladies – Lady Bertram, Mrs. Norris, Maria and Julia – were all gathered, as the chill and the gloom that accompanied the storm made the noble fire in that room's large hearth particularly inviting. The topic of conversation was mostly about Mr. Yates. Mrs. Norris was the most voluble. "Even if he is the heir to the Baron of Dexthorpe, his behavior is particularly odd. To leave a house in the middle of the night! Without telling anyone or even writing a note for people to find! It is most inconsiderate, especially to Sir Thomas, and to you, Sister, because of the worry it will cause you."

Lady Bertram, to whom this was chiefly addressed, stroked her pug. "I am certain we will discover where he is soon."

"Perhaps I am being uncharitable," mused Mrs. Norris. "Perhaps he went for a ride and was thrown by his horse and is lying injured somewhere. Maria, the stallion is rather spirited, is he not?"

Maria said she had never known that horse to throw anyone, but supposed it was possible, or that some other mishap might have occurred during a ride in the dark. She then addressed *her* sister. "Does Mr. Yates have a tendency to ride in the middle of the night?"

Julia was even less interested in the subject than her mother was. "I am sure that I do not know."

Susan informed the other ladies that she had made inquiries among the servants but had learned no intelligence.

Mrs. Norris peered at Susan. "A sensible thing to do," she said reluctantly, because she did not wish to offer that niece anything that could be mistaken for praise, "but I am sure you lack the necessary firmness to elicit complete answers. Certainly, one of them knows something. Especially someone in the stables. I could speak to them, Sister."

"Oh! I am sure that is not necessary. He has not been missing very long." The theoretical exertion, even offered by another, seemed to exhaust Lady Bertram, who was always a little more fatigued on rainy days.

Susan said that she believed Sir Thomas had sent someone to make additional inquiries in the stables; the information irritated Mrs. Norris, who wished to make the recommendation to the baronet herself. Before Mrs. Norris could vent more than two sentences to express her opinion about her niece's impertinence, their conversation was stopped by a loud disturbance in another part of the house.

Even Lady Bertram looked up, not exactly in alarm, but with more attention than usual. "Whatever is the matter?"

Mrs. Norris offered to go find out; her sister replied that it was surely not necessary. A few minutes passed, and then Lady Bertram's confidence was rewarded, as the male members of their family – Sir Thomas, Mr. Tom Bertram, and the Honorable John Yates – entered the drawing-room.

"We have found Mr. Yates," said Sir Thomas gravely.

"Oh, have you?" asked Lady Bertram.

"Where is he?" inquired Mrs. Norris. "Has he apologized for all the difficulty and trouble he has caused?"

"No, George has not apologized," said Mr. John Yates dramatically. "George cannot apologize. George will never apologize. We – we should apologize to him."

"Whatever do you mean?" pressed Susan.

"He is dead," said Tom. "Mr. Yates is dead."

"Oh!" cried Julia, and fainted.

CHAPTER NINE

The ladies in the drawing-room received this information in their different manners. Mrs. Norris and Mrs. Rushworth both exclaimed in horror and demanded particulars. What had happened? Had there been an accident? Had he been thrown from his horse? Mrs. Norris added that riding in the middle of the night was pure folly. Susan, although just as curious as her aunt Norris and her cousin Maria, first tended to Julia, who fortunately had swooned in a sitting position. Susan fetched a cloth from the poor basket, poured water on it and pressed it to Julia's temple and her wrists. Lady Bertram wondered if she ought to faint as well but could not manage it, and only thought of offering her younger daughter a whiff of her own sal volatile after Julia had been revived by Susan's ministrations.

Mr. John Yates stopped ranting and assisted Susan by going to his wife's other side, kneeling beside her and taking her hand. Julia's eyes fluttered open; even though she remained pale, she assured everyone that she would not faint again.

With Julia reanimated and entrusted to her husband's care, Susan could attend to the conversation around her.

Mr. Yates's body had been discovered in a corner of the stables, under a small mound of hay. Sir Thomas was no medical expert, certainly not a coroner, but he and Tom had looked at the body and discovered evidence of several blows to the head as well as a gash in his neck that looked as if it had been caused by a knife.

"His throat was cut?" inquired Maria.

"A knife wound!" exclaimed Lady Bertram, so interested that she sat upright on her sofa and put aside her pug. "How could a horse have done that?"

Lady Bertram was still operating on Mrs. Norris's conjecture that Mr. Yates must have been thrown from his horse.

"No horse slashed George Yates's throat," said Tom. "No horse dragged his body to the mound of hay and hid him under it."

"A man must be responsible," said Sir Thomas.

"My brother murdered! Foully murdered! I cannot believe it," said Mr. John Yates, and now it was Julia's turn to comfort her partner.

"But who would wish to murder Mr. Yates?" inquired Lady Bertram.

Lady Bertram, with her kindly disposition, could not imagine anyone wishing to kill another, but Susan discovered, to her consternation, that *she* was not particularly sorry that Mr. Yates was dead. A murder was dreadful, of course, but if anyone was to die like this, of all her acquaintance she would have chosen Mr. Yates. And then Susan was ashamed of herself for being so unfeeling and for rendering such a harsh judgment on a man she knew so little. Mr. John Yates was overcome by the sudden death of his brother, while Julia had been so affected that she had fainted, literally fainted!

Susan decided she would never, ever confide her own uncharitable thoughts to anyone, not even to Fanny, who would be horrified by their cruel, unforgiving nature.

Sir Thomas explained that Mr. Yates's horse – the one he had brought with him from Sotherton – was definitely gone. "Perhaps someone was trying to steal the horse and Mr. Yates discovered him in the process."

"A horse thief must be responsible," said Maria.

Tom said this was possible. The animal had been especially valuable; perhaps someone had noticed Mr. Yates with it, or had learned of its removal from Sotherton.

Mrs. Norris proclaimed, "Of course the culprit is a horse thief! Some man came into the stables, wishing to steal Mr. Yates's fine new horse, and Mr. Yates discovered the man and then there was a fight and poor Mr. Yates was murdered."

Mr. John Yates said that he could not bear to think of it, of what had happened, and of course continued to talk of nothing else.

When her brother-in-law paused for breath, Maria said thoughtfully: "If we discover the horse, we may discover the man who murdered Mr. Yates."

"Yes," said Sir Thomas, but added that he was not hopeful. "It is likely that he is already far away."

"But is that not a good thing?" inquired Lady Bertram. "We do not want a murderer in the neighborhood! Or even a horse thief!"

Mr. John Yates then interrupted to say that it was especially horrible that his brother should be murdered and that the guilty party should escape justice.

When his son-in-law was done, Sir Thomas agreed with him. "It is better for everyone for the man to be caught and punished. That way, he cannot kill again."

"What a dreadful thing to have happen at Mansfield Park! I am so sorry for you, Sir Thomas, that you should have that happen in your stables. The trouble it will cause you and Lady Bertram!" said Mrs. Norris.

Maria had more penetration than her aunt, and was not as determined to flatter her parents. "I grieve for you, Mr. Yates. I cannot imagine the tragedy of losing a brother or a sister."

Of course, Mr. John Yates was now Mr. Yates, as he no longer had an elder brother.

Mr. Yates spoke some more about his loss, the shock at the suddenness and the horror of how it had happened.

When Mr. Yates's soliloquy was done – and given his situation, his speech was tolerated with more patience than usual – Susan, practical, asked what needed to be done, and what she could do to assist. She found paper, pen and ink and began taking notes. They needed to notify the coroner – Sir Thomas said he had already sent a footman on that errand – and to send an express to the Baron of Dexthorpe. Perhaps Mr. Yates knew what should be done with the body of his brother? Mr. Yates mastered himself long enough to say that the body should be transported to his family estate in C—. He would accompany the body. Tom said he would go with his brother-in-law; Sir Thomas nodded approval.

Mr. Yates was profuse in his thanks, and he also hoped the others would take care of his dear Julia while he made this melancholy journey.

"Are you sure you do not wish me to come with you?" asked Julia.

Women often did not travel to funerals, and especially, given the circumstances and the suddenness, Mr. Yates thought his wife would be more comfortable staying in her father's house. Everyone assured Mr. Yates that Julia was in good hands.

Those most important items being settled, Sir Thomas, with Susan's assistance, arranged for the express to be sent to Lord Dexthorpe. Then there were the secondary, but still significant, matters to manage.

"We can be assured that much of the neighborhood is aware of what happened," said Sir Thomas, for two notes of condolence and concern had been brought in by Baddeley. The Mansfield Park servants had spoken to servants not on the estate, and the latter had related news of the death to their masters and mistresses.

Mrs. Norris opined that it was rude of others to speak about Mansfield Park, while Lady Bertram said that she did not suppose it could be helped.

Sir Thomas was more methodical. He wished to inform people more formally, to make sure that everyone was warned, and to determine if anyone knew anything.

"That is very sensible, Father," remarked Maria. "Perhaps other stables have been robbed."

"Or at least they may know of attempts," said Sir Thomas. "If other stables had been robbed, I should expect to have been informed – unless the theft was extremely recent."

Lady Bertram added that they needed to tell Fanny and Edmund. "How strange, to think that they do not know!"

Susan was not sure what practical assistance either Fanny or Edmund could offer – and then reproached herself; Edmund, as a clergyman, could condole with Mr. John Yates, while Fanny's good sense would support them all. And Susan agreed with her aunt that it was odd that Fanny, who had known every particular of their lives until just a few days ago, could be unaware of something so significant. Then she said, "I believe the coroner is arriving." Her excellent hearing alerted her to the fact that someone was approaching the house, while her position near a window let her discern who it was.

Sir Thomas instructed a servant to take the coroner to the stables. After that aspect of the investigation was done, the coroner could come up to the house and they would resolve whatever needed to be resolved.

The baronet's statement nearly provoked another speech from Mr. John Yates – and although Susan was sympathetic, she wished to forestall it – so she suggested that Mr. Yates go to the room in which his brother had been staying in order to prepare his things to be transported with him back to C—. Sir Thomas nodded with approval, for his former objection to an inspection of Mr. George Yates's personal belongings had died with him.

"Should I not meet with the coroner?" inquired Mr. Yates.

Sir Thomas assured his son-in-law that if the coroner needed to speak with him, that he would be summoned, but in the meantime, Mr. Yates could spare his sensibilities. Sir Thomas then asked a footman to accompany Mr. Yates to assist with packing and his son Tom to attend to Mr. Yates to support his spirits.

Tom frowned briefly, as if he did not relish the assignment, but Susan was glad to observe that her cousin then banished the expression of distaste from his face. "Come, Yates," Tom said, rising and compelling his brother-in-law to rise as well.

When the young men were safely away, Maria spoke. "I suppose it is too early to offer congratulations, Julia."

"Congratulations!" exclaimed Julia, as if the term alarmed her, and then she asked cautiously, "Of what do you speak?"

Maria explained. "Your husband, Julia, is now the heir of the Baron of Dexthorpe."

"One day you will be Lady Dexthorpe," added Mrs. Norris. "An elevation, indeed, but one you surely merit."

Julia's eyes widened. "I suppose that is true."

Lady Bertram beamed at her younger daughter. "How lovely, my dear! I am so happy for you."

"Yes, it is an elevation, Julia, but we must recall the current circumstances. You should not celebrate too soon," said Sir Thomas, but even he had to struggle to appear solemn.

"No, Father," said Julia, and indeed she did not look particularly happy. In fact, Susan thought she appeared to be the only one in the room who was not affected by her change in status, despite that change being great indeed. Julia could expect rank and fortune in the future; the match which had originally so disappointed Sir Thomas appeared to have turned out well after all.

Of course, Mr. George Yates had been Julia's brother-in-law; his death was so shocking to her that she had actually fainted. What was interesting to the rest of them was dreadful for Julia. Again, Susan chided herself for her indifference; why was she not more distressed? A man who had been alive yesterday, who had accosted her on the stairs, yes, but who had lived and breathed and laughed – he was dead, dead forever.

Before Susan could persuade herself to be as distraught as her cousin Julia, Tom entered the room carrying an object that everyone recognized as an important item in Sir Thomas's collection of curiosities.

Sir Thomas asked, "Tom, what are you doing with my snuffbox?"

Sir Thomas did not use snuff, but the item was a memento, constructed from the hoof of a famous battle horse in the previous century. Sir Thomas's treasure usually occupied a particular place in one of the halls, so why Mr. Bertram should be carrying it into the drawing-room was a reasonable question.

"I found it in Mr. George Yates's room."

"And what was it doing in Mr. George Yates's room?"

Tom said that he did not know, and that he had come downstairs to pose questions on that subject himself.

No one knew for certain; Sir Thomas had not given permission to Mr. George Yates to remove it from its position of honor. Lady Bertram suggested that perhaps Mr. Yates had wished to use some snuff, but as the hoof was empty, everyone doubted her conjecture. Lady Bertram then suggested that Mr. George Yates had not realized that it was empty, but it was even more possible that he had not realized that it was a snuffbox. Everyone denied having described the item to him during this visit, but the fact that it was one of Sir Thomas's possessions was general knowledge.

"Could someone else have placed it in Mr. Yates's room?" inquired Mrs. Norris. "Some servant, perhaps, wishing to impress Mr. Yates by showing him such a valuable object?"

Although Mrs. Norris was ready to suspect the servants of anything and everything, those who lived at Mansfield Park were less willing to find fault with the domestics.

"Perhaps," Sir Thomas conceded. "If Mr. Yates expressed an interest in examining it. But why would he not come to me to ask about it?"

"Mr. Bertram," said Susan, "where was it in the room?"

At the formality of her address, Tom raised his eyebrows, but he answered her question. "That is what is so odd, Miss Price. I did not find it on a table, but at the bottom of his traveling case. It appears that George

Yates, who was killed by a horse thief, was not above stealing horse parts himself."

The information took them all by surprise, except for Lady Bertram, who did not quite understand and needed to have the situation explained to her by Susan; then she was as shocked as the others. "Mr. Yates planned to steal your uncle's snuffbox? But why would he do that?"

"For money, I suspect," said Maria.

Sir Thomas, holding the hoof, said: "We should not be hasty. We do not know what happened exactly."

"You are too good, Father, but you are right, as always. We should not be hasty to judge the dead, for not only is it cruel, they can no longer defend themselves," Maria said, and then added that she had never trusted Mr. Yates, who was not as sweet and kind as their Mr. Yates, Mr. John Yates.

Sir Thomas inquired of Julia if she had ever suspected her brother-in-law of theft. Julia reflected. "I do not know. Certainly, he seemed to have more money to spend than we could comprehend. We were aware that he was a gamester, and by all accounts his wagers were generally profitable, but we always mistrusted that information, because it is easier to lose than to win. We believed that the Baron of Dexthorpe was simply generous with his elder son."

Sir Thomas then asked his younger daughter if her husband would be very distressed if he inquired whether or not his deceased brother could have taken the hoof. Julia hesitated, as if she did not wish to deny her father this but as if she knew very well that her husband, already so affected by what had happened, would be overpowered by the suggestion that the elder Mr. Yates could have been a thief.

"Let me make the inquiries," offered Tom. "The subject will be natural to introduce while we are traveling."

Sir Thomas was pleased by this, either because he was happy to see his elder son taking responsibility, or simply to be spared his son-in-law's rants. He handed the snuffbox to Baddeley, telling him to return the object to its position of honor, then excused himself and his son to meet with the coroner, and to give directions about the body.

CHAPTER TEN

The next few hours were very busy. Notes of concern continued to arrive from friends in the neighborhood; Susan read them to Lady Bertram, wrote her replies, including one to Fanny and Edmund, who had learned the dreadful news.

Mrs. Norris went to make inquiries of her own and reported that Cook was terribly agitated, for a loaf of bread was missing and had been missing ever since the morning. Cook had made her own inquiries, and all the servants denied taking the loaf. Cook was now convinced that the missing loaf of bread was connected to the murder of Mr. Yates.

Maria expressed doubt – the two crimes were hardly of the same magnitude, and one had taken place in the stables while the other had occurred in the kitchens – while Mrs. Norris maintained that the stolen loaf of bread was worse because it had actually been *inside* Mansfield Park, which meant that the murderer was inside Mansfield Park as well! Lady Bertram placidly said that she did not think that they had a murderer in the house, but that she did not like the possibility that Cook could be upset. Meals suffered whenever Cook was distressed. Julia, as if she could not bear listening to the discussion, excused herself to go upstairs, professing that she wished to be with her husband. Susan observed Mrs. Yates with curiosity as she departed. Did Julia just wish to get away from the conversations she was hearing? Or did she wish to mourn her brother-in-law in private?

"Perhaps Mr. Yates took the loaf of bread with him to the stables," said Susan, and although Mrs. Norris was reluctant to approve anything uttered by any Miss Price, the suggestion was so satisfactory that even Mrs. Norris could find no fault with it. If Mr. Yates had been planning a journey, then he might have wished to take a loaf with him. The bread could easily have been removed by the horse thief, or eaten by birds or mice or even the horses.

The coroner declared the death to be murder by person or persons unknown; meanwhile arrangements were made for the transport of Mr. George Yates's body to the Baron of Dexthorpe's estate in C— and for the two young men to accompany it. The next morning, the rain still falling, the two young men departed, the vehicle with the coffin following the young men riding in Mr. John Yates's chaise. Watching them leave, Susan experienced a sense of emptiness; now no young men remained at Mansfield Park.

Susan joined the ladies, applying herself to the neglected poor basket while the other ladies paired off – Maria was speaking with Julia, and Mrs. Norris with Lady Bertram – and then Sir Thomas asked Lady Bertram if he could borrow Susan for a few hours.

"If you must, Sir Thomas," said Lady Bertram while Mrs. Norris said that, while she did not see what good Susan could possibly do for Sir Thomas, she assured him that she would look after everyone, especially Lady Bertram.

Susan put away her needle – really, she was not making any progress on the shirt – and joined her uncle. When they were beyond the hearing of those in the drawing-room, he explained that he wished to call at the Parsonage and to speak with the Grants. As the house nearest to Mansfield Park, it was possible that someone associated with it might have noticed something.

"I want another pair of eyes and ears with me," said her uncle, "and now that Tom is away, you are the only one here I can ask."

Susan expressed her willingness to be of service, and her eagerness was augmented by her great curiosity. Susan had only met the Grants briefly when she had first arrived, as the elopement of Mrs. Rushworth and Mrs. Grant's brother had made everything awkward and had reduced the intercourse between the families to mere formalities.

The Grants were extremely hospitable, with Dr. Grant offering, *"Media vita in morte sumus,"* and other choice phrases in both Latin and English about the frailty of life. Mrs. Grant inquired after the health and spirits of everyone at Mansfield Park, and asked that her kindest regards be conveyed to Lady Bertram. Mrs. Grant's sister, Miss Crawford, joined them as well. Susan had never met Miss Crawford, but she knew that Edmund had been in love with the petite, dark woman, and hence was particularly interested in this former rival of Fanny's. When Sir Thomas introduced her as "my niece, Miss Price," Susan perceived Miss Crawford's start. Poor Miss Crawford! From what Susan had gathered, she had also been in love with Edmund, and had expected to marry him. Through no fault of her own, instead due to the shocking behavior of others, Miss Crawford was separated from Edmund forever. Despite her pretty face, good humor, and twenty thousand pounds – an income of 1000£ per annum, so much personal wealth Susan could not imagine – Miss Crawford was still unmarried, hinting that, despite the more than two years that had passed, the disappointment of her heart had not healed.

The inmates of the Parsonage were aware of everything that had happened at Mansfield Park, including details about the body having been found in the stables and a horse having been taken.

"It is all so extraordinary!" Miss Crawford exclaimed. "To think that Mr. George Yates could have been killed by a horse thief!"

Sir Thomas asked Miss Crawford if she had been acquainted with Mr. Yates.

"A little," Miss Crawford admitted.

"I understand he was a good friend of my brother's, was he not, Mary?" said Mrs. Grant.

Alluding to Mr. Crawford in front of Sir Thomas was especially awkward; Sir Thomas's expression darkened, and Miss Crawford quietly said she believed so. After that, Dr. Grant invited Sir Thomas to come with him to speak to the man in charge of the Parsonage stable; Mrs. Grant accompanied them. Susan found herself alone with Miss Crawford in the parlor of the Parsonage and was wondering how to begin a conversation with this woman when Miss Crawford began speaking herself. She said she was glad to have a moment to speak with Miss Price. "Mr. Edmund Bertram and your sister are now married, are they not?"

Susan said that they were; the service had taken place a few days ago.

Miss Crawford was so perturbed that she could not remain seated. She rose, walked to the window and stared in the general direction of Thornton Lacey, although of course it was too distant, too blocked by trees and hills and houses, for her to see anything of it. Miss Crawford said, without turning, "I wish them every happiness. I do indeed."

Susan said nothing, but stared at Miss Crawford's back with pity.

"If only one could go back in time and make other choices! Wisdom often comes too late. But I expect that Fanny – I mean, Mrs. Bertram – is very happy and he – Mr. Edmund Bertram – must be as well. Your sister will make an admirable clergyman's wife, far better than – but this is the past, and we must concentrate on the present. You will convey my compliments – *I* dare not write – but you can do it for me. Would you do that for me, Miss Price?"

Susan said she would.

Miss Crawford thanked her, and then, finally turning around, crossing the room again, said she wished to discuss another matter: Mr. George Yates. "As I said, I knew him a little; I sometimes met him at the theatre and dinner parties and I know many things were whispered about him."

Susan inquired as to the nature of these whispers.

Miss Crawford, despite her forthright nature, was reluctant to speak. "I have several reasons for hesitating. First, we are not supposed to speak ill of the dead; second, I am not certain in my information – and third, Miss Price, you are so young that I do not wish to sully your innocent ears."

Susan had heard many shocking stories during her time in Portsmouth – her father, Mr. Price, had not repressed his tongue – and even at Mansfield Park she was not spared tales of disgrace and infamy. She assured Miss Crawford that she was willing to listen to anything. "You have information about the character of Mr. Yates?"

"I do."

"Information more pertinent than the information that can be given by his brother, Mr. John Yates?"

Miss Crawford colored. "Possibly. Mr. John Yates may not be aware of all that has been said about his brother. Sometimes we are unaware of the deficiencies in our nearest relations – something I have experienced myself – and I could understand if Mr. John Yates were reluctant to speak ill of, or even to *think* ill of, his deceased brother. And if Mr. Yates was killed by a horse thief, as I understand Sir Thomas believes, then my information may not matter. On the other hand, it *may*" – hesitating – "and I think it may be important for you, or at least for Sir Thomas, to know more about Mr. George Yates. I do not know everything and cannot speak with authority – especially not to your uncle; I cannot even imagine that conversation – but I will write to Henry, my brother, to ask him what he knows. I know Henry was with Yates recently, and may be able to provide information useful to Sir Thomas. It is the least I can do."

"You do not think that Mr. Yates was killed by a horse thief?"

"I think it wise to be open to other possibilities," said Miss Crawford.

"I do not think my uncle would have much confidence in any letter written by your brother."

"I am aware of that. Still, is it not important to know if the killer is not a horse thief but some other guilty party? If someone dangerous is among us, should we not know?"

Susan did not have a good opinion of the late Mr. Yates, but nevertheless she wondered if Miss Crawford were inventing things. Miss Crawford could simply be wishing for a reason to be readmitted into the society of some members of the Bertram family. On the other hand, what if Mr. Crawford did have something important to convey? "I suppose it would do no harm for you to write to your brother and to ask him for particulars," Susan said cautiously. "If the information is irrelevant, there will be no need to show his letter to my uncle."

"Yes!" agreed Miss Crawford.

Hoping to put an end to the tête-à-tête, Susan suggested they join the others, and Miss Crawford led Miss Price to another room.

The information learned at the Parsonage was not conclusive. The only item of interest was that an unfamiliar horse had been observed by Robert, one of the manservants, in the early morning. Robert had noticed the animal because it was walking along the road without a rider. The sighting had been shortly after sunrise, with the bright rays reducing visibility, so the young man could not give a detailed description of the animal nor be certain that its owner was not walking nearby. Other than that, none of the Parsonage's inmates had anything unusual to report. No one had been murdered; no one had been hit on the head or stabbed in the throat. No horses were missing; no one had broken into their stables. Those who worked in the kitchen assured Sir Thomas and his niece that they could not even report a loaf of stolen bread.

The Grants assured Sir Thomas, however, that they and everyone at the Parsonage would remain watchful and would inform him of anything that they learned or observed in the future.

Sir Thomas thanked them and then he and Susan departed to walk back to Mansfield Park. During this walk – the day had become very fine – Susan told her uncle about Miss Crawford's offer to write to her brother to inquire about Mr. George Yates.

"I cannot see what will come of it," said Sir Thomas, brusquely, not pleased by the allusion to Mr. Crawford. Then his tone softened, and he asked about Miss Crawford. "She must have suffered a great deal, after – and she was completely faultless. That is a dreadful consequence of misdeeds – so often the innocent are punished."

Susan said that Miss Crawford's spirits seemed a little agitated but that could be attributed to the murder that had taken place. "This was my first time to meet her, Uncle, so it is difficult for me to judge."

"Sometimes I forget that you have only been with us a few years. You seem a fixture at Mansfield Park."

"I am most sincerely attached to Mansfield Park."

CHAPTER ELEVEN

The shocking murder of Mr. George Yates was no longer so shocking; the deed had apparently been committed by a horse thief who had stolen a valuable steed, and although everyone was determined to remain watchful and vigilant, other subjects took precedence. After her return from the Parsonage, Susan found herself quizzed by Mansfield Park's other ladies, who were curious about the inmates but who either could not or would not call on the Parsonage themselves.

Lady Bertram was the most at ease with the knowledge that the Grants had returned to the neighborhood, and accepted Susan's conveyed civilities from Mrs. Grant with a smile, while Julia Yates yawned and appeared indifferent. Mrs. Norris and Mrs. Rushworth, however, were less tranquil. Mrs. Norris wished to know how everyone appeared and if they were still living in a luxurious manner. Susan said she could not judge; they had not been offered a meal, only some tea, and that, Sir Thomas had declined.

Maria's agitation was palpable, but she waited until a private moment to make her inquiries. When Julia fell into a doze and Mrs. Norris was complaining to her sister about the housemaid Ann Jones, how she had heard that young woman playing on a pianoforte when the shelves so obviously needed dusting, Maria approached Susan, who sat by a window, sewing. Under the guise of pretending to examine her work, Maria asked whom, exactly, Susan had met at the Parsonage; Susan said she had met the Grants and Miss Crawford.

"Not – not anyone else?"

Susan mentioned the servants.

"I suppose it is just as well. I never counted on meeting him here, and I have no wish to see him again, I assure you."

Susan was aware that the *him* was Mr. Crawford.

"And he is not expected at the Parsonage?"

Susan replied that she had heard no mention of such an expectation, but that Miss Crawford planned to write to her brother to ask him about Mr. George Yates. "Evidently they were well acquainted," said Susan, "and Miss Crawford believes we would benefit from understanding Mr. Yates's character better."

Maria was silent for at least a minute after this. "But the murderer is a horse thief, is he not?"

"That is what my uncle believes," said Susan.

The clock struck three and Susan informed the others that she heard a carriage pulling up to the front of the house. Given the degree of activity they had recently experienced, the arrival of a visitor was not a surprise, but so far the vast majority had either been men of business on horseback or servants carrying messages of concern and condolence. Certainly, however, someone was arriving, although Susan did not recognize the carriage or the livery of the coachman and footman – but everything appeared very fine.

"*You* should look, Maria," said Mrs. Norris.

Maria was curious enough to turn her head, and then exclaimed, "Oh!" – turning pink. "The carriage is from Sotherton," she explained.

"Sotherton!" exclaimed Julia; the information was sufficient to startle her out of her lethargy. "You mean to say that Mr. Rushworth is coming *here*?"

"Apparently so," said Maria. "He is descending from the carriage."

"Perhaps he is coming to see *you*, Maria," suggested Lady Bertram.

Maria shook her head. "I cannot comprehend why he should."

"I agree with my sister, Mr. Rushworth has come to see you," said Mrs. Norris. "He now realizes he lost a treasure when he lost you." Mrs. Norris had been a great proponent of the match between Maria and Mr. Rushworth; the marriage had been her greatest success; its dissolution, her greatest failure. Mrs. Norris, unable to blame her darling Maria for anything, faulted Mr. Rushworth and Mr. Crawford.

"If he is not coming to see you, then why is he here?" asked Lady Bertram.

"We will learn soon enough," said Julia.

"Do you wish to meet him, Maria?" inquired Susan. "Or would you prefer to go to your room?"

"Why? Mansfield Park is her house – at least Mansfield Park is her father's house," amended Mrs. Norris. "It is not for *her* to go and hide."

Maria and the other ladies waited in a state of tense anticipation, but they were disappointed, for Mr. Rushworth was not announced.

"I suppose Mr. Rushworth is speaking with Sir Thomas," said Lady Bertram, turning her attention back to her pug, to whom she was more attached than to her former son-in-law.

Mrs. Norris suggested tea. "I do believe that Baddeley is a little behindhand. And if Sir Thomas and Mr. Rushworth are inclined to join us, then we will have refreshment to offer."

Lady Bertram had no objection, so Susan rang the bell. They all sipped their tea, wondering if they would be joined by the men. Maria, tired of worrying about Mr. Rushworth's entrance, asked Susan to fetch the backgammon table.

Susan obliged but before the game could begin, a servant entered and asked Miss Price to join Sir Thomas in his study.

"Her!" Mrs. Norris objected at Susan's appearing to be the most relied upon by her uncle and her aunt. "Why her? *She* cannot be the reason that Mr. Rushworth has called. The caller is Mr. Rushworth, is it not?"

The servant confirmed that Mr. Rushworth, indeed, was at Mansfield Park but confirmed just as stoutly that Sir Thomas had requested Miss Price.

Despite Mrs. Norris's protests, Susan rose and went with alacrity to Sir Thomas's rooms. Like her aunt, she could not imagine why Mr. Rushworth would wish to meet *her*. But to quote Julia, she would "learn soon enough."

Sir Thomas was sitting with Mr. Rushworth, a tall, heavy man dressed in the latest fashion. She wondered if he always took such care with his appearance – surely the green vest was made of satin – or if he had made an especial effort in order to impress the residents of Mansfield Park.

"Ah, there you are. Mr. Rushworth, this is my niece, Miss Price," said Sir Thomas. And then, because Mr. James Rushworth appeared confused, Sir Thomas explained that this was Miss *Susan* Price, the younger sister of Miss Fanny Price, who was now married to Edmund Bertram.

"Oh! Yes, yes. I did hear something about that." But Mr. Rushworth expressed no hopes of happiness for the newly married pair.

"Susan, I have asked you in here because I want another pair of ears to hear what Mr. Rushworth has to tell us."

"Yes, Uncle," said Susan.

"Mr. Rushworth has some interesting information to share with us. It concerns his horse."

"His horse!" exclaimed Susan. "You mean, the horse that Mr. Yates rode from Sotherton to Mansfield Park? The one that was stolen during the night that—?"

"Yes, *that* horse. Go on, Mr. Rushworth. Speak."

Mr. Rushworth was not accustomed to speaking, at least not coherently, and moreover his narration was broken by a frequent need to clear his throat, which made him even less attractive. Susan was forced to exert patience as he told about how Mr. Yates had tricked him out of the fine steed, or at least how he suspected the fellow of cheating, but as a man of honor himself he had given over the animal, although with great reluctance. Yesterday, however, the horse had returned to Sotherton, on its own.

"I thought Mr. Yates had felt guilty for what he had done and had returned the horse himself," said Mr. Rushworth, "but then yesterday evening we learned he was dead, actually murdered, at Mansfield Park! So – Yates could not have returned the horse."

"No," said Sir Thomas. "Mr. Yates did not return the horse to Sotherton. And as it returned to Sotherton, it does not appear to have been stolen."

"No one stole the horse!" Susan exclaimed. "Then, Uncle, how did it get out of your stables? And" — she did not finish her second question, because she was struck by a dark idea, and she was reluctant to express it.

"That is an excellent question," said Sir Thomas. "How did it get out of the stables?" Then he asked the question that Susan would not. "And if no one stole the horse, who murdered Mr. Yates?"

Mr. Rushworth did not quite follow, but he spoke anyway. He said that he did not know who had killed Mr. Yates and he could not know who had released the horse from Mansfield Park, but he was happy to see the animal again, as it had always been a favorite.

Sir Thomas and Susan tolerated Mr. Rushworth's irrelevant remarks, then Susan began again. She did not want to relinquish the possibility of a horse thief too easily. "Is it not possible that the thief was thrown by the horse?"

Mr. Rushworth provided information more to the point. "That horse has an excellent nature. He is spirited, yes, but not unmanageable. He would never throw anyone!"

"Not even if the animal were harmed?" inquired Sir Thomas.

Mr. Rushworth explained that one of his grooms had done a thorough examination of the horse and had found no evidence of injury or abuse. A shoe needed repair, but that was all.

"Perhaps you are correct, Uncle, and there was no horse thief. Consider what we learned at the Parsonage, how one of the servants observed a horse without a rider the other morning," said Susan. "And the Parsonage is so close to Mansfield Park! And the road so good!"

"I agree that it seems unlikely that an accident could have occurred, especially on that stretch," said Sir Thomas gravely. "Besides, most horse thieves would be too skilled to let such a valuable animal run off."

"I am not experienced in horse thievery," Susan remarked.

"No, but I am," said Sir Thomas, and then clarified this odd statement by saying that when he had served as a member of parliament, he had been compelled to learn many details on the subject.

"But then how did the horse reach Sotherton?" inquired Susan.

Mr. Rushworth explained that the horse was a very bright animal that certainly knew its way home. "We always treated it very well at Sotherton. Of course, it wanted to return to Sotherton."

"Yes, but who let it out of the Mansfield Park stables? Unless your horse is intelligent enough to open and shut a gate, some man must be responsible," said Susan.

"Yes, that is the question we wish to answer," said Sir Thomas.

Mr. Rushworth replied seriously that he did not think the animal could have opened and shut a gate on its own – the solemnity with which he spoke caused Sir Thomas to cough while Susan moved her hand before her mouth to conceal a smile. Then Mr. Rushworth inquired about the ownership of the steed. "Is the horse now *my* horse? I did not bring it with me, because I heard about the murder, so I was not sure who would inherit. And the horse was obviously happy to be home and a shoe needed fixing."

Sir Thomas replied that he did not know who, given the circumstances, was the animal's proper owner. The deceased Mr. Yates had a father and a brother; presumably one of them would inherit. Sir Thomas promised Mr. Rushworth that he would look into the matter and then inform him of the result. In the meanwhile, the animal could remain at Sotherton. It was content to be at what it considered its home, and Sir Thomas was content not to be responsible for stabling such an expensive animal.

That business settled, the immediate question became what to do with Mr. Rushworth. Sir Thomas was obliged to him for having brought such useful information, but the awkwardness of having Mr. Rushworth at Mansfield Park when Maria was in the house could not be emphasized enough. Yet it was too inhospitable to send him back to Sotherton – a ten-mile journey – without more attention from those who lived at Mansfield Park.

Susan suggested a room in which Mr. Rushworth could take refreshment before returning to his carriage. Then she would ask if any of the ladies in the drawing-room wished to speak with him during the remainder of his visit; if no one obliged, she would attend to him herself.

Sir Thomas approved of this approach, only requesting that she rejoin him in his study when she was released.

Mr. Rushworth was happy to eat and drink and to receive any of the ladies. Susan then went to the drawing-room where she was assailed by questions. She answered briefly, relating the fact that Mr. Rushworth had had a matter to discuss with Sir Thomas – she would let her uncle explain – and that the visitor was in another room – if any of them would care to sit with Mr. Rushworth before he climbed back into his carriage to return to Sotherton, Mr. Rushworth would welcome any of them.

"Why would I wish to speak with Mr. Rushworth?" inquired Lady Bertram, who could not be bothered to put aside her pug and to stir from her sofa. Julia, too, said she had no inclination to meet her former brother-in-law.

Mrs. Norris and Mrs. Rushworth exchanged glances. "*I* cannot speak with him," said Maria.

"Very well, *I* will go," said Mrs. Norris. "After all, it is inappropriate to leave him with only Susan."

Susan agreed with Mrs. Norris, although she suspected they had different reasons, and led Mrs. Norris to the room in which Mr. Rushworth sat, enjoying a plate of cold meat and salad. Susan could not imagine what they would say to each other, but she did not much care, and she returned to her uncle in his study.

Sir Thomas stood by a window, gazing in the direction of Mansfield Park's stables. He asked about Mr. Rushworth; Susan joined him and explained that the visitor was being entertained by Mrs. Norris.

"The distance between the stables and the Parsonage is not very great," said Sir Thomas, pointing. "I do not see how anyone could have fallen off the horse between here and there."

"Do you believe that there was no horse thief?"

"That is what I believe. But someone wanted us to *believe* there was a horse thief – to believe that it was a thief who had an altercation with Mr. Yates and who then killed him. I now believe it was a ruse to disguise what actually happened."

"And what do you think actually happened, Uncle?"

Her uncle answered that whoever had killed Mr. Yates must have done so deliberately. Mr. Yates had suffered a blow to the head, which suggested that he had been struck from behind, and then had cut his throat.

"The manner of his death means that it was murder," said Sir Thomas, "and not, for example, manslaughter."

Susan had never considered the distinctions between these crimes, but it seemed the wrong moment to ask for an explanation.

Sir Thomas had more to say. The deed had been done at Mansfield Park, in the stables, by someone who knew that Mr. Yates was staying there, and who knew that his horse was in the stables and by someone who then released the horse to make it appear as if the killer had left Mansfield Park.

"Uncle, does that mean" – Susan began, but her idea was too dreadful to put into words.

He answered the question she could not ask. "Yes. It is all too likely that the killer never left Mansfield Park, but remains among us."

CHAPTER TWELVE

Susan, feeling her knees shake, moved away from the window and sat down.

"I see you comprehend," said Sir Thomas. "That is one reason I wished for you to join me; you are quick. And you are discreet. The servants trust you; you can help me interview them. And, although you may be shaken now, I believe I can depend on you. You will not faint; you will not succumb to hysterics. If possible, you can keep this from frightening everyone. I do not want to distress Lady Bertram or my daughters."

Susan, honored by the confidence her uncle had in her, promised to do her best. "However, if we interview those in the house, word of the investigation will spread."

"I know, but with some effort we can reduce the terror and the tumult. In addition, I do not want to provoke Mrs. Norris."

That was a powerful argument for keeping their inquiries unobtrusive. Susan did not argue her point any further, and listened and took notes as her uncle discussed the steps he wished to take: speaking at greater length with everyone who had been, or who might have been, at the stables; and working harder to better determine the movements of everyone in the house that night. As she helped her uncle create a list of tasks on how to proceed, she wondered how much discretion they could manage – and was discretion even wise? If a murderer lurked among them, would not warning the household be prudent? No one took pleasure in being afraid, of course, but fear could prevent people from taking unnecessary risks.

Her uncle also discussed questions he wished to answer. Could they fix the time that the murder had occurred? Who might have wished to do violence to Mr. Yates – so much as to wish him dead? Who would have had the strength to kill him? Who could have been in the stables at that time of night? Why had Mr. Yates been in the stables? And finally, who could have released Mr. Yates's horse from Mansfield Park?

"I think these points will help focus my inquiries," said Sir Thomas, after Susan read them back to him. "Are there any that you would add?"

"Yes." She explained that the manner that he was killed seemed odd. "As you say, Mr. Yates was hit from behind with something heavy, and after that his throat was cut. Is it not strange for a killer to use two different weapons?"

Sir Thomas considered, then said: "Perhaps to be certain that he was dead. A blow to the head might not kill someone, but a slash to the throat"—Sir Thomas then paused, as he focused on his niece. "I should not be subjecting you to these ideas. Although you have a sturdy spirit, especially for such a young woman, I am afraid I will be giving you nightmares."

Her dreams were already likely to be tormented, she thought. Aloud she said although she would not deny that she felt some anxiety, she preferred to be useful if at all possible. But then she had to ask if he would not find better assistance elsewhere.

Sir Thomas said that if Tom were home, he might turn to him, but with his eldest son away, and with Edmund and Fanny seven miles distant, Susan, despite her youth and inexperience, was the most reliable person in the house.

Susan promised to do her best, but before they could continue, the door was flung open and Mrs. Norris entered.

"Mr. Rushworth tells me there was no horse thief – that the horse was never stolen! What does this mean?" Before Sir Thomas could reply, Mrs. Norris continued. "Yet there must have been a horse thief! If there was no horse thief, then who killed Mr. Yates?"

So much for Sir Thomas's wish not to alarm the household, thought Susan, as Mrs. Norris described her conversation with Mr. James Rushworth. Mrs. Norris had been curious, she said, about Maria's former husband and how he was faring – and to determine if he had come to Mansfield Park in order to apologize or to find some way to attempt a reconciliation. If so, she was ready and willing to serve as an intermediary.

"Mr. Rushworth never deserved our darling Maria," said Mrs. Norris, and continued along this vein for a minute or two – but as Sir Thomas seemed disinclined for this direction of conversation, the older woman finally returned to the subject of Mr. Yates's death and the horse thief or lack thereof. "I asked Mr. Rushworth why, if he had not come to Mansfield Park to make amends to Maria, he had made the journey from Sotherton. He said the black stallion had returned to Sotherton, without a rider, and that *you* believe there never was a horse thief."

Sir Thomas said that was indeed his conclusion. Mrs. Norris persevered for a while, arguing that the crime must have been committed by a horse thief – Sir Thomas steadfastly opposed her, explaining that he had other information that indicated that no horse thief had ever existed – and insisted that he had to make inquiries, because the possibility of a murderer being at Mansfield Park, although dreadful to contemplate, was too dangerous to ignore. Mrs. Norris yielded, and praised Sir Thomas's goodness in guarding them all in these terrible circumstances. She promised that she would do everything within her power to protect and support the spirits of Lady Bertram and her two dear nieces.

Susan was also a niece, but Mrs. Norris did not include her in her reckoning.

Sir Thomas thanked Mrs. Norris for her intentions and invited her to sit down. He wished to inquire if, given the new circumstance, she had anything to add about what she had noticed during the night of Mr. Yates's death.

"Very well," said Mrs. Norris, and as she chose a chair, she seemed to notice Susan for the first time. "And what is *she* doing here?"

"Susan often takes notes for me," explained Sir Thomas, and upon that, Susan picked up her pen again. "As Tom is not here, she is the person most suitable."

Mrs. Norris sniffed, but made no more objections to Miss Price, and Sir Thomas posed his questions regarding Mrs. Norris's movements from that evening. Mrs. Norris had nothing more to add to what she had said before. Then Sir Thomas asked her if she knew if anyone at Mansfield Park had had any reason to dislike Mr. Yates particularly – or if she knew if anyone would benefit from Mr. Yates's death.

Mrs. Norris reddened. "Sir Thomas! I do not know what you mean."

Sir Thomas continued. "For example, we know that Mr. John Yates is now expected to inherit the Barony of Dexthorpe. That means that Mr. John Yates, and even my daughter Julia, benefit significantly from the death of Mr. George Yates."

"My word! You cannot possibly think that dear Julia had anything to do with this."

"I am not accusing Julia. I cannot imagine a woman hitting Mr. Yates on the head, slashing his throat, and then dragging his body to a corner of the stables and covering it with hay," said Sir Thomas.

"No, indeed! So, Julia cannot be guilty," said Mrs. Norris.

"But that does not acquit her husband. Besides, I intend to be thorough. If anyone at Mansfield Park had a reason to wish for the demise of Mr. Yates, I need to know about it."

Mrs. Norris maintained that Mr. John Yates certainly had nothing to do with the terrible deed – he had been so distraught upon learning that his brother was dead, and besides his sweet nature would prevent him from ever committing such an act. Nevertheless, Sir Thomas insisted on an answer to his question: did she know of anyone at Mansfield Park who might wish Mr. Yates an early departure from his life?

Mrs. Norris was actually silenced for a minute or two as she reflected on her brother-in-law's words. Susan observed her aunt's expression change several times, as if she were struggling with what to say.

"I did not know Mr. George Yates very well, so I cannot be expected to know much about who would wish him dead," said Mrs. Norris. "But the last person I saw him speak with was Susan."

At this, Susan ceased taking notes. Of course, Mrs. Norris's statement was perfectly true; she *had* spoken with Mr. Yates on the stairs. Yet the tone of her aunt's voice made her suspect that worse accusations were coming. Susan hastened to defend herself. "And you saw me leave, Aunt, and go up the stairs towards my room."

"Yes, but nothing can prove that you did not turn around and come back down," said Mrs. Norris. "And your conversation with Mr. Yates appeared animated. As well as inappropriate! You were holding hands!"

"He was holding my hand! Against my will! He only released it when you appeared."

Sir Thomas defended his niece. "Susan went to her room and barricaded herself from within."

"Did she tell you that?" said Mrs. Norris, her tone implying that Susan could not be trusted.

"Yes, and so did the housemaid," said Sir Thomas.

Susan started; she had not realized that her uncle had verified her statement.

Mrs. Norris considered. "Susan could have barricaded her room afterwards, so that no one would suspect her of killing him. The furniture before the door may have only been a ruse."

"Nonsense! What reason would Susan, who only met Mr. Yates a few days ago, have to kill the man?"

Mrs. Norris glanced at Susan, raised an eyebrow, then continued. "Very well. Suppose Mr. Yates made her an offer, an offer that sounded like a proposal of marriage. Suppose Mr. Yates then changed his mind, and decided all he wanted was an illicit relationship. That might make Susan angry enough to kill him, might it not?"

"You have many supposes," said Sir Thomas.

"You asked for speculation," said Mrs. Norris. "And although I cannot prove that Susan is guilty of the deed, as I was not – was not in the stables when the murder occurred, that does not mean that she did not do the deed."

Sir Thomas shook his head. "The same argument that applies to Julia applies to Susan. I cannot imagine any young woman having the strength to hit a man over the head, to cut his throat, and then pull him to a corner of the stable."

Susan felt immense relief, and even Mrs. Norris did not protest.

"Perhaps," conceded Mrs. Norris. "But Wilcox and Cooper have both told me that Susan is good with horses – not timid like Fanny. She would have been able to release that horse, to divert suspicion from her."

Sir Thomas sighed. "Very well, Mrs. Norris, you have presented a case against my niece, although I do not see how she could have physically done the deed, or how, in the short time that she spent with Mr. Yates, she could have managed to have the illicit relationship that you describe. Do you suspect anyone else?"

Mrs. Norris continued to speak, but in veins that were less distressing to Susan. Men in the stables had to be most suspect, of course, as they were on the spot, and also because they were men. Only a man would have the strength and the violent nature to do what had been done to Mr. Yates.

Much of this contradicted what Mrs. Norris had said moments ago, but as Susan preferred these words to what her aunt had said before, she did not point out her aunt's reversal.

A footman entered to say that Mr. Rushworth was about to depart, unless Sir Thomas wished him to stay.

"I will say goodbye to him," said Sir Thomas. He rose, and with his gestures, indicated that Susan and Mrs. Norris should leave his rooms as well.

"Will you need me, Uncle?" asked Susan.

"No, Susan. Not right now." His manner was grave.

Mrs. Norris returned to the drawing-room. Susan, needing to refresh her spirit after Mrs. Norris's suspicions and accusations, hesitated in the vestibule and then, instead of joining the other ladies, went outside.

CHAPTER THIRTEEN

Susan ran to the gardens. Her eyes were full of tears, making it impossible for her to really see the flowers, but the fresh air and the perfume of the blossoms revived and calmed her a little. If only Fanny or Edmund or even Tom were here; her dear sister and the cousins whom she knew better than Maria or Julia. They would defend her from such monstrous notions! Then she remembered that she did not wish for Tom to be at Mansfield Park, because then Mrs. Norris would accuse her of scheming to marry him.

How much had Fanny suffered from Mrs. Norris? Fanny had dropped hints, had warned her of Mrs. Norris's unpleasant nature, but Susan had not comprehended how personal and cruel her aunt's attacks could be.

Susan was also astonished by the breadth and scope of Mrs. Norris's story about her, and how plausible she had made her ideas sound, with such passion that Susan almost felt guilty, although she knew she was not. Susan might have done no violence to Mr. Yates, but had she not been less than completely sorry about his death? How wrong, how very wrong she had been, not to feel with force and conviction that the murder of another human being was evil, absolutely evil.

Susan walked with such haste that she nearly collided with a gardener, who was pruning one of the hedges. He was the only one out in this weather, for dark clouds threatened.

"Excuse me, Miss," he apologized, as she started.

"It was my fault," she said, and after that she paid more attention to her surroundings and continued at a more reasonable pace.

As Susan paused beside a tree she watched Mr. Rushworth depart in his fine carriage, with Sir Thomas bidding him farewell. After that Sir Thomas walked in the direction of the stables. As he certainly did not intend to ride at this hour, he had to be planning to interview those who worked in them.

Susan wondered if Sir Thomas suspected *her* of killing Mr. Yates. Surely he thought better of her; besides, had he not said that a woman could not have done this? He had merely listened to Mrs. Norris out of necessity, for she had had to have her say about Susan before she would discuss anything else. Although Sir Thomas surely did not believe Susan had murdered Mr. Yates, he could suspect her of inappropriate behavior with the gentleman, and although he might not condemn her to prison or to transport, she could be exiled from Mansfield Park. And even if her uncle did not believe Mrs. Norris, what about Lady Bertram? Mrs. Norris certainly had influence over her sister. Or what if Mrs. Norris's stories spread around through the neighborhood; what if they were deemed credible by Fanny and Edmund? Edmund, a clergyman who needed to keep his reputation free of blemish, would never permit her even to visit, let alone to live with them. Susan could be compelled to return to her father's cramped and disorderly house in Portsmouth.

Even in this weather, with the dark clouds above, Mansfield Park had a serenity that made her love it. Large drops of rain compelled Susan to go back inside and to meet her relations. Perhaps it was better to face them, and to put a stop to Mrs. Norris's insinuations, and to make sure that Lady Bertram, especially, was not influenced by them.

Sir Thomas was still out, but the ladies were all gathered in the drawing-room. The idea that the murderer was not a horse thief – that there had been *no* horse thief – had been conveyed to them. The matter was so animating that even Lady Bertram and Julia were participating in the conversation.

"Have you heard, Susan?" said Lady Bertram. "Sir Thomas believes that Mr. Yates was not killed by a horse thief, but by someone else – that a murderer could be among us! It is very disagreeable."

"Yes, Mama," said Maria. "We shall have to be careful."

Julia addressed Susan. "My aunt believes that *you* may have had a reason for killing him."

Susan's agitation increased; if the languid Mrs. Yates could attack her, all her relations could be thinking ill of her. She felt herself grow hot, but she defended herself with all the firmness she could summon. "I did not kill Mr. Yates. In fact, I had very little to do with him. He took my hand; I did not take his. I was eager, in fact, to get away from him."

Susan surveyed her audience to see if her words made any difference to them. Julia frowned, but Susan could not be sure why; these days she seemed to find everything distasteful. Lady Bertram nodded and smiled, while Mrs. Norris appeared angry. Maria flushed, perhaps not liking the subject of improprieties committed by women, and unexpectedly came to Susan's defense. "I do not see how any woman could have been strong enough to commit the murder as described. The murderer needed enough strength to strike him on the head with a blow hard enough to disable Mr. Yates – possibly to render him unconscious. Then she would have to have the emotional fortitude to take a knife to his throat. And finally, she would have needed the strength to drag him – and he was a large, heavy man – to a corner of the stable and to cover him with hay. Nay, no woman could have done this!"

Maria's words were both reasonable and persuasive, and Susan felt a little relieved. Still, she seated herself beside the poor basket and took out a shirt to hem; an occupation for her fingers might reduce the tumult in her mind.

"Of course, Susan had nothing to do with Mr. Yates's murder," said Lady Bertram. "She only just met him! Julia had a much better reason for wishing him dead, but it is impossible that she killed him either."

"Mama!" exclaimed Julia.

"My dear, I just said your killing Mr. Yates was impossible. As Maria said, it must have been some man."

"But which man?" asked Maria.

They were all silent, but Susan's mind worked as busily as her fingers. She could not imagine what reason any of the manservants could have for murdering Mr. Yates – unless it had been some accident, where one of the grooms had believed him to be an intruder into the stables, and so had hit him over the head. But why then cut his throat? To disguise the first deed?

But finding a reason for one of the gentlemen to have murdered Mr. Yates was not so difficult. Mr. John Yates had the most obvious motive, for the death of his brother made him the elder son, with the expectation of becoming the Baron of Dexthorpe in the future. As for Tom, what if he had succumbed to temptation and had wagered with Mr. Yates and had lost? He might prefer for Mr. Yates to die than to have to pay him, especially given his promise to his father. As for Sir Thomas, what if he had somehow discovered that Mr. Yates had stolen his snuffbox? Could that have made him angry enough to murder the man?

Imagining her uncle as a murderer struck her as absurd, because surely Sir Thomas would have simply demanded the return of the snuffbox and then banished Mr. Yates from Mansfield Park. But Susan could not be as certain about Mr. John Yates or even about Tom.

She glanced at the other ladies, who also seemed to be plagued by uncomfortable notions, for all of them were quiet.

"It cannot be Tom or John," Maria said finally.

"Of course, Tom did not kill Mr. Yates," said Lady Bertram. "Tom had no reason to do such a thing."

The other ladies, more familiar with Tom's gambling history, exchanged glances but did not contradict her ladyship.

Then Julia defended her husband. "John could never do such a thing. And if he had, he could never have kept quiet about it."

Susan wondered if Mr. John Yates's voluble grief about his brother had been an attempt to conceal other feelings, such as remorse or consciousness of guilt, but this was another thought not worth sharing.

No one mentioned Sir Thomas as the possible perpetrator.

"One of the servants," declared Mrs. Norris. "It must have been one of the servants. Or even that horse thief. We have been too quick to dismiss the horse thief. Perhaps one of the servants has an arrangement with a horse thief and when he was releasing the horse he was discovered by Mr. Yates and so killed Mr. Yates."

"But the horse was not stolen," Susan objected. "It returned to Mr. Rushworth at Sotherton."

"Oh! I have an idea!" exclaimed Lady Bertram.

Everyone stared at Lady Bertram, who did not generally exclaim or have ideas. "What, Sister?" asked Mrs. Norris.

"Why, Mr. Rushworth, of course! He wanted that horse again – everyone keeps saying that it is an extremely valuable animal."

Maria, who as Mr. Rushworth's former wife, knew him best, shook her head. "That seems unlikely."

"I agree; I cannot imagine Mr. Rushworth coming to Mansfield Park in the middle of the night to fetch his horse," said Julia, who had stayed with Maria and her former brother-in-law shortly after their marriage, and so was also well acquainted with his personality.

"Given Mr. Rushworth's resources, why would he not purchase the horse back if he wanted it?" said Mrs. Norris. Then, remembering that it was her object to flatter Lady Bertram at every opportunity, continued with: "Still, it is an interesting idea, Sister. After all, we may *believe* that Mr. Rushworth's finances are sound, but we do not *know* that. In fact, when I spoke with him a little while ago, he struck me as a very troubled young man, one who has made nothing but wrong decisions during the last two years. A very interesting and most satisfactory idea, Sister."

It was especially satisfactory, thought Susan, in that it cleared those at Mansfield Park and blamed a man whom no one in the family much cared for. Because it was so convenient an explanation, the other ladies all made attempts to discover ways and means in which Mr. Rushworth could be culpable, even dismissing Susan's point that a horse without a rider had been seen walking past the Parsonage during the morning after the murder. And although Susan was not quite prepared to believe that Mr. Rushworth was responsible for the death of Mr. Yates, she was prepared to add him to the list of people who might prefer Mr. Yates to be dead rather than alive. Really, a man had to work hard to create so many enemies in such a short time and concentrated in such a small area of England. How many more were out there?

CHAPTER FOURTEEN

Sir Thomas, despite his fondness for Lady Bertram, was not persuaded by her theory that Mr. Rushworth had murdered Mr. George Yates. The baronet did not wish to cause alarm in the household, and to reassure everyone he reminded them that the death had taken place in the stables and not in the house. Still, he felt obliged to warn everyone to take care and to report anything suspicious. Sir Thomas's grave speeches, meant to calm people, actually made them all nervous, and the ladies lingered long in the drawing-room that night. No one wished to be alone.

But mortals cannot do without sleep, and eventually everyone, from the baronet and his lady to the least in the kitchens, was compelled to retire and rest. The next morning, they awoke to discover no murdered corpses in their midst; no one was even missing.

The full accounting of souls reassured the ladies and most of the servants, but Sir Thomas was not content; he still needed to determine what had happened. So that day, after dealing with other pressing matters, he again questioned the servants in the stables about the night of Mr. George Yates's death. Susan did not assist during his conversations with those in the stables, but she did help her uncle review the reports of those he interviewed.

The men and boys who worked in the stables had a routine, and on that day and night they reported that they had maintained their usual habits. They walked, fed, and watered the horses before nightfall, then put the horses in their stalls, after which the boys, who did not live on the estate, went home and who therefore had seen nothing. When darkness fell, all had been as usual. The men who cared for the horses slept in quarters close by, with Wilcox, the old coachman, having the nearest rooms, while the grooms shared an upstairs apartment. Wilcox would have had the best view of anything, but he was older and a little deaf. Wilcox said he had not seen Mr. Yates that evening or that night, but he *had* seen a young woman near the stables sometime after dark.

The old coachman explained that during the night at some point he had risen, had gone to a table to pour himself a glass of water, had glanced through the little window and had seen what appeared to be a young woman leaving the area. He did not know the time – perhaps midnight, perhaps a little after, he could not say exactly – and he was not certain who the woman was, only that she seemed to be walking in the direction of the main house.

Sir Thomas told Susan that he had encouraged Wilcox to guess who the young woman might have been.

The old coachman said that he had assumed the woman was the housemaid Ann Jones, coming to see Stephen Jackson, because they sometimes did spend time together. He was aware the pair had quarreled recently, and thought that they might have been attempting to reconcile. Wilcox reported that the woman had walked alone, which now that he thought about it, was rather strange. Jackson would have insisted on accompanying Ann Jones back to the house, no matter that the distance was only a hundred yards. On the other hand, if they were still quarreling she might have refused his protection, and besides, Wilcox was not completely sure that the woman *had* been Ann Jones. He could only say that she had had the gait of a younger, rather than an older, woman. It had never occurred to Wilcox that the young woman might have done anything to one of the horses, and although Wilcox had few details to offer about the young female, he could say with certainty that no horse had been with her when he looked out the window. Sir Thomas asked if the young woman might have been with Mr. George Yates – to the coachman, the murder victim was less important than the horses – and Wilcox answered no, he had not seen Mr. Yates that night. But he had only looked out the window for a minute or two, so he could not answer for what had happened the rest of the night.

The other men, including Stephen Jackson, said they had seen nothing that evening nor during the night. Stephen Jackson also said he had not spoken with Ann Jones that evening. Jackson shared a room with another groom, Cooper, who confirmed that Ann Jones had certainly not been in their room that night; that she had never, as far as Cooper knew, ever been in their room. As to whether or not Jackson had been in the room all night, Cooper could not say. He was a sound sleeper.

Sir Thomas related the substance of these interviews to Susan, who took notes, and then the baronet shook his head. "None of the men saw any other men; no one even saw Mr. Yates! Wilcox only saw a woman, and I do not see how a woman could have committed such a brutal act."

Susan assisted at her uncle's interview with Ann Jones. The housemaid said that she *had* been spending time with Stephen Jackson; he had been courting her; everyone was aware of that. But she had not been with Jackson on the night of Mr. George Yates's murder, and she had not gone to the stables on her own. Besides, Jackson usually came to the house, he did, and they sat in a room near the kitchens while she played the pianoforte for the servants. After all, meals were served in the house, not in the stables, and furthermore, as a housemaid she had to keep clean. In the stables, there was so much dirt, so Stephen and she usually met in the house.

But, as everyone could confirm, Stephen Jackson and Ann Jones had had a falling out, and they had not reconciled on the night in question, or any moment before or since. And then she burst into tears, such that the interview had to be terminated then and there.

Susan escorted Ann Jones to her little room on the top floor. Susan asked if there were anything she could do for her, but the housemaid refused; she said she would wash her face and then resume her duties. Susan went back to her uncle's study.

Sir Thomas remarked that he hoped the housemaid's spirits would soon improve. "I do not wish to be harsh, but we cannot have such tears. Who could imagine that Stephen Jackson could inspire such passion? However, as Jones and Jackson both affirm that she did not go to the stables that night, I do not see how she could have anything to do with the death of Mr. Yates."

Susan said that before this, Ann Jones had always been steady, and Sir Thomas agreed that Baddeley had told him that Ann Jones, up until the last few days, had been a model housemaid: diligent, capable and cheerful.

"If the woman Wilcox saw was not Ann Jones, then who was she?" was the question Sir Thomas wanted to answer.

Sir Thomas, with his niece's assistance, continued the interviews, but seemed to learn little of use regarding the movements of people the night that Mr. George Yates was murdered. He did learn from a scullery maid that a woman had been seen on the stairs early in the morning, but no one could say exactly who the woman was, only that the woman had appeared to be attired for sleep and not for going outside. But this was not exactly suspicious, for the house was full of women, and a woman walking on the stairs in a dressing gown shortly before dawn probably had nothing to do with a woman outside near the stables around midnight.

The only other interesting new piece of information from the servants came from Cook, who complained that this morning, this very morning, someone had taken three plain rolls from the kitchens, out of a set of rolls she had been saving for one of the servants' meals. Why not a cake? Or a fancy muffin? No, oddly enough, just three plain rolls. She could not understand it. Why would anyone commit murder for three ordinary rolls?

Sir Thomas did his best to calm down the cook – really, distressed servants were not good for keeping things comfortable at Mansfield Park, and the cook's agitation was perturbing the rest of the kitchen staff – and said he believed the two events were unrelated. Even if three plain rolls had been stolen from the kitchens, no new dead bodies had been found. Cook was not entirely convinced, however, and was certain dire deeds were about to be committed. There might not be a horse thief, but certainly there was a bread thief, and that thief was within the walls of Mansfield Park!

"It may not be my place to give advice on such things," said Cook, "but my opinion is, if we discover who is stealing my bread, we will discover a great deal – such as who is hitting people on the head and who is slashing their throats."

Susan, who was present for this conversation, recommended that Cook prepare a few extra loaves, to make sure that Mansfield Park was well supplied.

"That will mean using more flour," said Cook, but Sir Thomas said he was certain that Mansfield Park could afford to use a little more flour each day, at least until the bread thief was discovered.

"Take this as a compliment," Susan suggested. "Your bread is so delicious that someone is willing to steal it."

"Yes, your bread is excellent," said Sir Thomas, and the praise soothed Cook, especially as the baronet assured her that the matter would be investigated.

When Cook returned to the kitchens, Sir Thomas asked Susan what she thought; she replied she did not see how it could be relevant.

Over the rest of that day and the next, Sir Thomas interviewed all the Mansfield Park servants, with Susan taking notes. None of them reported anything unusual regarding the night in question; all claimed to have gone to their rooms and had not departed until their usual time to rise in the morning; no one, as far anyone knew, had any reason to wish for Mr. Yates to die. All of the women declared that they had been nowhere near the stables during that night, something they would certainly remember because it would be so unusual.

Finally, done with the interviews of servants, Sir Thomas spoke again with the ladies.

"Someone saw a *young* woman near the stables?" asked Mrs. Norris. "Who told you that?"

Sir Thomas said he did not wish to reveal his sources, a position that irritated Mrs. Norris, as her brother-in-law had apparently confided this information in their niece. After a pointed frown at Susan, as if she were considering suggesting that the young woman near the stables could have been Miss Price, Mrs. Norris chose another approach. "But you do not think that a woman could have done the deed."

Sir Thomas agreed that he still considered it unlikely. Nevertheless, the young woman, if she had been in the vicinity of the stables that night, might have witnessed something. At the very least she could assist in fixing the time of when the murder had *not* occurred.

Mrs. Norris nodded, then shook her head. "I cannot imagine what sort of business any of the young ladies of Mansfield Park could have near the stables late at night. As for the young female servants, that is a different matter. Perhaps one of them is lying. Or your witness, whoever he may be, is mistaken. Are you certain the young woman – if indeed there was a young woman – was from Mansfield Park?"

Sir Thomas said that, as the woman could not be identified, he could not be certain she was from Mansfield Park, only that she had been seen walking in the direction of the house.

Sir Thomas asked if Mrs. Norris had been on the stairs during the night. Mrs. Norris said that indeed she had, going through the house, making sure everything was in order, as she had been wont to do when she had stayed so many times at Mansfield Park before. She did not have confidence in the younger servants, and Baddeley was growing older. But as the murder had taken place in the stables and not on the stairs, she did not see how that was relevant.

The baronet sighed, dismissed Mrs. Norris with some difficulty and spoke again with the other ladies of Mansfield Park, including Lady Bertram, who, in the dark, thanks to her elegant figure, might have been mistaken for a young woman. Lady Bertram, Julia and Maria did not think they had left their rooms that night, although Lady Bertram was not certain – Pug sometimes wanted to leave her room and she rose to open the door, so the dog could go through it – but she did not remember if that had been one of the nights. Lady Bertram was positive, however, that she had not gone to the stables on that night, or on any other night. "If I had done that, I am certain I would remember," and both Sir Thomas and Susan agreed with her.

"We are not advancing," Sir Thomas said, after several hours had slipped by. "Mrs. Norris was correct about one thing: not everyone may be telling the truth. Susan, please ask Julia to rejoin us."

Julia, Sir Thomas thought, was most likely to know something – if not about the events of that night, then about her deceased brother-in-law. "Who is most likely to profit from the death of Mr. George Yates?"

Julia frowned. "I suppose we – John and I – are the most obvious beneficiaries. But I retired early that evening, and did not leave my room until morning. And I cannot imagine that John would do such a thing." Mr. John Yates had played at billiards with Mr. Yates and with Tom that evening, but when he had come upstairs, Julia had detected nothing unusual in his manner, and as far as she knew, he had not left their chamber during the night.

Susan could corroborate part of Julia's story. Mr. John Yates had passed her on the stairs as she was taking the poor basket back to the drawing-room, and she had encountered Mr. George Yates, still very much alive, afterwards.

Sir Thomas repeated his previous question, wanting to know if anyone else could have preferred Mr. Yates dead and not alive.

Julia sighed. Possibly. Probably. Mr. George Yates had not been especially respectable, and she knew he was disliked by many. He had ruined the reputations of several young women and the fortunes of several young men.

Susan remembered Julia's caution to her with respect to Mr. George Yates. Mrs. Yates's warning might have not been intended as a slight, but rather had been an attempt to guard her from an unscrupulous man. Susan felt a burst of gratitude towards her cousin.

Sir Thomas, on the other hand, was indignant. "Your husband invited this blackguard *here*, to Mansfield Park?" And he recounted Mr. Yates's offences: importuning Susan, making an effort to steal his precious snuffbox, repeatedly tempting Tom into a game and probably tricking the hapless Mr. Rushworth into making a foolish wager.

Julia attempted to defend her husband's invitation of Mr. Yates; the man had been his brother, the future Lord Dexthorpe, and his time at Mansfield Park was expected to last only a night or two. But Julia agreed with her father that she wished that Mr. Yates had not come. It would have been better for everyone, most of all for Mr. Yates, who might still be alive if he had not stayed at Mansfield Park.

Sir Thomas, perhaps conceding that the injury done to Mr. Yates at Mansfield Park was probably more severe than any inflicted by Mr. Yates, agreed that the visit had proved most unfortunate. Then, in a calmer tone, the baronet asked: "Can you think of any reason your brother-in-law would have to go to the stables late at night?"

Julia shook her head; she knew of nothing specific, then asked why anyone went to the stables, at any time of day. "Father, I am sorry for all the trouble this is causing, but I can answer few of your questions. I did not know my husband's brother well, and during his visit here, we hardly spoke. You would do better to speak to John. I am certain that John and my brother will return as soon as they can." She had received a letter from her husband, she said; they were already at C— in Lincolnshire, and would return as soon as they could.

Susan attempted to reckon when that could be. Mr. Yates and Mr. Bertram had only departed two days before – a day's journey there, a day's journey back, with time during the visit to bury the deceased.

Sir Thomas asked if Mr. John Yates would not remain a few days at C— in order to condole with his father. Lord Dexthorpe must be suffering severely; the loss of a child was a great grief; surely he would want the consolation of his younger son, now his only living child.

Susan was not so sure of this. She had never met the Baron of Dexthorpe, but she had heard that he was a hard, unforgiving, ungenerous man, very different from the sweet-tempered, tender-hearted Mr. John Yates.

Julia said that she still believed that her husband would return to Mansfield Park as quickly as he could, and in the letter she had received from him, he had written that was his intention. The county, Lincolnshire, was not far from Northamptonshire, and therefore she was certain that John and Tom would soon be back at Mansfield Park.

Sir Thomas asked his daughter several additional questions, but Julia was unable to offer any further intelligence. She asked if she could be excused and he allowed her to leave his study.

Susan remained, and asked her uncle how he would like to continue.

"You saw Mr. Yates on the stairs."

"Yes," Susan said, with a little anxiety. She did not like to recall that encounter, and she worried, too, that Sir Thomas could suspect her. She sat up straighter.

"You said that, as you came up the stairs, Mr. Yates was holding something in his hand, that he was examining the object by candlelight. Do you know what it was?"

Susan hesitated. "I could not see it well, but I believed it was his watch. It was small enough to be in his hand and it gleamed gold as if it were a watch. And before he placed it in his pocket he said it was a watch, a watch that needed repair."

"Do you know if a watch was found among his belongings?"

Susan did not know. "Why, Uncle?"

Sir Thomas shook his head. "If Mr. Yates stole my snuffbox, then perhaps he stole something else. But nothing else was discovered in his things, at least nothing that was recognized as belonging to Mansfield Park."

Sir Thomas rose and walked to the window and gestured in the direction of the stables. "Let us ask again: why did Mr. Yates go to the stables that night? Perhaps if we determine why he went there, we will understand why he was murdered. We should consider Julia's version: why does anyone go to the stables?"

Susan considered. "If one does not work or live at the stables, one goes there in order to get a horse. Usually, in order to go for a ride, or even to depart. The fact that his horse was saddled implies that he was doing this."

Sir Thomas agreed, but he had several objections. "That is true; that is the most common reason for going to the stables. But several things are unusual about Mr. Yates's behavior. First, it was late at night, a strange time to go for a ride, unless some emergency made it necessary. Second, he went to the stables, instead of asking for a groom to bring the horse to the front door. Third, if he were planning to depart Mansfield Park, why were his effects still in his room?"

With respect to the potential emergency, Susan suggested bad weather – after all, the following day it had rained excessively – or some appointment that Mr. Yates urgently needed to keep. Given the late hour, Mr. Yates might have preferred to go to the stables to fetch the horse himself, rather than to disturb the grooms. She could not explain, however, why he had left his possessions in his room. "Why else would one go to the stables, Uncle?"

The baronet said that was the question. "To examine the horse?"

They discussed this possibility. Mr. Yates had a new horse and was concerned about one of the shoes. But neither of them could see how this could lead to his being killed. Sir Thomas asked if Susan could think of any other reason Mr. Yates would go to the stables late at night.

"Perhaps he was wakeful, and wanted to take a stroll. His brother indicated that he kept late hours. Mr. Yates needed an object for his stroll, and the stables supplied one."

Sir Thomas agreed that Susan could be correct, but he did not see how that helped determine why Mr. Yates had been killed. And Mr. Yates had not just been killed, but murdered – first he had been hit on the head and then his throat had been cut. Mr. Yates would have had to have been extremely unlucky, for a casual stroll to lead to his death.

"What if he went to the stables to meet with someone?" asked Susan. Then she added: "But it would have to be someone that Mr. Yates could not have met with easily in the house, because the stables are not nearly as comfortable as Mansfield Park."

Sir Thomas agreed. The most logical people to meet in the stables were those who worked in the stables: the coachman, Wilcox, and the grooms, and a few stable boys. But the baronet could not understand what business – other than perhaps the hoof of Mr. Yates's horse – the murdered man could have had with any of them. "I do not see how Mr. Yates could have met with any of them before this visit, nor what business could have caused any of them to murder him." Besides, Sir Thomas knew all the men, had known them all for many years, and had confidence in their characters. None of the men would behave in such a manner. As for the stable boys, the baronet was less acquainted with them. Perhaps one of them was strong enough to do the deed, but why? And the boys did not live on the estate, but in the houses of some of his tenants, so Sir Thomas was at a loss to explain why any of them would have been in the stables after dark. "I will speak to their parents, but I do not see what that will gain. Perhaps Mrs. Norris is correct, and the murderer was a horse thief."

They discussed Sir Thomas's tenants. Perhaps one of the men had decided to steal the horse, and Mr. Yates had tried to stop him and had been killed during the altercation. And then the man, alarmed by what he had done, panicking, had made sure that Mr. Yates was dead in order to rid himself of a potential witness, and then had released the horse to give himself more time to escape.

"Has any horse ever been stolen from the stables before?" inquired Susan.

Sir Thomas said no, none ever had, but that could explain why this attempt had been so flawed. "Perhaps we are dealing with a first-time offender. An amateur." Presumably even horse thieves had to learn what they were doing. The baronet said he would meet with his steward to inquire if any of his tenants were likely culprits. And he sighed, because such suspicious queries were not likely to keep his tenants content; he would have to make sure his steward proceeded with the utmost tact.

Susan nodded then returned to their former topic. "What about the young woman seen near the stables? What if Mr. Yates had gone to the stables to meet with her?"

Sir Thomas pointed out they had already agreed that meeting in the house would be far more convenient for any of the ladies residing at Mansfield Park.

"Unless the woman does not live at Mansfield Park," said Susan.

"Whom do you have in mind?" asked Sir Thomas. From what he understood, Mr. Yates had never been in this neighborhood before; with what woman could he have arranged a meeting?

Susan then suggested Miss Crawford. "She and Mr. Yates were acquainted. And Miss Crawford would not have wished to come to the house."

This suggestion pleased Sir Thomas, because it was so convenient. Miss Crawford was not associated with Mansfield Park, whereas everyone else – residents, servants, tenants – would stain his estate with guilt. However, Sir Thomas was conscious enough to realize his bias. "A meeting with Miss Crawford – especially if they wished it to be secret – would explain why it took place in the stables. I will ask Wilcox if the young he saw that night could have been Miss Crawford. And if he is certain she was headed in the direction of the house."

"Do you think Miss Crawford, with her slight frame, could have dragged Mr. Yates into the corner?" asked Susan.

Sir Thomas agreed that would have been difficult for the lady in question – likewise, it was difficult to imagine Miss Crawford either overpowering Mr. Yates or cutting his throat – but Miss Crawford might still have been the woman Yates met in the stables – *if* Mr. Yates had met a woman in the stables – and Sir Thomas wished for Susan to speak with Miss Crawford again.

Susan said she was willing to do so; in fact, after two days of listening to interviews and taking notes in Sir Thomas's study, she was eager for a reason for a brief respite, even if it only involved calling at the Parsonage.

"Yes, make the call," encouraged Sir Thomas. "Perhaps you will discover something. Usually such matters, in my experience, are obvious, or at least they become obvious once you put the facts in order. We have heard a few facts, and listened to much speculation, but the criminal is not obvious. All we have so far is the dead son of Lord Dexthorpe, and a horse that was released from the stables, but which was not, as far as I can determine, stolen."

"And some missing bread," said Susan, attempting to cheer up her uncle with a little levity.

But Sir Thomas did not smile. "I truly do not believe that we are in danger at the house, but it is my duty to protect you, and I take that duty seriously."

CHAPTER FIFTEEN

The next morning, as soon as the hour was reasonable, Susan called at the Parsonage and was able to have a few minutes alone with Miss Crawford. Miss Crawford reported that she had written to her brother, but that so far she had only received a brief scrawl from him. Nevertheless, it was encouraging, as he promised her a longer letter in the near future.

"It would be easier if we could talk," said Miss Crawford. "Henry is far better at making speeches than he is at putting things down on paper. But he has promised to make an effort, and I am convinced that he will."

Susan, from what she knew of Fanny's opinion of Mr. Crawford's ability to keep promises, was not particularly sanguine that a letter would arrive from whatever gay place that Mr. Crawford was currently visiting. Susan only said she thought the letter would be most interesting when it arrived. She then asked Miss Crawford if there was anything more she could tell them about the night on which Mr. Yates was murdered, and even asked if Miss Crawford had gone to the stables to meet Mr. Yates.

"I! Trespass at Mansfield Park in order to speak with Mr. Yates! And in the middle of the night! In the stables! I assure you, I have done no such thing." Miss Crawford spoke with such indignation that Susan wondered if any further inquiries from Mansfield Park would be repulsed – if Miss Crawford would even share the letter – if it arrived – from her brother. Susan left the Parsonage within minutes, without even bidding adieu to Mrs. Grant. For this Susan was sorry, and wished she had been more tactful, as Miss Crawford, up until this moment, had been pleasant and amusing.

Moreover, when Susan returned to Mansfield Park, and spoke again with her uncle, she learned that the query had been unnecessary. The coachman said he could not identify the young woman from that night, but that he was certain that she had been rather tall and slender: Miss Crawford, whom he remembered from several years ago, was too small. The woman had been more the height of Mrs. Rushworth – a height that was similar to the height of Mrs. Yates, Miss Price, several of the housemaids, and even Lady Bertram and Mrs. Norris – although Wilcox did not think the woman could have been Mrs. Norris, as the widow was stout and the woman he had glimpsed had been slender. The coachman added that the woman seemed to be carrying something – perhaps a bag? – as she left the area of the stables.

"At least Miss Crawford is not guilty," said Susan, and explained that her questions had given great offense to that lady.

Her uncle advised her not to be too concerned with Miss Crawford's opinion; he did not think that Miss Crawford's irritation would last, and besides the Grants – and therefore Miss Crawford – would not remain in the neighborhood long. "Unfortunately, an inquiry into a crime of this nature is bound to unsettle people. One must ask questions one would rather not."

Susan also reported that Miss Crawford had written to her brother, and that Mr. Crawford had sent a line back promising to write at length on the subject of Mr. George Yates.

Like Susan, Sir Thomas did not put much reliance on Mr. Crawford's opinion, and also doubted that he would write at all. The baronet then changed the subject, and he and Susan discussed what he had learned from the coachman, but they could find no satisfactory explanation for the possibility that the woman might have been carrying a bag. A bag had not been used to kill Mr. George Yates. Nor had a bag been used to carry stolen goods away from the stables, because the only thing missing from the stables was the horse, and they knew where the animal was.

Sir Thomas continued his queries over the next two days, sometimes working with his steward to interview tenants, at other times asking Susan to take notes, but no one had any information to give. Sir Thomas was frustrated, but he had no more avenues of inquiry to pursue. Julia received a note from her husband that Mr. Yates had been buried, that Lord Dexthorpe was both angry and grieved. Instead of taking comfort from his second son, he was distraught about the loss of his first, and so John and Tom planned to return to Mansfield Park any day.

The neighborhood moved on to other topics: the making of hay, the repair of a bridge, and the engagement of Mr. Charles Maddox to a wealthy, much older widow. Mrs. Grant and Miss Crawford called on Lady Bertram, a visit that was made uncomfortable by the anger of Mrs. Norris and the resentment of Mrs. Rushworth. The well-bred Mrs. Grant made polite conversation with Lady Bertram, asking about acquaintances in the neighborhood, and sometimes answering her questions herself, as Mrs. Grant was already better informed than her ladyship. Miss Crawford confined most of her conversation to Mrs. Yates and Miss Price, asking Mrs. Yates what she thought of Lincolnshire, the county in which C— was located, and where she would presumably live, and informing the latter that the letter from her brother had still not arrived but she was confident that he would write soon.

Susan still doubted that the letter would ever arrive, but she was glad for the restoration of civility, no matter how strained, between her and Miss Crawford. She took a moment to apologize for the question she had placed, using her uncle's argument as her excuse.

Somehow, when the sun was shining, the inmates of Mansfield Park could no longer feel the terror that had gripped them several days before. A letter arrived from Fanny, offering to come if needed, but Lady Bertram's spirits were restored to their general tranquility, so Susan wrote back, thanking her for the offer but saying her presence was not needed. "Of course, Fanny is not needed!" exclaimed Mrs. Norris, who insisted on being informed of the contents of any correspondence. "I can look after my sister very well." Chapman, Lady Bertram's maid, sprained her ankle and Mrs. Norris insisted on applying a poultice made of cabbage leaves, which actually helped, and so Lady Bertram's elegance suffered no interruption. Ann Jones, although she said she could never reconcile with Stephen Jackson, and although still pale and unhappy, had at least ceased her copious weeping. Maria, with some assistance from Julia, read Shakespeare's *Antony and Cleopatra* to Lady Bertram, entertaining all in the drawing-room, and Susan, listening, finally finished several pieces in the poor basket.

A week after the death of Mr. Yates, in the late afternoon, a carriage arrived. Julia glanced out the window and announced that it was not her husband.

Susan's heart fell a little, for if Mr. John Yates was not arriving, nor was her cousin Tom.

"It must be someone else," said Lady Bertram, stating the obvious. "Susan, can you tell us who it is?"

Susan obligingly went to the window to get a better view. "Oh!" she exclaimed, in a tone with sufficient surprise in it to attract the attention of all the ladies. "My brother, William, is descending from the carriage."

"Lieutenant Price? Why would *he* come here?" asked Mrs. Norris, as if she could not bear to be invaded by yet another Price nephew or niece.

"If he wished to attend Fanny's wedding, he is too late," observed Lady Bertram. "What a pity that Fanny is not here."

Julia reminded her mother that a letter from William Price had arrived on the day of the wedding itself, in which William had congratulated Edmund and Fanny, so William must be aware that he had missed the ceremony.

Maria observed that that was correct, that William had written from Antigua. "How long does it take to sail from Antigua? He must have made very good time."

The ladies all naturally expected their curiosity to be satisfied soon, but there was a delay, as William first went to speak with his uncle in his study. Susan, deciding that it was too late for William to continue to Thornton Lacey that evening, told the housekeeper to prepare a room for her brother. She also ordered tea and then returned to the drawing-room.

"I do hope he will be able to see Fanny," said Lady Bertram. "She made such a pretty bride."

"Well, I think it was rude of him to come unannounced," said Mrs. Norris. "What if Mansfield Park were hosting a large party?"

"I expect he is coming on some business for my uncle," said Susan, but she, too, wondered why William had made the journey. Her curiosity was not required to suffer long. Sir Thomas entered, his expression unreadable, followed by Lieutenant Price, who carried a bundle in his arms.

"Lady Bertram, I have an important introduction to make to you," said Sir Thomas.

"An introduction? To whom? I know my nephew, of course," said Lady Bertram.

"Not to your nephew. No, he has brought someone important to us – our granddaughter."

Everyone exclaimed. Granddaughter! How could the Bertrams possibly have a granddaughter? Mrs. Norris was especially loud in her astonishment.

"Hush, you will wake her," said Sir Thomas.

The ladies fell silent.

On Sir Thomas's urging, Lieutenant Price approached Lady Bertram, and Sir Thomas gently removed a blanket from the bundle in William's arms.

Lady Bertram, who had the first chance to see the child in her nephew's arms, appeared bewildered. "I do not understand."

Mrs. Norris, crowding in, had the second good view, and she responded in horror. "Get that thing out of here!"

Lieutenant Price stepped backwards, protecting the young child.

"Why? What is the matter?" Maria demanded.

"That – that is a slave!" exclaimed Mrs. Norris.

CHAPTER SIXTEEN

Mrs. Norris's angry tones roused the little girl, who began to cry. Sir Thomas took the child in his arms, but that made matters worse, so he returned her to William, who was the only person in the drawing-room that the little girl had seen before. Susan, grasping at least some of what must have happened, went to assist her brother, guiding him and the little girl to a sofa.

Mrs. Norris was told by Sir Thomas to be quiet, and then Sir Thomas gave his family the necessary explanations.

Elissa, the name of the little girl, was Tom's natural daughter by a woman who had been a slave in Antigua. Tom had at first trifled with, then to his surprise had fallen in love with, the mother, but circumstances did not permit an alliance between the two. In fact, in order to put an end to the relationship, Sir Thomas had sent his elder son home from Antigua earlier than originally planned. But although Tom departed, Hetty was already with child, and this girl was that child.

"Although I was certainly not pleased by this – this liaison, my opinion of the mother improved after Tom's departure. I freed her so that her child would be born free, and arranged for her to be in a position where she could support herself and the child. And I promised her that if anything happened to her, that I would look after her child."

William reported that he had been instructed to visit Hetty and her daughter, and had discovered that the mother, unfortunately, had died.

Sir Thomas added: "If that were so – and if Elissa's living conditions were untenable – I authorized William to bring her here. I will not permit any grandchild of mine to be unprotected."

"My, my," said Lady Bertram, to whom this information was chiefly related and who actually sat up straighter in order to have a better look at her granddaughter. Elissa had calmed down and was staring at the room full of relations with bewilderment.

Everyone was astonished, and not all were pleased. Mrs. Norris expressed doubt. "Are you certain, Sir Thomas, that this – this creature is Tom's?"

"Yes," said Sir Thomas, in a voice that permitted neither contradiction nor discussion.

"Your first grandchild, Mama," said Julia.

"Yes," said Lady Bertram.

"She is not what you expected, is she?" remarked Maria.

"No," said Lady Bertram. "But that is not her fault." She then actually moved aside her pug, rose and went to William and introduced herself to Elissa, her gentle tones reassuring to the little girl, and observing that Elissa resembled Maria and Julia when they were that age, although Elissa was dark while they were fair. Then Lady Bertram returned to her sofa.

Susan's mind and heart were full of both astonishment and comprehension. Hetty – this slave woman back in Antigua – no wonder Tom considered himself unfit to marry anyone; his heart belonged to another. Susan, like Aunt Norris, wondered briefly if the child really were the daughter of her cousin – but the little girl's chin was exactly like Tom's. Susan did some reckoning, and decided the little girl could not be more than three.

What did she now think of Mr. Bertram? Natural children were a frequent occurrence; Susan knew of many cases in Portsmouth and even some in Northamptonshire, although she had only heard of one mulatto. Certainly, Mansfield Park was providing plenty of gossip for the parish this summer! Mr. Charles Maddox and his wealthy widow would soon be dropped from conversation. And then she looked at her uncle with respect; he was risking the approbation of his family and friends, in order to do what was right by this young child. Susan esteemed William, too, for having carried out the commission, and she told him so.

Those were Susan's feelings. What, she wondered, were the feelings of the others? Lady Bertram was tranquil, Julia seemed disappointed, Mrs. Norris angry, and Maria – Maria appeared resentful. Why? Then Susan realized that this transgression of Tom's would be, in many eyes, no worse than Maria's own – yet Maria was banished from Mansfield Park, while Tom was still the eldest son of a baronet, with the position and expectations that accompanied it.

"Does Mr. Bertram know?" Susan ventured to ask, wondering how Tom would react to discovering that the woman he loved had died and that he was now expected to act the part of a father.

Sir Thomas replied that Tom knew about the child, of course, but was unaware that she was at Mansfield Park. Sir Thomas had not decided, either, exactly what should be done with her; that decision had to be shared with her father. He would have to meet her, and then needed to decide what was to be done.

"But we will have to take care of her now," said Susan, wondering where to put the little girl for the next few nights. Now that she was past the shock from learning of Elissa's existence, she was able to study the girl. Mixed-race people, usually adults, were sometimes seen in Portsmouth; in fact, Elissa was a pretty honey color, with rich dark curls cascading down her back. However, in Northamptonshire she would be a novelty.

"Are you hungry?" Lady Bertram asked Elissa; the little girl nodded. Lady Bertram asked her nephew to bring her granddaughter over to her sofa. William did so, helping the little girl stand, and holding her hand as they crossed the room.

The next fifteen minutes were spent feeding the little girl, who liked the bread, jam and ham that been sent with the tea. When she had eaten, she stared with curiosity and longing at her grandmother's lap dog. Lady Bertram introduced Elissa to Pug, and Elissa petted her so gently that the grandmother's heart was conquered. "I am your grandmamma," she said, "and these are your cousins," indicating William and Susan, "and those are your aunts," gesturing towards Julia, Maria and Mrs. Norris; "and Sir Thomas is your grandpapa, and in a day or two you will meet your father. We are your family."

Lady Bertram was prepared to love her granddaughter, but the rest of the family were less ready. Mrs. Norris, struggling to sound reasonable even as the sight of Elissa made her angry, said: "Sir Thomas, do you think it is wise to keep her at Mansfield Park? She will cause a great deal of talk."

"Yes, she will," said Sir Thomas. "But that will not prevent me from doing what is right."

"The servants may object," said Mrs. Norris, who usually did not care for the opinions of the servants. "Some may even give notice."

"I will deal with the servants," said Sir Thomas. "The question is, what should we do with her now?"

William said that Elissa was afraid to be left alone, especially at night. Of all those present, he knew her best, of course, having taken care of her during the passage, but he had to leave Mansfield Park in the morning.

Sir Thomas glanced around at the ladies in the room; they were all silent, perhaps more aware than Sir Thomas was, of how much effort he was asking. Besides, Lady Bertram was too indolent; Julia could expect to be joined by her husband as soon as tomorrow; Maria might consider her reputation too sullied to care for a natural child; and Mrs. Norris – Susan could not risk leaving the little girl with Mrs. Norris. "She can stay in my room with me, at least until a more permanent solution is found," said Susan.

"Thank you, Susan," said Sir Thomas, his voice full of gravity and gratitude.

The others appeared uncomfortable at his words, especially Maria, who was attempting to regain her father's good opinion and realized she had just neglected an opportunity. "It is better for Elissa to be with someone who lives here," said Maria, and then added, "but I am willing to assist Susan."

Mrs. Norris frowned at her niece's offer. Julia said nothing.

"I agree Susan is the best choice at present," said Sir Thomas. "She has several younger brothers and sisters, and helped look after them in Portsmouth."

"Yes, Sue was always good with the little ones," said William.

Elissa gave a great yawn; after such a long day her fatigue was unsurprising. William said he would have the little girl's few possessions sent up to Susan's room, and Julia said that when Elissa was more comfortable at Mansfield Park, she could be moved to the nursery.

Sir Thomas arranged for some things to be moved to Susan's room. As Mrs. Norris predicted, some of the servants were taken aback by the small, dark child. All of them stared and many of them muttered, but they were too accustomed to obeying Sir Thomas to voice any audible objection. As dusk fell, Elissa fell asleep. William carried her up to Susan's room, Susan following, where they found Ann Jones putting a blanket and a pillow on a little bed.

"You will take good care of her," said William, after Elissa had been put into a nightdress and tucked into the bed.

"I will try," Susan promised.

Elissa slept at once, but the brother and sister were loath to go far away. They left Susan's room, but also left the door open, then went and seated themselves on the top of the stairs where they spoke in low voices.

"What can you tell me about her?" asked Susan.

William described Antigua in more detail than Susan had ever heard before: the heat, the squalor, the wretchedness of life on sugar plantations, the suffering of the slaves. Elissa had not been born a slave, because Sir Thomas had manumitted her mother, but without a parent or guardian she would always be in danger of being forced back into that life. She spoke English, but with an accent. After the heat of Antigua, Elissa probably would find Mansfield Park chilly; Susan needed to take care that she was warm enough and did not catch cold.

Susan had many more questions for her brother, but then the little girl gave a cry, and Susan remembered that her young cousin was waking in an unfamiliar room.

"Be good to her, Sue," said William. "I know you will, but she just lost her mother and came a very long way. I must go downstairs to speak with Sir Thomas."

Susan returned to her room and spoke gently to her little cousin, soothing away her fears, telling her that she should sleep now, and that tomorrow, if the weather was fine, she would show her the gardens. Elissa said she liked Susan's room much more than she did the boat or the carriage, her modes of transportation with William. She had never been in such a comfortable bed before! Then Elissa asked her to sing and so Susan sang until the little girl fell back asleep.

CHAPTER SEVENTEEN

Susan took care of Elissa during the night, helped her dress in the morning and then took her downstairs for an early breakfast. This time Elissa descended the staircase herself, clinging with her little fingers to Susan's hand.

Susan and Elissa said farewell to William, who had to return to Portsmouth. On the way, he planned to call on Fanny and Edmund, and he was obliged to Sir Thomas for making this possible. Sir Thomas replied that he was indebted to William for rescuing his granddaughter from a dangerous situation. Then William departed, and Sir Thomas went to his study, leaving the little girl with the ladies. "We cannot determine what to do with her until her father returns," said Sir Thomas. "I am sure you will treat her with kindness."

But the ladies were not prepared to take care of such a small charge. Maria and Julia had never been mothers. Lady Bertram was a mother, but many years had passed since her children were young, and besides, she had always had Nanny and then the governess to supervise the children.

Still, most of the ladies made an effort. Maria and Julia showed their niece the pianoforte, and Lady Bertram invited her granddaughter to sit with her and Pug on the sofa. The weather was fine, so all the ladies went outside for a while and Elissa explored the flower-garden, her exclamations and wonder at the pretty flowers charming nearly everyone. Only Mrs. Norris stayed at a distance, as repulsed by the little girl as if she were made of dirt or nettles.

Most of the burden, however, fell on Susan. Mrs. Yates and Lady Bertram quickly grew tired and sat down on benches, and were joined by Mrs. Norris, but Susan listened to the little girl's many questions and did her best to answer them as they strolled on the gravel walk.

As Susan and Elissa rounded a hedge, they encountered Maria, who stood on the spot in the garden with the best view of the Mansfield Parsonage. She was gazing in its direction, a frown on her face. Susan wondered if Mrs. Rushworth were thinking about the inmates. Did she still have feelings for Mr. Crawford? Or did she simply regret what had happened?

Maria sensed Susan's interest. "Why do you stare at me, Susan?"

Susan could not let her cousin know her true thoughts, so she found something else. "I was admiring your necklace," she said. "That is a sapphire, is it not?"

Maria's demeanor softened. "Yes, it is. It was a present from my father on the occasion of…"

Susan assumed "my marriage" were the words Maria would not say. "It must be very valuable."

Maria seemed to take offense, for she turned away and went to sit beside Mrs. Norris. Susan wondered if she should not have commented on the jewel's worth: did that show a want of taste and breeding, making her appear too conscious of money? And yet people thought about money quite a bit; pretending otherwise was nonsense. Susan had assisted her mother with the budget while in Portsmouth, and now she often took notes for her uncle on pecuniary matters. And certainly Mrs. Norris spoke frequently about money, and Maria seemed to sit contentedly beside her.

Susan plucked a daisy, gave it to Elissa, and told her to carry it to her grandmother, then took a moment to glance in the direction of the Parsonage herself. Had they learned of the addition to Mansfield Park? They must have, and the news must have also reached the village and the rest of the neighborhood. But unlike the day after the death of Mr. Yates, when many notes of concern had been sent to Mansfield Park, so far this day, no correspondence from their neighbors had arrived – only several letters of business for Sir Thomas, a note from Fanny to Lady Bertram that had been composed before the arrival of Elissa, and a note written yesterday from Tom to his father saying he and Mr. John Yates would return today. The neighbors were probably at a loss at how to treat this piece of information; should they send congratulations or condolences?

What, for example, would the vicars in their circle write? Dr. Grant had lived in London, and he must have seen every type of sin and many natural children, but he might hesitate to pen anything due to the awkward relationship with the family at Mansfield Park. Turning in the direction of Thornton Lacey, which William must have reached hours ago, Susan considered her brother-in-law. Edmund was a man with delicate sensibilities, horrified by sin, and still too young to forgive easily. Susan was aware that Edmund had strongly condemned both Mr. Crawford and Maria after their liaison. How would he behave towards his own brother, Tom, when he learned of his affair with a dark woman in Antigua? And how would he treat his out-of-wedlock niece, the indisputable evidence of his brother's guilt?

With these thoughts, and recollecting that she, too, was an indigent niece, Susan stopped gazing in the direction of Thornton Lacey and went over to Elissa, who was exclaiming over a pair of snails beneath a bush. From her position Susan could easily hear the talk of the other ladies, seated on benches nearby.

"Cook tells me that the thief stole something again during the night," announced Mrs. Norris. "A plain cake was missing."

"Really? How peculiar," said Maria. "If one of the servants is hungry, then why not ask for more?"

"The thief does not seem to be a servant," said Mrs. Norris.

"No?" asked Lady Bertram. "Surely you do not think that the murderer of Mr. Yates is stealing bread and cake from our kitchen."

"Mama, I am sure the matters are unrelated," said Julia. "Why would a murderer break into Mansfield Park to take bread?"

"Why do you say that the bread thief is not a servant, Aunt Norris?" Maria asked.

"Because Cook saw someone leaving the kitchens around two in the morning," said Mrs. Norris. "Cook could not sleep; she was certain someone was stealing from the kitchens, and she was right, absolutely right! Sometimes presentiments are valid." Mrs. Norris then launched into a story about her garden in Ireland, about how she had been convinced that something was digging in her flowerpots of foxglove only to discover that the culprits were living close by. A pair of magpies, nesting in a nearby cherry laurel tree, were responsible for the mess, but she had been able to stop them by placing several large stones in each flowerpot.

Maria interrupted her aunt to ask her about the bread thief.

"Oh, dear, did I fail to mention the person? Cook believes the person was a woman. And, when I asked her, she agreed that it *might* have been Susan."

Susan, although a little distance away, had heard every word; she turned and defended herself. "I did not steal bread or plain cake from the kitchen. Not last night, nor the other morning, nor any other morning."

"Perhaps Elissa was hungry," suggested Maria, "and you were so fatigued from looking after her, that you forgot that you went down the stairs."

Susan repeated her denials; during the night she had not left Elissa. "If I wished for bread, why would I take it but not tell people? Why would I behave in a clandestine manner?"

"To give to someone else," said Mrs. Norris. "To give, perhaps, to the murderer."

"Do you truly suppose, ma'am, that the murderer of Mr. Yates is hidden in my room?" asked Susan.

To Susan's relief, Julia came to her defense. "I do not see why Susan would be taking bread from the kitchen. And perhaps Cook was mistaken. She is not young; how well can she see, especially when it is dark?"

And Maria added: "No one here has reason to steal bread; should we want more, we need only ask."

Mrs. Norris, spurred by these words from her favorite niece, grudgingly yielded to the notion that Susan was neither stealing bread nor concealing an assassin in her chamber. "Perhaps you are right, Maria. The culprit could be one of the servants. Perhaps one of the servants knows where the murderer of Mr. Yates is hidden and is bringing bread to him."

"That is a possibility," said Maria. "Among the servants there are several young women; Cook may have mistaken one of them for Cousin Susan. We should search the grounds. Do you not agree, Mama?"

But Lady Bertram, a smile on her face, appeared to be contemplating something else. Maria and Mrs. Norris had to repeat their ideas and suggestions to her until she understood, and then, with a resolution uncharacteristic of her, she said it was better not to worry the servants with searches and accusations. "That will only distress them."

"But Cook is distressed about the missing bread!" exclaimed Mrs. Norris, and then proceeded to detail several faults she had noticed with recent meals: the gravy had had lumps; the slices of ham had been tough; and the potatoes overcooked. "I am sure Sir Thomas has noticed as well, my dear sister, and you should tend to him."

Lady Bertram stared at the ground for a moment. "Very well, I will tell Cook that *I* have been taking the bread. Susan and I are about the same height. In the dark, as you say, it would be easy to mistake one of us with the other."

"You have been taking the bread?" asked Mrs. Norris.

"But why have you kept it secret all this time?" inquired Maria.

At first Lady Bertram did not seem to understand the question, then she frowned a little as she considered. "I do not exactly know why I did not tell anyone that I have been craving bread during the night or the early morning. But does it really matter?"

Mrs. Norris was ready to support her ladyship. "No, you may do as you like, Sister, for you are the mistress of Mansfield Park."

Julia supplied another explanation. "Perhaps, Mama, you did not wish to worry Cook with odd habits and hungers."

Lady Bertram nodded. "That is a good point, Julia. Cook would be unhappy to learn that I was not content with my meals, and I did not wish to distress her. Now, I think it is time to go inside and have some tea. It is lovely to be outside, of course, but inside is lovely as well. Elissa, do you wish for some tea?"

Susan agreed that it was time to go inside, but as she turned, she saw a figure down at the Parsonage. She recognized Miss Crawford, who was looking in their direction, and who appeared to wave at her. Susan asked to be excused. "I see Miss Crawford in the distance and I believe she wishes to speak to me."

Maria reddened at the mention of Miss Crawford, a woman Maria had hoped that would one day be her sister-in-law. Susan heard her whisper to Mrs. Norris that it was most unfair: Susan had usurped her place, her parents and even her friends. "True, true," said Mrs. Norris and Susan felt her aunt's angry stare. Susan thought Maria was being unjust;

she and Miss Crawford were not friends; in fact, she had offended Miss Crawford during their last tête-à-tête. That was one reason that Susan felt it urgent to make a conciliatory gesture if she could.

Lady Bertram was oblivious to all this, but said that Susan could go to the Parsonage as long as she hurried back. Elissa was reluctant to let her go – the little girl had lost so many over the past few months – but Susan promised to return in an hour or two. Lady Bertram then told her granddaughter that she could play with her little dog and Julia said they could make flowers out of paper.

Leaving Elissa in the care of her grandmother and her aunt Julia, Susan took the path to the Parsonage.

CHAPTER EIGHTEEN

Susan was correct; Miss Crawford *did* desire a conversation. After the usual greetings, Miss Crawford spoke briskly.

"Everything is so very awkward. I would not have ventured to this part of the country, except that I wished to support my sister during this visit. Dr. Grant has made progress with his affairs, but Mr. Hawk's dying parent still lingers among the living, so I cannot tell you how long we will inflict ourselves on the Bertrams and Mansfield. I suggested to Dr. Grant that he leave my sister in London, but he refused; he is completely dependent on her."

Susan assured her that it was no infliction, at least not for her, and as for the other residents of Mansfield Park, they would manage.

"You are too kind. I am aware how difficult it must be when you do not feel as if you can walk out of your own front door without being confronted with uncomfortable recollections. Sir Thomas was such an attentive neighbor! And now we are strangers, nay, worse than strangers, for we can never become anything better."

Miss Crawford seemed to have forgotten that she and Mrs. Grant had called on Lady Bertram only a few days ago, but Susan supposed that an awkward half hour of conversation was nothing compared to the many evenings of laughter and games they had shared before. Miss Crawford then asked if she might inquire about her former friends; Susan gave brief answers about them all.

Miss Crawford said, "I understand there is an addition at Mansfield Park."

Susan colored a little at this – and she did not know why she should, because *she* had done nothing wrong to create Elissa – nevertheless she kept her voice steady. "Yes, I am certain that she is a topic of much conversation."

"I did not think Sir Thomas would permit such a person at Mansfield Park."

"Elissa is his granddaughter."

"True, she is, but Sir Thomas has always been so upright and strict! And the rest of the family – how are they treating the mulatta?"

"They only met her yesterday."

"You are very discreet, Miss Price. I understand, their emotions must be mixed, and anyway I know most of the household well enough to imagine how all of them would respond. Sir Thomas means to be kind, but is so imposing that the little girl is terrified of him. Lady Bertram is kind when she thinks about it, but she bestows more attention on her dog. Mrs. Yates and Mrs. Rushworth do not know how to behave, and Mrs. Norris is as disagreeable as she was to your own sister. There, have I not done well? There is no need for me to call at Mansfield Park, when my former friends live so perfectly in my imagination. I am curious, however, about those we have not yet mentioned. Mr. Bertram – how does he behave with his daughter? And Mr. Edmund Bertram? He has to consider his position as a clergyman. How will he reconcile Christian charity with severe morality? And what about your tender-hearted sister, Miss Fanny Price – I mean Mrs. Bertram?"

Susan, although she thought Miss Crawford's descriptions rather apt, would not gossip about her relations. "I thought you wished to speak to me about something else, Miss Crawford. I have not much time, and so if this is everything, you must excuse me."

"I am sorry, Miss Price. Stay, Miss Price, please stay; I apologize for my words; I understand they may make you uncomfortable. I do have something for you; I have finally received a letter from my brother about the recently deceased Mr. Yates. Before I show it to you, I must excuse Henry's language – I can see that his language may be inappropriate for a young lady – but I feel compelled to show it to you. And if you judge it relevant, I beg you to carry it to Sir Thomas."

Miss Crawford took a letter out of her reticule and read aloud.

Dear Mary,

As you are well aware, I hate writing letters and avoid the practice whenever I can. But for you, my dear sister, I will make an exception.

So, George Yates is dead! An amusing fellow, if he respected you, but he did not respect many. You ask if anyone wished to kill him? I can think of several who might smile at learning of his end. Of course, John Yates benefits most from being the elder son, but George Yates made plenty of other enemies throughout the kingdoms. He was a gamester who won, which creates far more hatred than a fellow who obligingly loses, and a seducer as well.

A seducer, thought Susan. She was most relieved that Yates had not managed to enter her room that night. Oh, how fortunate she had been, that Mrs. Norris had appeared when she had!

So, both gentlemen and ladies could want him dead. The most recent dupe, from my understanding, was Rushworth, as Yates managed to get a valuable horse away from the master of Sotherton. This, however, you already know. Also, I saw George Yates with Tom Bertram at the theatre in London last year, and I believe that Yates pressed Bertram into a game. I expect George Yates went to Mansfield Park in order to collect from Bertram.

Susan felt ill at the idea that Tom could have been so weak as to have yielded to Mr. Yates's pressure, thus breaking his solemn word to his father not to wager. "Is your brother certain? Absolutely certain, that Mr. Bertram was in debt to Mr. Yates?"

"In my experience, Henry's observations are usually accurate," remarked Miss Crawford. She continued:

As for other details relating to our former friends at Mansfield Park, I am at a loss what more to say. I could write many pages about the sordid affairs of George Yates, but that would take hours, even days, would be mostly irrelevant, and require my writing down the names of people who would rather not be mentioned. If I were at the Parsonage, I am certain that I could be of assistance in resolving this puzzle, but I know that I am generally unwelcome. I hope, Mary, that you are enjoying your time in the country. At least it does not sound dull! Give my love to our sister, and my regards to Dr. Grant.

"That is all," said Miss Crawford. "It may not seem like much, but my brother does not care to write letters, and he has a point about not involving those who have nothing to do with the matter."

Susan, still reflecting on her cousin Tom's possible guilt – only with respect to wagering; she could not imagine that Tom had killed Mr. Yates! – said nothing.

Miss Crawford folded the letter. "Miss Price, will you be so good as to carry this to Sir Thomas? I have ventured once to Mansfield Park; the formal call was a necessity and my sister did not wish to go without me. I will not trespass again without a particular invitation."

Susan suspected that Miss Crawford would rather like a particular invitation to Mansfield Park, but she did not offer one. She agreed, however, to take the letter to her uncle, although she disliked its words about Tom. "If that is all for now, you must excuse me. I know I am needed back home."

"Ah, yes, the little girl! Mr. Bertram, when he returns, will find much requiring his attention."

Susan excused herself again, and departed hastily. She knew that Fanny had never liked Miss Crawford but had always believed her dislike had been due to jealousy. But now *she* was irritated by Miss Crawford, and she struggled to comprehend why. *She* did not envy Miss Crawford – well, Miss Crawford had 20,000£, so perhaps she envied her fortune – but Susan did not believe that she and Miss Crawford were both interested in the same gentleman.

No, her disquiet was due to her disappointment in her cousin and her distress about him. Tom had warned her that he was unworthy; probably because he knew he had fathered a child, and possibly because he knew, too, that he had a weakness for wagers. Could he also be a murderer? No, at that point, he could not have been a murderer; Mr. Yates was not yet dead.

Her thoughts and mind were so full that Susan found herself entering the house without realizing how quickly she had walked. She went straight to her uncle's rooms and handed him Mr. Crawford's letter.

Sir Thomas asked her to wait while he perused the dark handwriting. Afterwards, he inquired if she were aware of its contents. Susan explained that Miss Crawford had read the letter to her.

"Then you know what it says. Little that I did not know or fear – although this George Yates seems an even worse character than I imagined." He sighed, surely wondering about his eldest son, but did not mention Tom, and thanked her for bringing the letter from the Parsonage.

Susan went to the drawing-room, where she discovered that the ladies had exhausted their resources in entertaining little Elissa. Lady Bertram had let her pet her pug; Julia had told her a story; Maria had played the pianoforte; and Mrs. Norris had lectured her on how she should sit up straight and still and not talk. But each of these diversions, though they took active imagination on the part of the ladies, only amused the little girl for a short while. Hence, all of the ladies – as well as little Elissa – were relieved when Susan entered the room. They were especially happy when Susan offered to take Elissa upstairs, where she and the little girl would play with some of Maria's and Julia's old toys.

"Make sure she does not break anything valuable," said Mrs. Norris with a sniff, as Susan took her young cousin's hand and led her away. "Make sure she does not even *touch* anything valuable – she could soil whatever she touches."

Susan quickly removed Elissa from the contemptuous remarks of Mrs. Norris. Her aunt's last communication could be interpreted charitably as the strong probability that a three-year-old's hands might not be especially clean, but Susan believed Mrs. Norris implied something far worse.

Poor little girl, thought Susan, as they made their way through the house to the nursery. Given her circumstances, Elissa's future would be difficult, although remembering what William had told her about the conditions in Antigua, Elissa was probably safer here than there. Susan did not know what could be done to improve her young cousin's situation, but it was in her power to give the girl a pleasant hour, and so they sang, Elissa explored the toys, and they ate rice pudding from a tray brought to them by Ann Jones. Afterwards, Susan read to the girl from a book. Elissa wanted to know how Susan could tell what to say by looking at the pages and Susan found herself explaining the alphabet to her young cousin.

The activities were welcome, for Susan did not wish to dwell on what she had heard at the Parsonage. That letter from Mr. Crawford! Her cousin Tom was implicated in so much! What if it were all true? It could not be true, she thought, and yet she had to admit that it was not impossible. Tom *could* have been tempted to cards the last time he was in London. Gambling, as Susan had observed in Portsmouth, was very difficult for young men to refuse, and Susan did not think that the upper classes were any better at resisting temptation than the lower. If Tom had broken his word to his father, and had lost, then he could have owed Mr. George Yates a great deal of money. Mr. Yates could have come to Mansfield Park in order to collect. Then Tom, to avoid having to confess to his father, could have killed Mr. Yates.

The thoughts made her wretched, but the more Susan attempted to push them away from her, the more she tried not to think on the subject, the more her mind dwelt there. Her thoughts were only diverted by the unexpected arrival of Maria, who observed Susan's activities with Elissa, and then rummaged in the nursery until she found a box of letters – each letter was on a card, a little smaller than a playing card, and they could be arranged to spell different words. Soon the little girl was busy discovering the members of the alphabet, especially the E, the first letter of her name.

Susan thanked Mrs. Rushworth for the attention.

Maria said she had another motive for coming to the nursery. "I wanted to satisfy my curiosity. You went down to the Parsonage, did you not? And brought back a letter that Mr. Crawford wrote to his sister?" Maria then quizzed her at length about what the letter did and did not contain.

"The letter implicates my brother? Implies that Tom may have had a reason to harm Mr. Yates?" Maria looked troubled at the notion.

"Yes. If you wish to know exactly what it says, why not ask my uncle to show it to you? But it is not very long. Mr. Crawford wrote that he could say much more in person."

"I hope Mr. Crawford will not come here," said Maria. "It would be too much, too bold. He would not dare. But he was always very bold."

Susan said she had no opinion on the matter.

"I am aware of how much you are doing for this family," said Maria. "My aunt may have trouble perceiving it, but I do. I wish to assure you that she is very loyal to my family as well."

To *some* parts of it, thought Susan, but a noise spared her having to utter unkind truths or generous falsehoods about Mrs. Norris. "I hear a carriage," she said.

"It is too late for a caller," remarked Maria, for it was nearly time for dinner.

"Cousin William?" asked Elissa, remembering the carriage ride she had taken.

"I do not think so," said Susan, as her heart beat more quickly. In a few minutes they all heard the male voices echoing in the vestibule: Mr. Tom Bertram and Mr. John Yates were returned!

CHAPTER NINETEEN

Susan felt for her eldest cousin, with all the difficult news that he was most certainly hearing at this very moment, from suddenly acquiring the responsibilities of fatherhood to being suspected of murder, and even Maria appeared concerned. "What should we do? Should we take Elissa downstairs to meet her father?"

The little girl's dark eyes opened wide with anxiety, and Susan replied that she thought that would involve too many people. She suggested that Maria go down and ask Sir Thomas and Tom how they wished to proceed.

The introduction was a matter of great anticipation, and several messages went up and down the stairs before it was decided that the awful meeting should take place in the privacy of the nursery rather than in the public of the drawing-room. But all was settled quickly, and in a few minutes Tom Bertram tapped at the door and entered. The little girl stared apprehensively at the tall, fair man who announced he was her father; Tom looked down with wonder at the child whom he knew to be his daughter. Sir Thomas lingered for a few minutes in the doorway, to make sure that his son was doing his duty, and then, satisfied on that point, said he would leave Tom alone with Elissa for now.

Susan made a movement to depart as well, but both father and child appealed to her. "Stay," pleaded Tom, "just while we get acquainted."

So, Susan remained and helped these two converse, haltingly at first, for Elissa had both an accent and the elocution of a very young child, and Tom was at a loss what to say. She prompted them to talk about carriages and traveling, as that was something they both had experienced recently. Tom then asked about the sea journey that Elissa had taken from Antigua, and explained that he had made that journey himself.

Susan found a copy of *Tommy Thumb's Pretty Song Book* on a shelf, and suggested that Tom read aloud to his daughter. This occupation proved excellent, for his reading was amusing, and they were all laughing at his rendition of "Hickory, Dickory, Dock." They spent a pleasant half-hour, and finally Elissa fell asleep, her small fingers clasping one of her father's fingers.

"My daughter," Tom whispered, and his voice was hoarse, as he permitted himself to have the emotions that he had suppressed while the little girl was awake. "How could I have left her alone?"

Susan reminded him that Elissa had not been alone; she had been with her mother, but that Mr. Bertram was all she had now. She asked if he had partaken of any refreshment since his arrival; he said he had not but that he did not want to leave his daughter. Susan arranged for another tray to be brought up; while the child slept, they spoke in low voices. She asked about the journey, the funeral, and the reaction of Lord Dexthorpe to the death of his eldest son. The bereaved father had been angry, distressed and downright disagreeable, but Tom, experiencing paternal love for the first time, was charitable in his description. Tom then sent Susan away, saying that he was certain that most of the responsibility for his daughter had fallen on her shoulders during the last two days. Susan confessed that it had been so, and she went downstairs and joined the other ladies in the drawing-room; Sir Thomas and Mr. John Yates were in conference in Sir Thomas's study.

Everyone was curious about the meeting between Tom and his daughter; Susan spoke only briefly, saying she thought Tom should describe it himself.

"Does he know what he plans to do with her?" asked Mrs. Norris. And before anyone could answer, Mrs. Norris held forth, not understanding how even if Tom wished it, Sir Thomas could consider keeping the little girl on the estate. Elissa, with her dark skin, was evidence of wickedness, and would diminish Mansfield Park's standing in the neighborhood. Given how Sir Thomas had banished his dear daughter in similar circumstances, how could he permit the presence of an illegitimate granddaughter?

Julia yawned. "I do not think Father would have arranged for Elissa to come here if he did not have several ideas, even if we do not know them yet. As for Maria, she is here, is she not?"

"Yes, I am," said Maria.

"It *is* pleasant to have a grandchild in the house," said Lady Bertram. "Oh, that reminds me!" she exclaimed, and she told the other ladies that she had spoken with Cook about the bread and plain cake and had arranged for a plate of it to be available for her in the kitchen if she or anyone else became hungry during the night. Then she informed everyone that Pug was a grandmother as well; she had received a note from a friend, Mrs. Otway, telling her how one of Pug's daughters had just given birth, and wanted to know if Lady Bertram could suggest possible owners for the new puppies.

"Perhaps the new Mrs. Maddox, if she is agreeable, would like a pup," suggested Maria.

"Or Mrs. Grant, if she is not too busy," said Julia.

Susan, fatigued from caring for Elissa, was content to sit in silence while the other ladies chatted. Her respite was short, for Mr. John Yates soon appeared in the drawing-room and informed her that her uncle wished to speak with her.

Susan went to her uncle's study, expecting to report on Tom and Elissa. But Sir Thomas did not dwell on his son and his granddaughter; he had another matter to discuss.

"Mr. Yates brought a letter from his father. Perhaps you would read it, Susan. Read it aloud, please; I need to be certain I know every word."

Susan took the letter, repositioned several candles, and read the correspondence from Lord Dexthorpe. The bereaved father did not express sorrow but anger. How could Sir Thomas have allowed his son to be murdered? Why had the baronet not discovered and punished the criminal? Despite the alliance of their children, the baron was most dissatisfied and would make trouble for Sir Thomas's business affairs unless certain steps were taken.

Susan put down the letter – the extravagance of expression reminded her of Mr. John Yates – but the contents had the potential to be serious. "The baron holds you responsible for what happened to his son."

"Yes. And, as I am master of Mansfield Park, I am morally if not legally responsible."

Susan asked several questions. The threats were vague; did her uncle think Lord Dexthorpe could actually do anything? Sir Thomas said that the baron did have the ability to take several actions that would seriously injure his income, and hence create difficulties for everyone at Mansfield Park. The plantation in Antigua was at risk, as well as several trading arrangements. "There is no guarantee that he will take these actions, but he has the ability, and from what Mr. John Yates just told me, the resolution. Over the years, Lord Dexthorpe has ruined at least two other families because of his anger with them."

A cruel man, thought Susan, and wondered if Mr. George Yates had inherited this tendency from his father. Aloud she said: "But you have been making inquiries, Uncle! What more does the baron expect you to do?"

Sir Thomas said that the expectations were not just in the letter from the baron, but had been conveyed to him by Mr. John Yates. Mr. Yates had been most troubled by the additional communication he had been compelled to make, as it placed him between his father and his father-in-law. However, refusing to tell his father-in-law of his father's suspicions would not alter them, and warning Sir Thomas would give him the ability to take all possible precautions.

"What suspicions?" asked Susan.

Lord Dexthorpe believed Sir Thomas was hiding the truth because his own eldest son, Mr. Bertram, was the murderer.

CHAPTER TWENTY

Sir Thomas told Susan of the case against Tom – the reasons for the baron's suspicions – with far more concision than had been employed by Mr. John Yates. First, given what had happened, the killer had to be a man. Second, it seemed unlikely, that in the space of only two days, that anyone could have developed such a hatred of Mr. George Yates that he would make the effort to murder him. Only two men at Mansfield Park had been acquainted with Mr. George Yates *before* his arrival; those men were Tom Bertram and Mr. John Yates. Lord Dexthorpe was certain, from his knowledge of his younger son, that *he* had not killed his elder brother; besides, Mr. John Yates had an alibi in Mrs. John Yates. Third, Tom was strong enough to kill Mr. Yates and to move the body, and had the ability to saddle the horse that had returned to Rushworth. Fourth, Lord Dexthorpe was aware that Mr. Bertram had lost a considerable sum to his elder son in the past. If Tom had owed Mr. Yates money, then he would have had motive for murder.

Even though Susan had had some of these thoughts herself, she protested that it could not be true, that Tom could not have gambled, but she and her uncle agreed that the letter from Mr. Crawford indicated that it was at least possible. And then Susan recalled another point that seemed to confirm the baron's assertion. The previous winter, Tom had gone to

London but had come back to Mansfield Park several weeks earlier than expected. He had claimed that he had not been feeling well – Tom had once suffered a serious illness and had learnt to be careful – but what if Tom had come home in order to avoid paying his debts to Mr. Yates?

Sir Thomas recalled his son's return back in January. Distressed by their conversation, he rose and walked to the window. After a minute he found his voice. He hoped, he *hoped,* that Lord Dexthorpe's assertions were not true, because if they were, it meant that Tom had broken his word and had lied about it afterwards. The baronet turned back from the window. "But guilt even in one's own family must be faced."

Susan sensed that the possibility of Tom's not keeping his word to his father distressed Sir Thomas more than the possibility of Tom's being a killer; however, she was certain that the baron's priorities would be different. She listened to her uncle's speech, and made a suggestion. Was not the case against Mr. John Yates just as robust? His motive, to become the eldest son, would be just as strong, and Julia could have been asleep while her husband was out of their room.

"Or she could be lying to protect him," said Sir Thomas, and Susan could tell that this alternative was a little better, because it meant his daughter, and not his son and heir, was deceitful. The baronet agreed that Mr. John Yates might have the physical ability to murder his elder brother, and material motive to do so, but he apparently had had no opportunity to commit the deed. Mr. John Yates had quitted the billiards game earlier than the other men in order to go upstairs to his wife, a move corroborated by Tom, who had reported earlier that Mr. John Yates had ceased playing at billiards for a good three quarters of an hour before he and Mr. George Yates had left the room, by Susan, who had seen Mr. John Yates go upstairs, and by Julia, whom he had joined in their chamber. Sir Thomas said that perhaps it was not impossible for Mr. John Yates to have left his bed chamber to go to the stables to murder his brother – but why? If John Yates wished to kill his brother, why would he choose to perform the act at Mansfield Park? (Susan could tell that her uncle thought that Mr. John Yates could never be so inconsiderate.) Sir Thomas could perceive no urgency in Mr. John Yates's situation, whereas Tom's position was potentially more acute. And, as Julia had reminded them, Mr. John Yates was not a man who suppressed his feelings; if he were guilty, someone would have noticed. Alas, Sir Thomas had to accept the possibility that his own eldest son, his firstborn, his namesake, was the most likely person at Mansfield Park to have murdered Mr. George Yates.

Susan was horrified and struggled to keep her composure as she considered her uncle's reasoning – with which, alas, she could find no fault; much of it had occurred to her before. She asked Sir Thomas what assistance he required from her.

"Of course, I do not want Tom to be a murderer, so if anything occurs to you, any avenue that will convince Lord Dexthorpe of Tom's innocence or of another's guilt, then let me know." Susan promised to do her utmost, and asked her uncle how he would proceed.

"I will allow Tom this evening with his daughter. I do not wish to disturb that. But tomorrow I must question him." Sir Thomas then thanked his niece for listening and for her support in all the difficulties that were paramount at Mansfield Park.

Susan departed from her uncle's room, and as he had asked her not to reveal anything, decided not to return to the drawing-room where she could be assailed by the inquiries of her relatives. She rather envied them and their lack of knowledge and recalled Gray's, "Where ignorance is bliss, 'tis folly to be wise." Despite her fatigue, that night she slept little, as she worried about the burdens on Sir Thomas, the threats of Lord Dexthorpe against Mansfield Park, and most of all, the terrible suspicions that were about to befall her cousin Tom.

Tom learned of the accusations soon enough. Susan was not present at the interview – Sir Thomas had a tête-à-tête with his son – and yet afterwards somehow everyone at Mansfield Park knew exactly what had been said. Sir Thomas wanted to know if Tom had broken his word and had gambled during the previous winter with Mr. George Yates, and if he had owed Mr. Yates money. Tom at first denied this. Sir Thomas told his son about the letter from Mr. Crawford and asked if him he wished to remain with his story. At this Tom became indignant, for why would his own father believe Mr. Crawford, the man who had led Maria to her ruin, over his own son? Sir Thomas repeated the question a third time. Tom said he recollected encountering Mr. George Yates at the theatre, and that Yates had invited him to a game, but that he had refused. Sir Thomas pressed him, repeating that Mr. Crawford had it on good authority – several others, including Mr. Rushworth, had been present – and so the details could come out. At this point Tom conceded that he had played, and that he had, indeed, lost money to Mr. George Yates.

Sir Thomas was angry. "You broke your promise, and, what is worse, you lied to me about it."

Tom said that he was ashamed that he had broken his promise, and so he had paid the money to Mr. Yates and had departed from London the following morning, returning to Mansfield Park so that he would not succumb to further temptation.

"You paid the money to Mr. Yates before you left London? He did not come to Mansfield Park in order to collect from you?" inquired the baronet.

Tom averred that he had paid his debt before his departure, and that Yates had not been at Mansfield Park to collect from him – although Yates had attempted to persuade him to wager more money during his visit. The baronet, however, was not convinced. "Why should I believe you, when you have just demonstrated you are willing to lie to me? How can I have confidence in your word?"

Tom reddened but repeated that he was telling his father the truth. Sir Thomas demanded to know exactly how much money his son had lost to Mr. Yates the previous winter; Tom hesitated, then named a significant sum.

"And you paid the entire amount to Mr. Yates before you departed from London?"

Tom repeated that he had, and in fact it was in consequence of suddenly being without funds that had necessitated his abrupt return home the previous winter.

The baronet shook his head. He then explained what others, especially others with influence, might believe. That Tom had lost more than he claimed to Mr. George Yates; that Mr. Yates had arrived at Mansfield Park to collect the remainder from Tom; and that, in order to avoid paying the amount, Tom had killed Mr. Yates. Sir Thomas then told his eldest son what he had explained to his niece the previous evening: that he was the only man – other than Mr. John Yates, whose time could be accounted for – who had been at all acquainted with Mr. George Yates before his arrival at Mansfield Park. Tom had been with Mr. Yates for most of the evening. And to Tom it would be easy to ascribe a motive.

Tom spoke with warmth. "I repeat, sir, that I owed Yates no money; I paid my debt in full last winter. As for the other motive, to conceal my broken promise and my loss from you, let me say that I value your good opinion, but not so much that I would kill a man rather than confess a wager."

The speech moved the baronet. "I wish to believe you, but given everything else—. Is there any way to prove what you maintain? Some other witness, whom Lord Dexthorpe would accept as impartial?"

Tom, calmer, said several others had been with him and Mr. Yates at cards back in London. He was not sure how to locate all of them, but one of the men had been Mr. Rushworth. "He may not remember the amount that I paid Yates, but he should be able to confirm what I have told you, especially that I left the game early, after I decided that I had given away too much."

Sir Thomas was somewhat appeased. "Perhaps we have a means of determining the truth. I hope it will clear you, Tom, although Mansfield Park will not be secure until we discover who murdered Mr. Yates." The baronet said he would sent a message to Sotherton to ask Mr. Rushworth for information about the card game back in January, then ordered his son to go spend the next hour with his daughter. Tom protested that he was not certain that he would be good company for her at the moment; Sir Thomas said that it was his duty; paternal responsibilities could not be shirked simply because they were inconvenient.

Tom, unwilling to offend his father, joined Susan and Elissa as commanded, but his humor was dark. "Do you know I am my father's favorite suspect?" asked Tom. Susan said she did not believe that, but that her uncle had informed her of Lord Dexthorpe's speculations and intentions. Then, because it was not the time for this discussion, Susan suggested he show Elissa more of Mansfield Park. Walking outside might refresh his spirits, and the animals would entertain the little girl: the fish in the fish pond, the hunting dogs, the poultry-yard with its geese and chickens. Elissa laughed as a pair of hens fought over some food, with the result that the grain was nabbed by the rooster.

"The rooster makes a lot of noise in the morning," explained Susan.

"He crows the rest of the day as well," Tom added. "I am not sure the rooster knows when morning is."

Their conversation was interrupted by the sound of hoofbeats; someone was arriving on horseback. "Perhaps the bailiff," said Tom, "come to take me away."

"That is not amusing," said Susan.

"No, it is not. Let us go see who it is."

The man on horseback was not the local bailiff, but Edmund, who had ridden over from Thornton Lacey to see how they were. "I should have come before," he said, but everyone excused the new husband. His parents were especially happy to see him: Sir Thomas, because his second son often had good sense, and Lady Bertram, because Edmund brought a letter from her dear Fanny. Edmund listened to Mr. John Yates, who was happy to have a new audience to describe his utter wretchedness at his brother's shocking murder; Edmund tolerated a few arch remarks from his sister Maria, who informed him that Miss Crawford had called at Mansfield Park; and Edmund could not help but hear the many opinions of Mrs. Norris, from her certainty that a horse thief must be responsible for the death of Mr. Yates, to her deep concern that Sir Thomas was committing a grave error by bringing Elissa to his estate. What did Edmund, as a clergyman, have to say about Elissa? Edmund kept his answer to his aunt brief, but he said the child – he had seen her with Tom and Susan when he first arrived – seemed pretty and healthy, and that he was certain they would find a suitable situation for her in time.

Edmund knew Mrs. Norris too well to furnish her with additional arguments to use against his little niece, but when he finally had time alone with Sir Thomas, he was less reserved. His concerns were the same as hers, with an additional reflection due to his own situation. A clergyman, expected to preach and to practice morality, would be injured by such an example in his own family. "Even allowing Maria to remain at Mansfield Park raises questions," he said.

"Elissa is my granddaughter! I cannot leave her in Antigua. You have never been to the West Indies; you cannot be fully aware of the dangers. Besides, whether or not Elissa and Maria are at Mansfield Park or in distant lands will not alter the sins that have been committed by my own children. But I have more pressing matters to discuss with you." And Sir Thomas related Lord Dexthorpe's threats and his own concerns about Tom's possible guilt.

Edmund was at first skeptical; he did not believe that his good-natured brother could be violent towards anyone. But when he learned of Tom's gambling last winter and his consequent deceit about it, Edmund's confidence in his brother weakened. Moreover, he had something to add. "The snuffbox – the one made from the hoof of a battle horse – Tom told plenty of others about it. He even once spoke to a curio dealer to determine its worth. I expect that Mr. Yates learned about it from Tom."

This bit of information was intriguing, and Tom was summoned to his father's study for additional interrogation. Sir Thomas wished to know if Tom had described the snuffbox to Mr. Yates – if he had perhaps given the snuffbox to Mr. Yates so that Mr. Yates could collect on Tom's debt.

Tom admitted that he might have described the snuffbox to Mr. George Yates; he conceded that Edmund was correct that he had once spoken to a curio dealer about its worth, but only in idle conversation. While at Weymouth, Tom had met an expert in rare items and had wondered how those items were valued; as an example, he described his father's snuffbox. But he had not given the snuffbox to Mr. Yates; he had not owed Mr. Yates money. Why the snuffbox had been found among Mr. Yates's things, Tom could not say.

Sir Thomas said, "I can only hope that we will hear from Mr. Rushworth soon. I sent a servant to Sotherton six hours ago."

Edmund was confused by this; when the situation was explained, he was still skeptical. "I would not wish to rely on the memory of Mr. Rushworth to prove my innocence. Was anyone else at that game?"

Tom said another man had been there, a fellow whose last name was Smith, but Tom did not know much about him. It might be possible to track him down, but it would not be easy.

Sir Thomas concurred that Mr. Rushworth was not an ideal witness, but that the question to be posed to him was so straightforward that they should hope for the best. And, even if Mr. Rushworth could not remember how much Tom had lost that night last winter, perhaps he could help to identify and to locate Mr. Smith.

Tom, standing near the window, informed his father and his brother that the man Sir Thomas had sent to Sotherton was returning. "Now we shall learn something," said Sir Thomas.

The messenger, despite his ride of twenty miles – he was one of Mansfield Park's grooms, so a long ride was not especially fatiguing for him – insisted on reporting to his master immediately. "Well, Cooper, what information have you brought us?" asked the baronet. "Have you brought us a message from Mr. Rushworth?"

No, Sir Thomas, he had not.

"Is Rushworth traveling?" asked Edmund. "Do you know where he is?"

No, Mr. Rushworth was not traveling. Mr. Rushworth was still at Sotherton.

"Then why did he not send a reply?" inquired Tom.

"Because," Cooper explained, "Mr. James Rushworth is dead."

CHAPTER TWENTY-ONE

The news of the death of Mr. Rushworth startled everyone in Sir Thomas's study. After shocked exclamations, Sir Thomas asked for all the information that Cooper could give, but the man only had a few details. There had been no accident, no blow to the head, nor any slash of his throat. Mr. Rushworth had simply been found dead in his bed this morning.

"Poor devil," muttered Tom.

Sir Thomas still wished to know more. Was Mr. Rushworth's death natural, or had he been murdered?

The groom did not know, but could report that the local coroner – not the one who had recently visited Mansfield Park, but another man, much closer to Sotherton – was making inquiries. Mr. Rushworth had complained occasionally about a sore throat, but had appeared to have no illness nor weakness of consequence.

Sir Thomas asked the messenger several more questions, but soon came to the end of the man's knowledge. Cooper departed in order to seek refreshment.

"I do not know what to think," said Sir Thomas. "Rushworth! Dead! Could there be any connection between his death and the death of Mr. Yates, do you think?"

Tom and Edmund considered this, but could see little that linked the two deaths. Sir Thomas rose. "I do not think Maria will be especially affected, but I must inform her before she learns about Mr. Rushworth's death from the servants." As all the servants were certainly discussing the subject, the men hastened to the drawing-room to speak with the ladies at once.

Sir Thomas did not attempt to deliver the news to his daughter in private. Maria was shocked, certainly, and exclaimed, "Poor James!" but although she trembled, she neither fainted nor wept, and she asked what exactly had happened.

The other ladies were also startled. "How terrible!" Julia exclaimed. Lady Bertram pitied Mrs. Rushworth – not her daughter, but Mr. Rushworth's elderly mother – who would now be quite alone, and wondered if she would be a good prospect to be the recipient of a puppy. "Not immediately; it could seem as if she were trying to replace her son with a dog," Susan counseled, although she added that she thought the gesture might prove kind later. Mrs. Norris, like Maria, wanted to know how Mr. Rushworth had died. "Could he have been murdered by the horse thief?"

Sir Thomas said that seemed unlikely; he was aware of only a few details regarding the death of Mr. Rushworth, but this morning the man had been found dead in his bed.

Nevertheless Mrs. Norris persisted with her idea. "The horse that was in the Mansfield Park stables the night Mr. Yates died – it is now in the stables at Sotherton."

"An unlucky omen," said Mr. John Yates, then added: "The pale horse of death."

"The horse is black," Maria objected.

"Surely the horse had nothing to do with either death," said Susan. "Its presence must be a coincidence."

"Do not say that, Susan," said Tom. And then he explained that some people considered *him* to be the most likely murderer of Mr. George Yates. As he defied the world to discover or even to invent a reason for him to kill Mr. James Rushworth, he preferred the deaths to be connected, as that would clear him of involvement in the death of Mr. George Yates.

"Surely you did not kill Mr. Yates, Tom," said Lady Bertram. "Or Mr. Rushworth!"

Tom said he was glad that at least his mother believed in him; the men in the room all seemed rather ashamed of their lack of confidence in Mr. Bertram. Sir Thomas suggested they seek other topics of conversation. Edmund said he must go soon, and asked his mother if she had any message for Fanny. Lady Bertram employed Susan to write a note for her, which occupied Susan for a quarter of an hour. By the time she was done, tea was arriving, and the conversation was returning to the subjects that Sir Thomas had counseled against. Julia and her husband were trying to explain to Sir Thomas how seriously they should take the threats of Lord Dexthorpe, and Maria was attempting to comprehend how Tom could be a suspect in the death of Mr. Yates.

After the tea was drunk, Edmund rose to depart. He bade them all farewell, advising Tom, in particular, to tell the truth and all would be well.

"I am telling the truth," Tom protested, "but now my story cannot be confirmed by Rushworth."

"I suppose we should send a note of condolence to Mrs. Rushworth," said Lady Bertram, and again Susan's services were required.

Mrs. Norris patted the hand of her eldest niece. "You should not grieve, Maria. Mr. Rushworth never appreciated you."

Susan thought, from everything that she had heard, that Maria had never appreciated Mr. Rushworth, but she kept her ideas to herself. When Lady Bertram's letter to the elder Mrs. Rushworth was done, to be sent with the post the next morning, Susan sat quietly, studying Tom. She could not believe that he had murdered Mr. Yates – she could not! And what about poor Mr. Rushworth? How could he possibly be dead? He had been in good health when she had met him eight days ago! Except for his tendency to clear his throat, she thought, but surely he could not have died from that? Yet if he had been found in his bed, there could have been no accident nor any foul play.

Unfortunately, the death of Mr. Rushworth made the clearing of Tom's name more difficult. Tom was speaking with Mr. John Yates, trying to determine which Smith could have taken part in that card game – the first name had either been Robert or Richard – but Tom was not certain; that was the only occasion that they had met. "Crawford might know," Tom muttered to his father, but no one wanted to contact Mr. Crawford.

Mrs. Norris still spoke about the horse, how that had to be the key to all the mysteries of the last two weeks. Perhaps, suggested her aunt, Mr. Rushworth had sent someone to steal back the horse, but something had gone wrong, and then that someone – some manservant, Mrs. Norris supposed, at Sotherton – had feared the death would be discovered and he had killed his master.

Maria, familiar with the servants at Sotherton, thought this unlikely, but Mrs. Norris continued to promote her conjecture, until Lady Bertram said that she hoped servants were not murdering their masters.

Susan learned from a housemaid that she was wanted by Elissa; she went upstairs to care for her young cousin.

CHAPTER TWENTY-TWO

The next morning, upon the request of Sir Thomas, Susan called at the Parsonage. She explained that she had a favor to ask of Miss Crawford, to write to her brother to ask if he could help identify the Smith who had been at that card game with Tom Bertram and Mr. George Yates last winter. Then, if Mr. Crawford could identify the Smith in question, Sir Thomas would like assistance in locating him.

Miss Crawford made sure she understood exactly what Susan wanted, and then said: "Miss Price, I will do as you ask, as long as you grant me a favor – do not be alarmed, I want nothing more than a half-hour of chat. With all that has been happening, you must understand that we are all extremely curious, and any information that you can give me will provide everyone in the Parsonage with conversation for the rest of the day."

Susan agreed, but cautioned that she could spare no more than thirty minutes, as she would surely be needed at home.

Miss Crawford's initial questions concerned the death of Mr. Rushworth. How were those at Mansfield Park, especially Mr. Rushworth's former wife, responding to the news? Susan replied that Maria had seemed both surprised and shocked. Miss Crawford shook her head. "Poor Mrs. Rushworth! If she had endured only three years of marriage to him, and especially if she had managed to produce a son, she would have a pretty settlement for the rest of her life. Now I understand the property will go to a cousin, a Mr. Walter Rushworth who has been living somewhere in Switzerland. A happy day for the new proprietor, but not for my former friend. Ah, well, we all have regrets. Tell me, Miss Price – do those at Mansfield Park, in particular, does Sir Thomas – believe that the deaths of Mr. George Yates and Mr. James Rushworth are connected?"

Susan said that although it was tempting to believe that the deaths of two wealthy young men – so near each other in time, and both with ties, albeit in Mr. Yates's case, trifling, to Mansfield Park – were connected, Sir Thomas did not see how they could be. The horse seemed to be the only link, and although it could have played a part in the death of Mr. George Yates, who had died in the stables, it was difficult to see how the animal could have had anything to do with the demise of Mr. James Rushworth, who had died in his bed.

"This is a point where my intelligence is more to the purpose than yours, Miss Price," said Miss Crawford triumphantly. She explained that just that morning, Dr. Grant had learned from an acquaintance that poison was suspected in Mr. Rushworth's death!

This intrigued Susan, and she asked for whatever details Miss Crawford could share. Miss Crawford first warned Miss Price that the details were gruesome, not necessarily appropriate for such a young lady's ears, but Miss Crawford could not restrain herself, and so continued. She explained that the skin of the deceased Mr. Rushworth had had a strange color; he had smelled strange as well.

"Do you have a description of the smell?"

"Burnt nutmeats."

Susan did not understand the significance, but she committed the detail to memory. "My uncle will be interested in this, I am sure, but if Mr. Rushworth was poisoned, does not that make it even less likely that the deaths were committed by the same person? The deaths are so different."

Miss Crawford said that, as she had no murderers among her acquaintance – at least not that she was aware of – she could not speculate with any confidence on how they might behave. The clock struck the half hour, and Susan said that she appreciated the information, but that she really had to go. Miss Crawford promised to send the letter to her brother with the inquiries about Mr. R— Smith that morning, and walked Susan to the door. On the threshold she said: "I thought I saw Mr. Edmund Bertram yesterday, on his horse. Is that possible, or did my imagination play tricks on me?"

Susan confirmed that her cousin and brother-in-law had ridden to Mansfield Park yesterday. He was well, and her sister Fanny was well, but they were concerned by all that was happening at his father's estate.

"Of course, very natural, very attentive," said Miss Crawford. "I am happy to learn that all is well with Mr. and Mrs. Bertram of Thornton Lacey. I will detain you no longer, Miss Price, and will attend immediately to the letter to my brother."

Susan returned to Mansfield Park and went at once to her uncle's study with what she had heard from Miss Crawford about Mr. Rushworth's death. Sir Thomas made inquiries, and discovered that what Miss Crawford had told his niece was correct. He learned several other interesting details, including the fact that the coroner in Sotherton had determined that the poison, whatever it was, had acted quickly, probably in only a few minutes, information that, when it reached Cook, greatly reassured her, as the food he had consumed while at Mansfield Park several days before could not have had anything to do with his decease.

The inquiries into Mr. Rushworth's death ruffled few at Mansfield Park. The magistrate from Sotherton came to speak to them, especially to Maria as Mr. Rushworth's former wife, but Maria, although she had turned pale when she heard that James had been murdered, could tell her interlocutor little about Mr. Rushworth's recent visit. "I had no conversation with my former husband; I was never even in the same room with him, so I can tell you nothing of his state of mind." Sir Thomas explained that Mr. Rushworth had come to see him about the horse that Mr. Yates had won in a wager, as it had somehow reappeared at Sotherton, but that they had discussed little else. The baronet had not noticed anything unusual about his former son-in-law's spirits. Miss Susan Price had met with him briefly, but as this was her first introduction to Mr. Rushworth, she could not judge if his behavior were any different than it was on other occasions. Mrs. Norris had spoken with Mr. Rushworth as well, and she had a little more to say about her niece's former husband. "Mr. Rushworth had dressed in his finest clothes when he visited Mansfield Park. Obviously his intention was to make a good impression. After all, he had not needed to ride ten miles in order to let us know about the whereabouts of an animal; he could have sent the information by a servant. My opinion is that he missed my niece greatly, and after his visit here he realized winning back her heart was impossible, and so he found a way to take his life."

The Sotherton magistrate, who had already spoken with the servants on Rushworth's estate, confirmed that Mrs. Norris was correct in that Mr. Rushworth had taken great pains with his appearance that day, but what that said regarding his state of mind was inconclusive.

Over the next few days the inmates of Mansfield Park learned that Sotherton was in even more disarray than Mansfield Park. The last proprietor was dead from poison, but how that had been administered was not clear. Excepting those who had dealt with Mr. Rushworth's dead body, no one else at Sotherton had died or had even displayed any symptoms, so the poison could not have been in his food or drink. A clue was found on the floor of Mr. Rushworth's bedroom, a tiny, plain vial that no one in the household claimed to recognize. The vial was empty, so its contents could not be tested on an animal, but it smelled of burnt nutmeats, and so most believed that the poison must have been in that vial. Everyone at Sotherton denied having anything to do with it, and besides, if the vial had contained the poison that the killer had used to murder Sotherton's master, why had the murderer not taken that clue away? Destroying the vial would have been easy; one only had to crush it and leave the shards on one of the gravel walks.

"Perhaps the murderer was not very bright," said Mr. John Yates, as the inmates of Mansfield Park tried to comprehend what had happened at Sotherton. All but Sir Thomas, who was reviewing papers in his library, and Elissa, who was being cared for by Ann Jones, were gathered in the drawing-room on a rainy afternoon.

"James Rushworth was not very bright," said Julia.

"But why would Mr. Rushworth take his own life?" asked Lady Bertram. "He was young, healthy and rich!"

"Perhaps, after visiting Mansfield Park, he realized how much he missed Maria," said Mrs. Norris, still forwarding her idea.

Maria shook her head. "Aunt, I do not see how that is possible. James and I did not even speak."

"Perhaps he had financial problems we do not know about," suggested Susan.

Tom, still suffering from the suspicions that were burdening him with respect to the death of Mr. Yates – Miss Crawford had written to her brother, but Mr. Crawford had not yet replied, so there was no confirmation from the mysterious Mr. Smith – Tom had another idea, one that had been suggested and rejected before, but which now seemed to him more likely. "What if Rushworth followed Yates here and killed him in the stables? Rushworth must have been angry about the loss of his horse. He was also a large fellow, and could have managed it. Then, later, out of remorse, *he* took his own life."

For a minute, everyone contemplated Tom's theory. "That would be convenient," remarked Julia.

"Yet is it not reasonable?" argued Tom. "Everyone has assumed that the deaths were connected through Mansfield Park. But what if they were connected through Sotherton?"

His audience was pleased by his remarks. "Of course, those deaths had nothing to do with Mansfield Park!" exclaimed Mrs. Norris.

"If Rushworth took his life from remorse, why did he not leave a letter explaining what he had done?" asked Mr. John Yates.

The matter was discussed by everyone in the drawing-room. One theory, offered by Mrs. Norris, was that Mr. Rushworth had not wanted to distress his mother by being a suicide. Suicides were considered scandalous; the deceased were not even permitted burial in hallowed ground.

"I think it is all unlikely," said Julia and explained that, in her opinion, Mr. Rushworth had not been capable of such planning or consequential thought.

"You should not speak ill of the dead," said Mrs. Norris, and Susan wondered which was unkinder to Mr. Rushworth's memory: to think him stupid or to think him a murderer. Of course, it was possible for Mr. Rushworth to have been both stupid *and* a murderer.

Tea arrived; Sir Thomas joined them. He listened to the current speculations, expressed his hope that one of them was true, but was there any proof? First, of course, they would all feel more secure if they could be certain that the murderer had nothing to do with Mansfield Park. Second, if Lord Dexthorpe could be convinced that Mansfield Park had had nothing to do with Mr. Yates's death, that would be a great relief.

Until Lord Dexthorpe's threats could be checked, and Sir Thomas could be assured that his income would not be attacked, the baronet was reluctant to make several decisions. Maria and Mrs. Norris: should they return to Ireland? And what should be done with little Elissa? Their situations depended on Sir Thomas's future income.

"I do not wish to disappoint Lady Bertram," said Sir Thomas, who had been able to provide her ladyship with every luxury during their married life. Susan thought her ladyship and her dog could sit comfortably on a sofa in a much smaller room, if required, but she appreciated her uncle's fondness for her aunt.

A carriage, pulled by four horses, was coming up the drive. Mr. John Yates looked out the window and told his father-in-law and brother-in-law that they would have the opportunity to make the case very soon, for his father, Lord Dexthorpe, had arrived.

CHAPTER TWENTY-THREE

Lord Dexthorpe was ushered into the drawing-room at once. His elder son, although several inches taller, had been very similar to him in appearance; his younger son, Mr. John Yates, had inherited the baron's jaw.

Even though Lord Dexthorpe's estate was in the neighboring county of Lincolnshire, and their children were married to each other, Sir Thomas and Lady Bertram had never met the father of Mr. John Yates. If Julia Bertram and John Yates had married in the traditional manner, there would have been a wedding at which the parties could have effected an introduction – but Julia and John had eloped. Although more than two years had passed since that event – an event that had not pleased any of the parents when it occurred – neither the baron nor the baronet had expressed a desire to meet. Her ladyship, ever indolent, had not even considered issuing an invitation.

Now murder, not marriage, brought them together. As Mr. John Yates made the introductions, Sir Thomas, aware of Lord Dexthorpe's intentions with respect to the income of Mansfield Park, had to summon all his dignity in order to welcome him with civility, while the words of Lord Dexthorpe, who held the baronet responsible for the death of his eldest son, were full of hostility. Everyone appeared deeply uncomfortable, with the exception of Lady Bertram, who was the only one able to manage a smile. Lord Dexthorpe accepted a cup of tea, and Susan departed briefly to give instructions about the rooms. When she returned to the drawing-room she discovered that Lord Dexthorpe, with the highest rank, was doing most of the talking; and she detected another trait that Mr. John Yates had inherited from his father – his tendency to express his feelings.

"Decided had to come here and determine why you, Sir Thomas, have not yet found the murderer of my son. My son died here, a fortnight ago, and yet nothing has been done about it. Nothing!"

Susan wanted to contradict him, but she was just an indigent niece, so she stayed silent. Others, however, attempted to reason with the baron. Mr. John Yates said he was aware that Sir Thomas had interviewed many people in his attempt to discover the truth. "But Sir Thomas has not discovered it, has he? That is why I am here!" Mrs. Norris, a little subdued in the presence of a lord, ventured her opinion that the murderer was a horse thief, but Lord Dexthorpe dismissed the suggestion. "No other horses in the neighborhood were taken, while the horse that departed from the Mansfield Park stables just made its way back to Sotherton. Someone opened the gate for it, but I see no evidence of a horse thief." Tom advanced the notion that Rushworth was responsible – and that Rushworth might have taken his life out of remorse.

"James Rushworth! Impossible," pronounced the baron. He had met that late young man, and could not believe that Rushworth could have come to Mansfield Park in the middle of the night without being detected, especially not in order to murder George. Besides, George had been clever, and Rushworth a fool; it was inconceivable that Rushworth had overpowered George. The baron continued to say that, on the other hand, Sir Thomas was not a fool. "*You* must know more about the murderer, Sir Thomas, and I suspect you are trying to protect the blackguard."

Lord Dexthorpe did not name Tom Bertram, but his direct stare made his accusation clear.

Tom flushed with anger, but he spoke clearly. "Lord Dexthorpe, I did not kill your son."

The baron was not convinced. "You say that, but can you prove it? I know you were in debt to him before, why not last month?"

"My lord, I" – Tom started to defend himself, but his father, wishing to avert a scene, suggested to the baron that they go to his rooms to discuss this in private.

The baron refused; he wanted everyone in the drawing-room. "If you do not find and punish the murderer of my son, Sir Thomas, I will ruin you. I will start by making sure that you cannot sell your sugar through M—."

Susan, who assisted her uncle with his correspondence, was aware that M— was an important distributor. She did not know what influence the baron had with M—, but she was aware that the income of Mansfield Park relied heavily on a good business relationship with M—.

Sir Thomas repeated that the baron should come with him into his library, so that he could review all that the baronet had done to find the killer of Mr. Yates. Lord Dexthorpe finally consented to be led out of the room, accompanied by Mr. John Yates.

The others remained in the drawing-room; at first silence reigned, then Tom repeated that he had not killed Mr. Yates.

"Of course not," said Maria quickly.

"No one in his right mind could think such a thing!" agreed Mrs. Norris.

"My uncle will convince him of that soon," said Susan stoutly, with confidence that she did not feel.

"I am not sure of that," said Tom.

Lady Bertram was the least perturbed. "Lord Dexthorpe is simply upset about the loss of his son. His situation is very understandable, and we will have to find some way to restore his spirits."

Julia reproached her. "Mama! Nothing could compensate for the loss of a son."

"If you say so, Julia," said her ladyship, who then stopped speaking. Everyone was silent, as they wondered what the baron and the baronet were discussing in Sir Thomas's rooms. Tom, especially, was concerned. Then Lady Bertram turned to Susan. "With a baron here, I will want to dress in something nice for dinner."

Maria wondered if, with most of the men involved in an important discussion, they should postpone the meal. Mrs. Norris said that would inconvenience Cook, and hoped the men would be considerate.

Fortunately for Cook, dinner was served at its usual hour. Lord Dexthorpe had no interest in showing any consideration to anyone connected with Mansfield Park, but after his journey from Lincolnshire he was hungry. During the meal, the baron held forth, and informed everyone that he had already visited the stables where his son had died, had spoken with the coachman and the grooms, and had also inspected the room in which his son had stayed. He was convinced that *his* industry would soon lead him to the discovery of the murderer. Although Susan thought privately that the baron was treading the ground her uncle had already covered, no one contradicted the baron. As soon as the gooseberry tart was consumed, the ladies withdrew to the drawing-room; the men remained to discuss everything over Sir Thomas's best claret.

The servants, like before, were interested in the visit of the baron, although a little less eager than they had been with his eldest son, as Mr. George Yates's visit had ended so badly. "That is his father?" asked Ann Jones, with whom Susan spoke after she left the table. The housemaid continued: "Think he would want to stay away from the place where his son died. This place is unlucky."

"Lord Dexthorpe is also the father of our Mr. John Yates," said Susan.

The housemaid said nothing to this, but changed the subject, reporting that Elissa had eaten her dinner. Susan thanked her for all the care that she had recently shown the little girl; the housemaid said she was happy to do it, especially now. Susan supposed that caring for Elissa gave Ann Jones the excuse to avoid everyone, especially Stephen Jackson, with whom she had not reconciled. Susan went upstairs to the little girl's room – Elissa had been moved to the nursery – and read her a story and tucked her in bed. She was joined by Tom, and they spoke in whispers as the child closed her eyes. Tom reported that the other men were still speaking over dinner, but that the baron had requested that *he* depart.

"He still believes you are responsible?"

"Yes, he does." And Tom detailed Lord Dexthorpe's threats against the Mansfield Park estate, threats he claimed he would turn into reality if he were not satisfied. The baron would make it difficult for the baronet to sell sugar, compelling Sir Thomas to use inferior distributors. If that did not ruin the Bertrams, Dexthorpe would encourage the military in Antigua to ignore Sir Thomas's plantation and inspire the slaves to revolt.

"Would the military do that?" asked Susan.

"My father does not think so. Encouraging the slaves to revolt on one plantation could encourage them to revolt on the next, and no one wants that."

Susan thought that, from William's description of Antigua, that a revolt would be understandable. But she supposed a less violent solution would be better, if one could be found. She expressed some of this to her cousin.

"You are correct," said Tom. "The situation is abominable, but what can one do? At the moment, all I can do is to try to help her," he said, pointing at his daughter. "If Dexthorpe does not hang me for murder, perhaps I can do something more." He added that he would do much to keep Mansfield Park safe, but he would not go to the executioner for a crime he had not committed.

Elissa slept, so Tom and Susan went downstairs, where they found that the other men had joined the ladies in the drawing-room.

Mrs. Norris sniffed when Tom and Susan entered together, and said she hoped Tom would finally learn to make wiser choices. Tom looked pained and Maria implored Mrs. Norris to leave her brother alone.

As Tom and Susan took seats in the drawing-room, Julia informed them that her husband, Lord Dexthorpe and Sir Thomas planned to visit Sotherton tomorrow.

"Yes," said Sir Thomas. "We wish to determine if the two deaths are connected."

"It seems highly unlikely," said the baron, "but I wish to be fair."

"If they are, Tom, that would clear you, as it seems impossible for you to have had anything to do with Mr. Rushworth's decease," said Maria.

Tom wanted to join them; Lord Dexthorpe refused, saying that would taint the inquiry. Tom protested: "You are considering my guilt or innocence, considering my future, whether I have one or not. I will not remain behind in ignorance."

Susan wanted to applaud Tom's eloquence, and even Sir Thomas seemed impressed. The baron's eyes narrowed, but he acquiesced. Mrs. Norris encouraged Tom to do everything possible to find a horse thief – and also to investigate Rushworth's pecuniary situation.

The following fine morning, the men, who had to cover ten miles to reach Sotherton, departed early. That day, Susan was busy, attending to her aunt, the household, and her little cousin. When she ran up the stairs to fetch a doll for Elissa, she found Ann Jones putting away things in the nursery, tears sliding down her face.

"Ann, what is wrong?" asked Susan, the doll in her hand.

"Nothing," said the housemaid. "You cannot help me."

"If you like, I could speak to Jackson for you."

The housemaid shook her head. "No, just let me do my work. If you like, I can help look after Elissa today. She sings very prettily for one so young."

The hours passed slowly, as they all waited for the men to return from their excursion. Mrs. Norris busied herself with wandering the grounds and insisting on the application of a certain type of mud to a bee sting received by a gardener. Mrs. Rushworth attempted to work on items in the poor basket, but could not concentrate, and persuaded Julia to play backgammon with her. Lady Bertram yawned and fretted over dear Pug, who, her ladyship discovered, had several gray hairs on her muzzle. "We're both growing older," she said to her dog, "both grandmothers now," and her ladyship smiled at her daughters. Susan wrote notes for her aunt and applied herself to the poor basket, and tried not to worry about Tom.

The sun's rays were slanting deeply by the time the men returned from Sotherton. They refreshed themselves with a late supper and then joined the ladies in the drawing-room to make their report. The men had met Mr. Walter Rushworth, who had just arrived from Switzerland; his wife, a native of that country, would be joining him shortly. He was about forty, fit, and, as a man of strict habits and modest expectations, had never thought much about the property in Sotherton. Despite the fact that he inherited after his cousin, Mr. James Rushworth, Mr. Walter Rushworth's long absence seemed to clear him from any involvement in the former proprietor's death. Mr. Walter Rushworth had never met Mr. George Yates, although he had heard of him.

There was always the possibility that Mr. Walter Rushworth was lying, but even the suspicious Lord Dexthorpe and the highly motivated Tom Bertram detected no falsehoods. Instead, Mr. Walter Rushworth spoke at length about the cattle of Switzerland, and asked Sir Thomas if he thought the herds that grazed on the slopes of the Alps would do well in Northamptonshire.

The party from Mansfield Park had spoken with the servants, but found again, no one suspicious. No one else had taken ill. No one knew how Mr. James Rushworth could have consumed anything unusual, except from the empty little vial that had been discovered in Mr. Rushworth's bedroom. Sir Thomas asked, and Lord Dexthorpe demanded, if they could inspect the vial. The housekeeper showed it to them. None of them recognized it; it was small, white, and plain, with no distinguishing marks.

Tom asked to speak to Mr. James Rushworth's old valet, who was now in service to Mr. Walter Rushworth. "What was Rushworth wearing the day he died?"

"How could that possibly matter?" objected Lord Dexthorpe, but Sir Thomas insisted that the valet answer the question. Mr. James Rushworth had been wearing some of his finest, his favorite black coat and a green satin vest.

"And before that, when was the last time that Rushworth wore that attire?" Tom inquired.

The valet considered. The wealthy Mr. Rushworth had had many garments, and it was the manservant's duty to take care of them all. The last time the late master had worn those clothes was the day on which Mr. Rushworth had visited Mansfield Park, to inform Sir Thomas about the horse having reappeared, on its own, at Sotherton.

Lord Dexthorpe wished to go see the horse; as his son's next of kin, did not the animal now belong to him? But the others insisted on speaking with the valet for a few additional minutes. "I recall the green satin," said Sir Thomas. "Very interesting, Tom."

"But why does this matter?" asked Mr. John Yates.

"What if someone at Mansfield Park gave the vial to him?" asked Tom. He then asked the valet if the vial could have been in one of Mr. Rushworth's pockets ever since his visit to Mansfield Park.

The manservant hesitated. He had always taken his master's watch out from one of the pockets. But the vest had several pockets that Mr. Rushworth rarely used, and the valet was not certain he had checked them all. Therefore, it was *possible* that the vial, so small, could have been in one of the vest's other pockets for a while. Considering, he thought there had been a small lump in one of Mr. Rushworth's vest pockets on the day of his death.

"Could it have been the vial?" asked Sir Thomas.

"Possibly. Possibly," said the old valet.

The men wondered how the vial had come to be in Mr. Rushworth's pocket. The old valet swore that he had no reason to harm Mr. Rushworth, who had always been a good master.

"No one suspects you," said Sir Thomas, attempting to reassure the manservant.

Lord Dexthorpe objected. "We have no reason to suspect you more than anyone else," said the baron. "But *you* were the last person to see Mr. Rushworth alive, were you not? And *you* were the person who discovered Mr. Rushworth dead in his bed, were you not?"

The old manservant became extremely anxious, and protested his innocence. Sir Thomas suggested that they go see the horse, and en route apologized to Mr. Walter Rushworth for upsetting the old valet. "Please let him know that unusual deaths require difficult questions. I am sure he is innocent."

"I hope so," said the new proprietor. "I do not like the idea of a manservant who murders his master."

The black horse, its shoe repaired, was in fine fettle. Mr. Walter Rushworth said he had no objection to letting Lord Dexthorpe take the animal, as long as he could prove that Mr. George Yates had won the horse in a fair wager. This demand of proof annoyed the baron, but Mr. Walter Rushworth now had an income of £12,000 per annum and was ready to protest the claims of Lord Dexthorpe.

Susan had to hide her smile when she heard this, especially as it inclined the baron to suspect Mr. Walter Rushworth of the murders, as he apparently had motive. Alas for Lord Dexthorpe, additional inquiries at Sotherton made it clear that Mr. Walter Rushworth had been on the continent when both Mr. James Rushworth and Mr. George Yates died.

"Father, it seems impossible that the new Rushworth could be culpable," said Mr. John Yates. "Of most interest is the vial. When and how did James Rushworth acquire it?"

Sir Thomas and Tom Bertram had pursued the matter while at Sotherton, but none of the servants admitted to knowing anything about its provenance. They consulted with the coachman, who explained that Mr. James Rushworth had made no detours on the day he had visited Mansfield Park, and that in the week before his death, he had only been out a few days, as he had been suffering from a sore throat.

Sir Thomas wanted to know if Rushworth could have received the vial at Mansfield Park. Mr. James Rushworth had met with Sir Thomas, Mrs. Norris and Susan, and had interacted with several of the servants. All denied giving Mr. Rushworth a vial of poison, and none of them seemed to have any reason to wish for Mr. James Rushworth to die. Maria, the only one with a possible motive, stoutly claimed she had not met with him, but had remained in the drawing-room with the other ladies during the entire time of Mr. Rushworth's visit.

Lord Dexthorpe was not convinced that the deaths were connected. He only cared about who had murdered his son, and wanted to punish someone. He maintained that Tom Bertram was still the most likely perpetrator.

Tom protested. *He* had not lost a recent wager to Mr. George Yates; Mr. Rushworth was the most recent victim. Tom repeated his idea that Rushworth could have ridden to Mansfield Park that night, could have taken the life of Mr. George Yates, and then have killed himself from remorse. And if James Rushworth had performed the deed, that would explain the riderless horse, as he could not have ridden both horses back from Mansfield Park to Sotherton.

Mr. John Yates objected. "We know that James Rushworth was at Sotherton the night my brother was murdered. I spoke both to the servants and to the coachmen. Although George could have easily saddled a horse for a night ride, none of them had ever seen James Rushworth saddle a horse."

"Then, perhaps Rushworth hired someone to steal the horse, or at least to let the horse out of the stables, knowing it would return to Sotherton on its own," argued Tom. "*That* man then killed Mr. Yates."

"Is that not enough for reasonable doubt?" asked Sir Thomas. "Both deaths probably had nothing to do with anyone at Mansfield Park."

"I do not want reasonable doubt," fired back the baron. "I demand certainty. I demand that someone be punished for the death of my son. And unless you find someone, all of Mansfield Park will suffer." And the baron rose and left the drawing-room.

Lord Dexthorpe may have departed, but the tension remained; enough tension for even Lady Bertram to remark on it. "My, my," she murmured.

Mrs. Norris was indignant, and voluble on the baronet's behalf. "I know he is a baron," she said, "and your father, Mr. John Yates, but how can Lord Dexthorpe expect hospitality from you, Sir Thomas, when he is planning to injure Mansfield Park?"

Mr. John Yates apologized and Sir Thomas said he would deal with the matter, somehow. He had taken care of everyone at Mansfield Park for years and promised to continue to do his utmost. It would be easier, of course, if he could discover the murderer of Mr. George Yates, but even if he could not, he would protect them all.

"I am sure you will, Sir Thomas," said his lady.

CHAPTER TWENTY-FOUR

Eventually everyone retired for the night, with the hope that conditions in the morning would somehow be better, but with no reason to think that they would. As Susan prepared for bed, she looked around her little room, which for Mansfield Park was not at all luxurious, but which, compared to her situation back in Portsmouth, was spacious, comfortable and, most of all, clean. She had been here for more than two years, and had stopped wondering at the coverlet without holes and the water jug without chips a long time ago. She regarded these items with renewed appreciation, as well as the quality of the feather mattress on which she slept. What if Sir Thomas's income was severely reduced? Her uncle could not be expected to keep her; she would have to return to her father. And what about her aunt and her cousins, who had never known deprivation in their lives? How would they manage?

When Susan rose the next morning, the situation was no better than it had been the night before, and the unity that had prevailed the previous evening seemed to have vanished. Mr. and Mrs. John Yates conversed frequently in low voices, but Susan's keen ears discerned some of their words. Julia wanted Mr. John Yates to persuade his father to stop threatening her father, while Mr. John Yates said she ought to take action herself. Mrs. Rushworth and Mrs. Norris sat in a corner, quietly discussing some urgent matter; Susan was curious, but she only caught something about Maria's necklace, and she did not understand what that could mean. Was Mrs. Rushworth considering selling her necklace if they needed funds? Tom, especially anxious, had dark circles under his eyes, evidence that he, too, had slept poorly. The servants, from the highly starched Baddeley down to the red-fingered scullery maids, were likewise glum, because if Mansfield Park failed, how would they live? Sir Thomas and Lord Dexthorpe sat in the baronet's rooms, reviewing evidence, bringing in one person after another for conversation. The baron went to the stables many times, irritating the men and making even the animals nervous.

Only two people in the household seemed to be at ease: Lady Bertram and her granddaughter, Elissa. Elissa, of course, was too young to understand what was happening, but despite her ladyship's better comprehension, Lady Bertram continued to smile, doze on her sofa, and speak placidly to anyone near her. "I know it is unpleasant now, but I am certain everything will work out."

Susan had sometimes wondered why Sir Thomas had married her aunt; had it been for her serenity? Certainly, Susan did not feel serene; nor did she see how their situation could improve. They needed answers to questions, but discovering those answers seemed impossible, and she could not imagine what other approaches they could take. And even though the house was full, Susan felt alone. She usually spent several hours a day with Sir Thomas, but Lord Dexthorpe was with her uncle, and her attendance was not needed. If Susan attempted to amuse her aunt, Mrs. Norris or Mrs. Rushworth soon appeared. Mrs. Yates avoided everyone except for Mr. Yates; Tom stalked around the garden by himself. Elissa clung to Susan, but Elissa was a child, and Susan longed for adult conversation. If only she could go to Thornton Lacey for a visit, but given her responsibility for Elissa, and the general trouble at Mansfield Park, she could not ask her uncle to let her take the carriage for such an excursion. Susan, her heart full but with no confidant, added to the letter that she had still not posted. She had decided that she would never send it, for it was too revealing, and she even considered burning it. But with the warm weather, she had no fire in her room, and she dared not use the fireplace in the drawing-room. With so many people in the house, someone could easily see her and want to know why she was burning a letter. Besides, the words in it reminded her of what she wished to discuss with Fanny, whenever the opportunity arrived.

Susan could not go to Thornton Lacey, but she could walk to the Parsonage. To her surprise, Susan's best respite was a chat with Miss Crawford in the shrubbery. As the whole neighborhood seemed to be aware of the troubles at Mansfield Park, Susan was not betraying secrets when they spoke, and she could also talk of her feelings. "Only two days have passed since Lord Dexthorpe arrived, but they seem like the longest days I have ever known," said Susan. "Yesterday was a little better, because the men went to Sotherton to speak with the new proprietor, but they only learned that the new Mr. Rushworth has a deep interest in cattle. Mr. Walter Rushworth, who was away in Switzerland until recently, appears unlikely to have had anything to do with the death of Mr. James Rushworth, and had never met Mr. George Yates at all."

"Nevertheless, I am in agreement with her ladyship," said Miss Crawford, who had heard, too, that Lady Bertram was the only calm person on the estate. "So many things may change. For example, Lord Dexthorpe may grow tired of seeking revenge on Mansfield Park. He is grief-stricken now, but eventually he will see that whatever he does will not restore his son to life, and that he would do better to cultivate those who could be friendly to him. Listen to me, Miss Price! I could preach an inspiring sermon, could I not? If only I could attend to my own counsel."

Susan realized that she had been pouring out her own heart without giving Miss Crawford the same satisfaction. "Is there anything you wish to confide in me?"

"No – no, my regrets are old and not worth revisiting; it is just the return to Mansfield that has brought them to the fore. I could wish that some things had been different. But although my sister does well as the wife of a clergyman, I do not believe that I am suited for that position. How fare the Thornton Lacey Bertrams?"

Susan said they received pleasant reports from Edmund and Fanny, only that Mrs. Bertram was very busy becoming acquainted with everyone in the parish.

"I am happy to hear it. And I am positive, Miss Price, that something will happen to relieve those at Mansfield Park. I know, for example, that my brother is working on your case. Henry does not like to write letters, but in other ways he is diligent, and I am certain we will hear from him soon."

Susan was not as sanguine with respect to Mr. Crawford, but this she did not say. Their tête-à-tête was ended by Mrs. Grant, who came out to examine the apricot tree, which was infested with some sort of pest and would have to be cut down. "It is not a great loss; the fruit is not very good," she said. "Ah, well, not every tree can be the best." Susan stayed only a few minutes longer, then returned to Mansfield Park.

Although Susan had not placed any reliance on Mr. Crawford's utility to their situation – perhaps he even hated everything associated with Mansfield Park and wished them ill! – Miss Crawford's knowledge of her brother proved better than Miss Price's. Mr. Crawford did not write, but that evening at Mansfield Park they learned that Mr. Crawford had arrived at the Parsonage. A message was brought by a servant of Dr. Grant's, with the request that Mr. Crawford and his sister be allowed to call at Mansfield Park in the morning.

Normally Sir Thomas would not grant Mr. Crawford's request, but Lord Dexthorpe, who said that Mr. Crawford had been one of his dead son's true friends, wanted to see him, and both Tom and Mr. John Yates wished to hear what Mr. Crawford might have to say.

The ladies were also curious about Mr. Crawford, and as he would be accompanied by Miss Crawford when he called – the presence of the feminine intended to encourage civility in the men, who given the situation, could be tempted to anger – they also urged Sir Thomas to permit the visit. Even Lady Bertram said she would not object to their calling.

Sir Thomas finally agreed. "The more witnesses we have, the less likely anything will be distorted."

The awkward event was planned for mid-morning. The only lady who would not attend was Mrs. Rushworth, whom Mrs. Norris escorted away; Maria placed herself in her room at a window, so she could watch her seducer and his sister walking up the path from the Parsonage to her father's house.

Even without Mrs. Rushworth, no one was at ease. The Crawfords greeted everyone; Miss Crawford was introduced to Lord Dexthorpe; then Mr. Crawford seated himself on the sofa beside Lady Bertram.

"I know that I am not welcome here," said Mr. Crawford. "But after I learned of Rushworth's death, I felt that I had to come and to shed whatever light I can on the situation."

"I want to know who murdered my son!" said Lord Dexthorpe. "Can you tell me who it was? Was it this Rushworth?"

Mr. Crawford's answer was delayed by the reappearance of Mrs. Norris, announcing that she had told the servants to bring in tea and cake. Mrs. Norris sat next to Mr. Crawford on the sofa, compelling Lady Bertram to sit up straighter and to move her dog on to her lap. Mr. Crawford stretched out his hand to Pug; the animal sniffed it then licked it.

When they were all resettled, Mr. Crawford spoke. "My lord, I do not know who murdered your son, but I did know George Yates very well and I believe my knowledge may help you determine who killed him. But I must warn you, that you may learn things about your son that will not please you."

"I have already read your letter about him, and I know your opinion. I have mine. At least George loved life! And if your information helps me discover his killer, I am ready to listen to anything you tell me."

The only other person who had any reason to object to the blackening of the deceased's character was Mr. John Yates, and he indicated that Mr. Crawford should continue.

"Very well. I warned you, I cannot do this without speaking ill of the dead. You know that George Yates won most of his wagers. This is because he cheated."

The bereaved father protested, accusing Mr. Crawford of slander, but Sir Thomas reminded the baron that they had told Mr. Crawford that they would listen to what he had to say. Mr. Crawford had much to tell, and explained that Mr. George Yates had used a well-placed mirror to take advantage of Rushworth at cards.

Tom said that was the solution that he had always favored, that Mr. James Rushworth had murdered Mr. George Yates and then had taken his own life out of remorse. This solution, alas, retained the same objections that it had before. The servants at Sotherton claimed that Rushworth had been at home the night that Mr. Yates had died at Mansfield Park. And none of them had detected any symptoms of remorse on the part of Mr. Rushworth; he had not been upset at all by the death of Mr. George Yates and had been pleased to have the horse back in his stables.

"What more can you tell us, Mr. Crawford?" asked the baronet.

Mr. Crawford kept them interested, as he finished speaking of the cheating that Mr. Yates had done and then moved on to theft. Mr. Yates had visited great houses, and then robbed them of precious items that could be easily carried away and then sold: jewelry, silver, and other articles of value. In fact, Mr. Yates was known to leave great houses late at night, with his pockets full of stolen goods.

"You lie!" protested Lord Dexthorpe. "My son was not a thief."

But several gathered in the drawing-room offered evidence supporting Mr. Crawford's assertion. "I discovered my father's snuffbox in your son's bag," said Tom, while Mr. and Mrs. John Yates both said they had heard rumors to this effect, and added that they had always wondered how George had lived the way he had. "I thought you were giving him a larger allowance," said Mr. John Yates, but Lord Dexthorpe said he had not given his elder son any extra funds.

"That is not all," said Mr. Crawford. "Mr. Yates was engaged in blackmail as well, particularly of women of means." He described how Yates had been a frequent seducer of women, and then, to add insult to injury, would extort them for money or threaten to expose them.

"That cannot be true!" objected the baron, but then Susan, in a halting voice, explained how Mr. Yates had accosted her on the stairs, and how she had been so unsettled by what had happened that she had barricaded her door.

In this case, Mr. Crawford was reluctant to give any names, because he did not want to cause additional pain to those who had been harmed by Mr. Yates, but he knew of more than one case and he had to assume there were others.

"But what if one of them murdered my son?" said Lord Dexthorpe. "A woman was seen that night by the coachman!"

Sir Thomas still said he did not see how a woman could have managed the deed: hitting Mr. Yates on the head, cutting his throat, dragging his heavy body into a corner.

"That is true, Sir Thomas," said Mrs. Norris. "No woman could have moved Mr. Yates. Ah, tea! Baddeley, bring it here; I will pour."

Lord Dexthorpe said that he did not know how they were to discoverer his son's murderer if Mr. Crawford did not reveal which women were being blackmailed, while Mr. Crawford said that Yates had been rather secretive about such information but that he did have some ideas. In the meantime, Mrs. Norris created a bustle of activity, pouring tea and slicing cake and insisting that everyone partake; Susan carried around cups and plates to those not seated by the sofa.

The conversations broke in many directions. Some thought the mysterious woman to be important; others thought those who had been cheated in wagers to be most likely to be angry enough with Mr. Yates to kill him, while a few – Lady Bertram especially – took interest in her tea and cake. Mr. Crawford, seated between Lady Bertram and Mrs. Norris, resumed speaking. "You must understand that many people had reason to kill him." And he hazarded that one of the women, at least, was in the neighborhood.

"Henry has not told me who the woman might be," said Miss Crawford, "but from his hints, I believe that the woman planning to marry Mr. Charles Maddox could be a candidate."

"Oh, no!" cried Lady Bertram. "Oh, dear, no!"

All the attention that had been engrossed by Mr. Crawford was now directed towards her ladyship, who had never, in Susan's memory, spoken with such alarm.

"Lady Bertram, what is the matter?" asked Sir Thomas.

"Pug – something is wrong!" Her dog, Pug, had suddenly become ill. Before anyone could do anything other than comprehend what was happening, the little dog trembled violently, then lay still.

"My dear, I am afraid she is dead," said Sir Thomas.

"No! Poor Pug. How can that be?"

"A sudden seizure," said Tom. "She was not a young dog."

"But she was fine just yesterday, when we strolled in the garden. She seemed quite her normal self."

Mr. Crawford was distressed. "I fed her some of my cake. Could that have hurt her?"

Tom Bertram said he did not see how; the dog had been eating bits of cake her entire life.

"Poor Pug," said Lady Bertram, and tears slipped down her face. "Ever my sweet friend." Sir Thomas gently took Pug from her, then assisted her to her feet. "You must excuse us," he told those in the drawing-room, and escorted his wife out of the room, supporting her with one arm while he carried the lifeless animal in the other.

Lord Dexthorpe said that cake was not good for dogs, and that he would never allow his animals to consume anything of the sort.

"But Tom is correct, Pug has eaten cake all her life," said Mrs. Norris. "Unless *you* poisoned the dog, Mr. Crawford?"

"I beg your pardon?" asked Mr. Crawford, stunned by the accusation. His shock quickly transformed into anger. "Why, in God's name, would I wish to poison Lady Bertram's poor dog?"

Everyone in the room looked at Mr. Crawford with suspicion, but most made exclamations of doubt. Then Miss Crawford, in a much sharper voice, asked her brother if he had eaten any of the cake or if he had drunk any of the tea; Mr. Crawford answered that he had been too busy talking to do so.

"Then, Henry, I advise you not to touch anything," said his sister, and Mr. Crawford set his plate and cup down on a table, and wiped his hands on a napkin.

Everyone else in the room put aside their cups and plates. "Mansfield Park is dangerous – cursed," said Lord Dexthorpe; his son Mr. John Yates agreed with him.

Tom, however, was dubious. "It is impossible that Cook would send up poisoned cake. Besides, many of us have eaten and are not suffering."

"Then it was only *my* slice of cake," said Mr. Crawford. "Mary, let us quit this place. I am even less welcome at Mansfield Park than I had thought." The Crawfords hastily departed, with Miss Crawford pausing to give Susan a message for Lady Bertram, expressing how very sorry she was about the loss of her dear pug.

Mrs. Norris rose as well, saying she wished to comfort her sister, and Julia turned to her husband and said she was fatigued and wished to take a nap.

The drawing-room, that had been so crowded only a short while ago, was now almost empty: only Lord Dexthorpe, Tom and Susan remained. For a minute, they were quiet, all considering the recent events, then the baron said: "What if the cake is poisoned?"

Both Tom and Susan objected. The dog had been old; no one else had fallen sick; no one would want to harm Lady Bertram's dog.

"Not Lady Bertram's dog – Mr. Crawford. Young men of means have been dying in the area. What if the target was Mr. Crawford? He has a good income, has he not?"

Tom answered that Crawford had an income of about 4,000£ per annum.

"You are another young man with expectations," remarked Lord Dexthorpe. "You should be careful."

The baron's observation was sufficient to make Tom glance at the crumbs on his own plate with trepidation, and to make Susan study her cousin with concern. "I feel fine," Tom said, partly in order to convince himself, and Susan assured him he showed no symptoms.

Lord Dexthorpe was insistent. "Nevertheless, we should examine the cake – the slice that belonged to Mr. Crawford. We should feed it to some other animal. If the animal dies, the cake was poisoned."

Tom considered. He averred that it was most probable that his mother's dog had simply died, but he was willing to test Lord Dexthorpe's conjecture. If, in the unlikely situation that Mr. Crawford's slice of cake contained poison, he would only risk giving it to an animal that he did not wish to live. "I have an idea," he said, and carefully picked up Mr. Crawford's plate that contained the rest of the slice of cake. Lord Dexthorpe insisted on accompanying him. Susan watched them depart, hoping that even if the baron's speculation proved untrue, that the cooperation between the baron and her cousin would at least improve Lord Dexthorpe's attitude towards Tom and would dissuade him from implementing the threats he had made to ruin all of Mansfield Park. Then Susan quitted the empty drawing-room herself. She contacted the servants, told them to be careful – that Lady Bertram's dog had died after eating a piece of cake – and went upstairs to play with Elissa.

CHAPTER TWENTY-FIVE

As details of the event spread through the estate, Mansfield Park was in confusion. Lady Bertram was in tears about the death of her dog, while everyone else was perturbed about the possibility of poison.

"I never poisoned anyone," declared Cook, terribly distressed, and all work in the kitchens ceased.

Sir Thomas attempted to console his wife, and when she was a little calmer, turned her over to the ministrations of Chapman. He then questioned the servants, first speaking with Cook, and assuring her that even if the cake had been poisoned, which was not a certainty, it could not have been her doing, as no one else in the drawing-room had suffered any ill effects. Nevertheless, Cook was unable to resume her duties, and her assistants could only promise a simple supper. Sir Thomas questioned Baddeley, who had supervised the tea service. Baddeley had served at Mansfield Park for many years; the notion of him poisoning part of the cake strained credulity. Perhaps he had resented Mr. Crawford on Maria's behalf – that was possible – but how could he have known which slice of cake would reach Mr. Crawford? Baddeley, although he had brought in the cake and the tea, had not handed the plates and cups around, but had left it for the gentlemen and ladies to serve themselves.

As Sir Thomas had been in the room himself, he had confidence in the veracity of the butler's words and assured him that he, too, was not under any suspicion. Sir Thomas interviewed everyone who had been present, with the exception of the Crawfords who had already left for the Parsonage. No one had seen anyone adding anything to Mr. Crawford's cake, so it was not possible to determine the guilty party – if there were a guilty party – with certainty. However, it was possible, given the recollections of everyone, including Sir Thomas's own, to reduce the number of possible suspects. Lady Bertram had been at one end of the sofa, Mr. Crawford in the middle, and Mrs. Norris at the end. Susan was the only other person who had even approached that part of the room.

Lady Bertram *could* have poisoned her dog herself, but Sir Thomas dismissed this as impossible. Lady Bertram had loved her little dog and would never have harmed it deliberately. Besides, Sir Thomas did not believe that his wife had any toxic substances in her possession. He conveyed this opinion to Susan and Mrs. Norris, after inviting them to join him in his study.

"I agree, Sir Thomas," said Mrs. Norris. "Lady Bertram would never have hurt her dear pet."

"I also agree, Uncle," said Susan. "First, if someone wished to kill Pug, doing it in a drawing-room full of people seems a very odd time and place. Besides, who would want to kill a dog?"

The only person, Susan reflected, with any motive to murder Pug had been Sir Thomas, as Lady Bertram often bestowed more attention on her pet than on her husband. But Susan suspected that her uncle, who was so busy, did not object to sharing his lady's affections.

"Perhaps Mr. Crawford?" suggested Mrs. Norris. "He may have a desire to do harm to this family."

Sir Thomas said that it seemed unlikely, although he could not completely dismiss him as the culprit. Mr. Crawford may have had no particular love for those residing at Mansfield Park, but murdering the dog would be not just cruel but peculiar, and Sir Thomas could not understand how it could possibly benefit Mr. Crawford.

"Mr. Crawford was the center of attention," Susan objected. "Everyone was observing him and listening to what he had to say. I do not see how he could have poisoned even his own cake without being noticed."

Sir Thomas said Susan had made an excellent point, praise that caused Mrs. Norris to bristle, but before she could oppose the compliment, Sir Thomas continued. "That leaves the two of you," said Sir Thomas. Mrs. Norris had sat on the other side of Mr. Crawford and had sliced and served the pieces of cake, while Susan had carried the small plates around the room.

Then, who had touched Mr. Crawford's plate of cake? Susan said she had not; she had carried plates to those not sitting on the sofa, but that Mr. Crawford, sitting by Mrs. Norris, had been handed his plate by Mrs. Norris herself. Mrs. Norris denied this, maintaining that Susan was lying.

Susan defended herself. She had not handed Mr. Crawford anything. And even if she had, why should she wish to harm Mr. Crawford? He might have done injury to the family at Mansfield Park, but never to her personally; in fact, Mr. Crawford had been of great assistance in getting a promotion for her dear brother William. Besides, *she* had no poisons, no harmful substances.

Mrs. Norris maintained that Susan was clever and could manage to procure poison if she so wished. Besides, this was all speculation and they did not know if Pug had died from eating the cake. Lady Bertram's dog might have had a sudden seizure from some natural cause, poor thing. It was distressing, especially to her dear sister, but not proof of any malevolence.

"We are attempting to discover that," said Sir Thomas. Both Mrs. Norris and Susan wished to know how, so the baronet explained that Tom, accompanied by Lord Dexthorpe, had gone to an area in the stables which was plagued by rats and had placed the questionable remaining piece of cake in a trap. The rats were usually only active at night, so the experiment might not be concluded before the following morning. However, if a rat consumed some of the cake and then died, they would have evidence that the cake contained some harmful substance.

"By morning we should know," repeated Sir Thomas.

"I see," said Mrs. Norris. She asked the baronet if he had any additional questions; he said he did not, and Mrs. Norris excused herself so that she could comfort her sister.

Susan remained with her uncle and asked what he thought had happened.

Sir Thomas shook his head. "I cannot imagine that anyone would wish to kill Lady Bertram's dog. I could understand that several members of my family may resent Mr. Crawford, but I cannot believe that anyone would actually attempt to murder him! Except for Mrs. Rushworth, perhaps, but she was not in the room. Mrs. Norris is the widow of a vicar, and my own sister-in-law – I cannot comprehend it! So, what I expect is that poor Pug died of natural causes, for the dog was not young, and we simply had the bad luck to witness it. As long as Lord Dexthorpe is here I must at least attempt to investigate, but I expect that tomorrow we will discover that the stables still have as many rats as they do today."

Susan was about to remark on that likelihood – that Mr. Crawford's cake had not been poisoned at all – when a maid entered and said that Elissa needed either Mr. Bertram or Miss Price, for the little girl had just learned that Pug was dead and was in tears. As Mr. Bertram was in the stables with Lord Dexthorpe, Miss Price was required. Sir Thomas told Susan to go console his granddaughter.

Elissa, although young, remembered the death of her mother and so was perturbed by the death of her grandmother's dog. Susan sat with her little cousin and did her best to comfort and amuse her. They sang, Susan read to her, and then they took turns hiding, and then finding, a doll in various corners of the nursery.

Ann Jones brought up a tray with bread, cheese, cold meat, pickles and celery. "Cook is too vexed to make a proper dinner."

"Is there news from the stables?" Susan inquired, and then, as she saw the young housemaid appear alarmed, for Stephen Jackson worked in the stables, she added: "I mean, with respect to the rats."

Ann Jones understood that Mr. Bertram and his lordship were still waiting for a rat to take the cake. Susan thanked her, and the housemaid departed. After the meal, Elissa grew drowsy. The day was long, so the sun was still up when Elissa went to sleep. But as the girl was still distressed by the death of the dog, Susan remained long after dark, returning to her own room quite late.

When Susan entered the breakfast parlor the next morning, only Sir Thomas was at the table. He informed her that a rat had died during the night, immediately after consuming part of Mr. Crawford's cake.

"We have a poisoner," he said abruptly.

Susan swore that she had had nothing to do with it; her uncle assured her that he did not suspect her. She was hungry, but the news made her reluctant to eat. Her uncle understood her apprehension and recommended the soft-boiled eggs, which could not be tampered with, and the bread, which he had already consumed without ill consequences.

Their tête-à-tête was interrupted by others, as Lord Dexthorpe, Mr. John Yates, Tom, and Maria all appeared. All yawned as if their nights had been short on sleep, but Lord Dexthorpe wore the expression of satisfaction of a man whose judgment has proved correct.

"One less rat in the stables," said Lord Dexthorpe. "I knew it!"

Tom confirmed Lord Dexthorpe's account. "As I do not think anyone would want to kill my mother's dog, or that I had the opportunity to, we must assume that the baron is correct and someone is targeting gentlemen."

"Young gentlemen of means or with expectations," continued Lord Dexthorpe. "My son George, Rushworth and now Crawford. John and Bertram should be cautious - or leave Mansfield Park immediately."

"Are we certain those three cases are linked?" inquired Sir Thomas. "Mr. Rushworth was probably poisoned, and apparently someone attempted to poison Crawford – but your son's death was different. In my experience as a magistrate, murderers do not usually change their methods."

"You originally believed my son was killed by a horse thief," said the baron, his tone making it clear he did not think much of the baronet's experience.

"Where is Mrs. Norris?" inquired Mr. John Yates, in an attempt to stop his father and father-in-law from arguing. "Has she already breakfasted?"

Sir Thomas had not seen her; nor had anyone else at the breakfast table. Sir Thomas sent a servant up to see if his sister-in-law required anything; the maidservant did not return, but in a few minutes Baddeley entered, his face pale. He leaned over to whisper something to his master, but Sir Thomas's hearing was not that good while Susan's was excellent, and as she understood what was said, she gasped.

Everyone at the table demanded to know what was the matter; Susan looked to her uncle.

"What is it, Sir Thomas?" asked Lord Dexthorpe. "Is Mrs. Norris dead too?"

Lord Dexthorpe's speculation was correct; Mrs. Norris was, indeed, dead.

CHAPTER TWENTY-SIX

Sir Thomas excused himself; both his son and daughter asked if he needed any assistance. The baronet said he would let Tom and Maria know if either were required, and Mr. John Yates decided to make sure his wife was safe and left the table as well. Susan expressed concern for Lady Bertram. "She will be terribly distressed." Those still at the table debated whether to inform her immediately or to let her sleep.

"My father will know what to do," said Tom, and they decided not to interfere.

"So, I was wrong," said Lord Dexthorpe. "Not only young men of means and expectation, but small dogs and the widows of vicars are being murdered at Mansfield Park."

"We do not know that my aunt was murdered," said Maria.

Lord Dexthorpe glanced at Mrs. Rushworth with scorn and spoke at length about how absurd it was to imagine that anything besides murder had happened. "And although I told Sir Thomas that I would not leave Mansfield Park before I saw justice for my son, this plague of untimely deaths may force me to flee, and to take John and Julia with me."

No one protested his potential departure.

They were all anxious for details; those details soon arrived. Mrs. Norris had been found dead, wearing her dressing-gown; apparently she had taken some medicine that had ended her own life. On her desk was a note for the general public, as well as several sealed letters: a thick one addressed to Sir Thomas, another to Lady Bertram, and a third to Mrs. Rushworth.

The contents of the note that had been prepared for all were soon discussed by everyone at Mansfield Park. Mrs. Norris said she wished to live, but her heart, which had been weak for some time now, required that she take an extract of foxglove. It was possible that the medicine would either restore her to health or take her to Heaven; she did not know; her future was in God's hands. Mrs. Rushworth confirmed that Mrs. Norris had been suffering from what she believed was heart trouble and had learned to make the medicine from foxglove flowers while in Ireland.

Lord Dexthorpe opined that Mrs. Norris had clearly taken her own life but did not want her death classed as a suicide, as that would be a scandal for the widow of a vicar, an embarrassment to Sir Thomas, and would require the forfeiture of her estate, not that she had been especially wealthy. "If it can be ruled an accidental death, then none of these penalties will apply. The verdict depends on how friendly the coroner is with Sir Thomas. But I want to know what is contained in the other letters."

"Father, we may never know," said Mr. John Yates. "The recipients may choose not to reveal their contents."

Lord Dexthorpe said that he was certain that the information of the other letters would be revealed, as the coroner – summoned to Mansfield Park again – would demand it. The baron was correct. The first letter to be shared with those at the estate was addressed to Lady Bertram.

My dearest Sister,

Susan, when she saw these words, considered that they were true, that Lady Bertram had been Mrs. Norris's dearest sister, as she had not cared sixpence for her other sister.

I must apologize for the great grief that I have caused you in removing one of your dearest companions. The death of your dog was an accident, but I know I am responsible.

Lady Bertram was less affected by the death of her sister than she had been by the death of her dog. She was shocked, certainly, but her grief was less acute. After all, Mrs. Norris had been living apart for the past two years, while Pug had shared her sofa for many hours of every day. "Poor Pug!" she said, brushing away a tear, when Susan read her aunt Norris's letter aloud to Lady Bertram.

Mrs. Norris did not confess to having attempted to kill Mr. Crawford, but that was implied, as she wrote that the infusion from the cherry laurel leaves had not been intended for her sister's canine companion. The remainder of Mrs. Norris's letter to Lady Bertram emphasized her affection for her dearest sister, and her hope that no one would impose on her. Susan believed that Mrs. Norris was attempting to imply that *she* was the one taking advantage of Lady Bertram, but her ladyship did not look for insinuations, and only said that her sister had always attempted to protect her, but now Mrs. Norris was gone, and Lady Bertram would have to rely on others, such as her nieces.

The letter to Maria declared that Mrs. Norris was deeding all her worldly goods to Mrs. Rushworth, whether or not Mrs. Norris lived or died. She explained that of her nephews and nieces, Tom, Edmund and Julia all had excellent expectations for the future; only Maria's situation was in doubt (Susan noticed that she and her brothers and sisters were again completely forgotten by their aunt). The rest of the letter was an account of the goods that Mrs. Norris was giving to Maria, from a reticule full of bank notes and coins – a considerable sum, handed to Maria before Mrs. Norris's death – to her few jewels, her clothes and her favorite shawl. As Mrs. Norris had given the reticule to Maria before her death – a deed witnessed by Chapman and Ellis, which they confirmed when they were asked – the chance of forfeiture due to a judgment of suicide was lessened. Few cared about the older woman's clothes, although Lady Bertram asked Maria if she might take the shawl, to which Maria agreed. Lady Bertram was fond of shawls, and Mrs. Norris's had originally been a present from Sir Thomas.

But the contents of the third letter, the thick letter addressed to Sir Thomas, were not revealed so readily. Rumors of what was written spread through the estate – that in it Mrs. Norris had admitted to accidentally killing the dog while attempting to murder Mr. Crawford, perhaps to poisoning Mr. Rushworth as well when giving him a small vial that she recommended taking against sore throats at bedtime (Mr. Rushworth's sore throats were cured; he would never have another again). These two men had ruined her darling Maria and Mrs. Norris believed they deserved the severest of penalties. But Mrs. Norris declared that she had not killed Mr. George Yates. She had hit him with a shovel on the head, to prevent him from stealing from Mansfield Park, but she had not slit his throat and she had not dragged his dead body to the corner of the stables and hidden it under a pile of hay. After all, how could she, a weak old woman in poor health, have been capable of such deeds?

These passages caused Sir Thomas some difficulty because the one murder that he most needed solved was the murder of Mr. Yates, and because Mrs. Norris's other words were also disturbing. For two hours the baronet consulted with no one but the coroner and Dr. Grant, then walked around the grounds, revisited the stables where he frowned but did not speak, and finally returned to his study. He sent for Susan, and she had just sat down when Lord Dexthorpe entered and demanded to be told exactly what was in Mrs. Norris's letter to Sir Thomas.

The baron, who had already learnt some of the letter's contents and was guessing at the rest, ignored Susan and began speaking at once. "I believe that Mrs. Norris could have poisoned Mr. Rushworth, although from what I understand, his death occurred several days after his visit here." Lord Dexthorpe had made himself familiar with many details. "And that she could have poisoned your wife's dog when she meant to murder Mr. Crawford. But I do not see how or why she would have murdered my son, either by hitting him on the head or by taking a knife to his throat." The baron enumerated the reasons for his doubts. Firstly, Mrs. Norris had been a woman, and not even a young woman, while Mr. George Yates had been a strong, large, heavy young man and he had not died from poisoning. How on earth could she have overpowered him? Secondly, the baron could not understand why Mrs. Norris would be in the stables so late at night.

Mr. George Yates had late habits, and he might have wanted to inspect his new horse, but Mrs. Norris's going to the stables after dark seemed very unlikely. Sir Thomas had known her better than the baron had, but in their short acquaintance the vicar's widow had shown herself to be a rational woman. Thirdly, although Mrs. Norris may have been bitter towards Mr. Crawford and Mr. Rushworth, for the roles they had played in Mrs. Rushworth's disgrace, she had no grounds for wishing harm on his son George.

But Sir Thomas demurred, explaining that Mrs. Norris had written that she had been in the stables that night, but that he wished to investigate further before sharing the letter with others.

"I am tired of waiting for your investigations, Sir Thomas!" cried the baron, and snatched several sheets of paper from Sir Thomas's desk. "If Mrs. Norris was in the stables she must have at least seen what happened to George!"

"My lord!" protested the baronet, but the baron refused to return the pages. The baron took them to the window, put on his spectacles and began to read.

"I am sorry," Sir Thomas said to Susan. "But he would have to see everything eventually."

Susan did not understand why her uncle was apologizing to *her*.

"Not what I expected," concluded the baron, after perusing the pages twice. "But Mrs. Norris says she offers a knife and a letter as evidence. I want to see everything, Sir Thomas."

Sir Thomas shook his head, but he could not gainsay the angry father. He took several sheets of paper out of his desk, carried them over to the baron, and said he would let him examine the knife momentarily. The baron again stood by the window, reading and frowning and exclaiming, "Good God!" more than once.

"And where is the knife that was used to murder my son?"

Sir Thomas opened the drawer again and took out a knife.

"*That* is the knife?" asked the baron.

Susan experienced bewilderment as she recognized it. "Impossible," she said, but she had such difficulty speaking that her word came out in a whisper and neither man heard her.

"According to Mrs. Norris, yes, it is," said the baronet, answering the question posed by the baron.

Lord Dexthorpe was grimly triumphant. "Then we know who the murderer is – Miss Susan Price."

CHAPTER TWENTY-SEVEN

"What?" cried Susan, now finding her voice. "I have not murdered anyone!"

Lord Dexthorpe asked if the knife was hers.

Susan conceded that the silver knife was hers, given her by one of her sisters back in Portsmouth. Then she protested: "But I never used it to harm anyone, let alone your son."

"There is no proof that *this* was the knife used to murder Mr. Yates," said Sir Thomas. "It is not even particularly sharp. Besides, many people have knives."

Lord Dexthorpe agreed that many people did but that Mrs. Norris had found *this* knife hidden in Miss Price's room and that she believed Miss Price had used it to murder Mr. Yates. "A young woman was seen near the stables that night, a woman too tall to have been Miss Crawford. Could that young woman have been Miss Price?"

Susan was grateful that she was sitting down, for what she was hearing made her knees tremble. Still, she attempted to defend herself. She explained that she had not gone to the stables the night Mr. Yates was murdered. She had not even left the house, but had spent the entire time in her room.

Her uncle supported her by reminding the baron that the coachman's description of the woman could match several persons.

"Your niece, Miss Price. Your daughter, Mrs. Rushworth. Even your other daughter, John's wife," said Lord Dexthorpe. "They are all about the same height, all fair, and I doubt that they could be distinguished from each other at night. Which would you blame, Sir Thomas? One of your daughters, or your niece? My son John was with his wife that night; he assures me that she did not leave the house. Mrs. Rushworth and my elder son barely knew each other. Besides, Miss Price seems healthy and capable; I expect that she had the strength to murder him. She could have dragged his body to the corner of the stables and could have buried him beneath the hay. Or perhaps he was in the corner of the stables when Mrs. Norris hit him on the head in the first place! That means that any person, small or large, could have cut my son's throat and killed him. What strength does it take to do violence to an unconscious man?"

Sir Thomas acknowledged the truth in at least some of what Lord Dexthorpe was saying, that many persons were capable, physically at least, of killing Mr. George Yates in those circumstances.

The baron said that the fact that Susan had *hidden* the silver knife in her room was more evidence that she was guilty; Mrs. Norris had found it hidden at the back of a shelf, behind several books.

Susan shook her head and attempted to explain. The silver knife had been a gift from a sister when that sister was dying, another sister, Betsy, had perpetually tried to take it from her in Portsmouth. Susan had grown accustomed to hiding it. If they needed confirmation in her story, they could ask Fanny. "Besides," she concluded, "why would I wish to harm Mr. Yates?"

Then Lord Dexthorpe put a letter before her, a letter written in her own handwriting – the letter that she had written to Fanny, and then had not sent, because several of the paragraphs described sentiments too embarrassing to imagine being read by even her dear sister. Now Susan realized that those words, words describing her shame at being matched with Tom, had been read by the baronet and the baron. Why, oh why, had she not burnt it?

But Lord Dexthorpe pointed to other sentences, sentences which offended him.

I hope that Mr. Yates leaves Mansfield Park as soon as possible. He is such a rude, unpleasant man, I cannot believe what he suggested to me.

Susan burned when she read this; the baron said that she had obviously hated his son and had taken advantage of a moment of opportunity to murder him.

Sir Thomas attempted to use the words in Susan's letter to clear her. "Is this not evidence that Miss Price would try to avoid Mr. Yates? Why would she follow him to the stables in the middle of the night?"

"That is a question that only Miss Price can answer," said Lord Dexthorpe, but when Susan attempted to repeat that she had not ventured to the stables that night, the baron simply talked louder. Lord Dexthorpe emphasized what Mrs. Norris had written: that Mrs. Norris said that she had followed Miss Price when she left the house, because she suspected Miss Price of impropriety, and that that was when she hit Mr. Yates on the head, to prevent anything dreadful from happening, which implied too that the baron's deceased son had been attempting to force his attentions on Miss Price, but certainly Miss Price should not have been in the stables in the first place, and the greater crime lay with the baronet's niece, not the baron's son.

"I was not in the stables that night!" Susan protested.

"Do you think Mrs. Norris lied in this letter?" retorted Lord Dexthorpe.

Sir Thomas conceded that it would be a serious matter for Mrs. Norris to have lied, a serious matter indeed, especially in her situation, when she was expecting her life to end shortly – whether or not by her own hand, she had been ill – and to have to stand before the heavenly maker to be judged. "It would be bearing false witness," said Sir Thomas.

"Yes. Exactly so," said Lord Dexthorpe triumphantly. "Mrs. Norris, the widow of a vicar, would never have done that."

Susan lost her temper with his lordship. "Your acquaintance with Mrs. Norris was of short duration. How can you possibly know what she would or would not do?"

The baron was not accustomed to being challenged this way, especially not by a young woman, and his fury was expressed with both volume and volubility. The fact that Miss Price, a woman of neither rank nor fortune, would dare to speak to him in this manner – would write about his dear departed son using the words that she had – was evidence of her guilt. The baron was certain that she had followed Mr. Yates and then had wielded that knife when Mr. Yates had refused to do whatever she demanded.

Sir Thomas intervened. "Susan, perhaps it would be wiser if you left my room for a while."

"*I* should leave?" Susan was indignant.

Lord Dexthorpe counseled against this as well. If Miss Price left Sir Thomas's room, perhaps she would run away. Criminals, especially murderers, should not be permitted to stroll around estates but should be placed in the deepest, darkest dungeons.

But in this Sir Thomas prevailed, first by extracting a promise from his niece that she would not leave the estate, and also, upon the baron's insistence, ordering a footman to take a message to the stables that, until hearing otherwise from him, no one was allowed to take out a horse or the carriage without his express permission. Miss Price should leave them for the following hour, while they discussed the contents of Mrs. Norris's last written words.

CHAPTER TWENTY-EIGHT

Susan escaped into the gardens. The day was fine, but the clement weather did not lift Susan's spirits. She walked past the blossoms without perceiving them; she did not respond to the respectful greeting of a gardener; she barely noticed where she was. Deciding to avoid everyone, especially her relations, for as long as she possibly could, she chose an alcove nearer the kitchen gardens instead of her usual spot near the roses, and seated herself where she could not be seen.

The scene that she had just witnessed was incomprehensible. *She* had not murdered Mr. Yates! She had gone to her room that night and had pulled furniture before her door, in order to escape from Mr. Yates. Why on earth would she have followed him outside?

Mrs. Norris had to have been mistaken. Or had her aunt composed deliberate falsehoods about her? But why would she do something so terrible? Had her aunt hated her that much? Susan felt that Mrs. Norris *had* hated her, a conclusion that Susan had reached long before this moment, and she tried to comfort herself with the reminder that Mrs. Norris's resentment had been based on the fact that Susan was the sister of Fanny, another young woman she had greatly disliked. Susan, a mere niece, had been making her home at Mansfield Park, while Mrs. Norris and Mrs. Rushworth, sister and daughter, closer relations, were banished to Ireland. Somehow the scorn and dislike were easier to endure when they were based on Susan's position and not on Susan's personality. But had Mrs. Norris's hatred been such that she would write down lies?

Susan had not seen the actual letter itself; perhaps the words implied her guilt but did not directly accuse her. She had been compelled to leave Sir Thomas's study without reading it.

Could she convince her uncle that she had not killed Mr. Yates? Could her uncle convince Lord Dexthorpe that she had not killed his son? Or would she be arrested and sent to prison, even executed? The fact that her uncle had sent her away, willing to listen to Dexthorpe and not to her, was a very bad sign indeed.

And that was not the only matter that distressed her; there was the rest of the letter that had been discovered by Mrs. Norris. Obviously at some point, Mrs. Norris had searched her room, another cause of vexation, to realize that her aunt had not respected her privacy, but had decided to inspect her possessions without permission. Susan did not know how often Mrs. Norris had been in her room, because housemaids entered to clean, and so occasionally her possessions were moved, but Mrs. Norris must have been in her room last night, while Susan had cared for Elissa. Unfortunately, the letter that Mrs. Norris found was undeniably written by Susan's hand. Assuming that Susan managed to convince everyone that she had not killed Mr. Yates – and the notion that she had killed him seemed so absurd, so extraordinary that she could not believe that the accusations of Mrs. Norris and Lord Dexthorpe would be deemed credible by anyone else – that letter would still exist, would still require explanation, would still cause embarrassment. Such indiscreet, warm phrases! About Tom! About everyone, including Mrs. Norris!

Lord Dexthorpe had implied that she would run away, and for once Susan admired his penetration, for at the moment she longed to do just that. She could not, of course, for she had promised her uncle that she would not leave the estate, and besides, she did not have the means to do anything of the kind. Besides, where could she go, assuming that the bailiff did not arrive to lock her away for murder? The Parsonage was within view, and possibly she might find comfort in a conversation with Miss Crawford, if she could bring herself to confide in that gentlewoman. But Mr. Crawford was also at the Parsonage, and Susan had a strong desire *not* to see him. He was too intelligent, too cutting, and he reminded her too much of Mr. George Yates. What if she were compelled to depart from Mansfield Park altogether? Could she make her home at Fanny's? Edmund would certainly not welcome her if the neighborhood believed her to be a murderer, but even if that were not the case, if she were merely exiled from Mansfield Park, she must consider Thornton Lacey closed to her as well. She could find refuge in Portsmouth, but recalling the cramped quarters and her father's drunken oaths, that was unappealing. Where did she wish to be? Her heart told her, Mansfield Park. But a different Mansfield Park, where she was entertaining her aunt and assisting her uncle and singing duets with her cousin in the evening. Not *this* Mansfield Park, where people and dogs died and her nearest relations believed her a criminal. Susan remembered how, just a few short weeks ago, she had anticipated the visits of her cousins with pleasure, how she had thought that their company would bring animation and gaiety to Mansfield Park. Now she wished she could return to the earlier Mansfield Park; the former dullness now struck her as sweet and tranquil. Oh, for an evening spent reading to Lady Bertram, playing backgammon with her uncle, or even chatting with the servants!

Susan was certain it was the hour for tea, and she longed for a cup, especially as clouds were gathering, but she lingered outside. She simply could not enter the house and face the disapproval, the anger, the suspicion, and especially not more ranting from the baron. She berated herself for being a coward, but she seemed affixed to the bench.

But Mansfield Park was home to many, and despite her choice of seat in a less attractive area of the estate, placed between the flower-gardens for the master's family and the kitchen-gardens for the servants – an area which usually received less traffic than others – eventually Susan heard footsteps approaching along the walk. Susan attempted to compose her features as a small face peeked around the shrubbery.

Elissa announced triumphantly that she had found Cousin Susan; the child was soon followed by Mr. Bertram. Tom congratulated his daughter on her discovery, then sent her to the care of a gardener who promised to show the little girl the vegetable garden. Susan said that she hoped Tom would excuse her, for she preferred to be alone, but Tom said that he did not believe that solitude was a good idea at the moment, and instead of departing, seated himself next to her on the bench. He remarked that he did not think he had ever been so impatient to see cabbages and onions as Elissa seemed to be, but of course he did not recall what it was like to be so young. After this bit of levity – designed, as Susan perceived, to raise her spirits – Tom continued speaking, informing her that his father and his mother had missed her at tea. Furthermore, there was a funeral to plan. The coroner had determined that Mrs. Norris's death could be considered accidental – Sir Thomas's influence had prevailed – so Mrs. Norris would lie in rest next to Reverend Norris in the parish cemetery. "My mother, contemplating my aunt's funeral, is rather low."

Susan felt a pang for her favorite aunt, but Lady Bertram had her daughters with her; her presence could not be necessary. Besides, why would Sir Thomas and Lady Bertram wish for the company of a murderer?

"Do you not think I am a murderer?" asked Susan.

Tom told her that he did not. He reminded her that recently *he* had been Lord Dexthorpe's preferred perpetrator and he was aware of how unpleasant the position was. *He* had always known that he had not killed Mr. George Yates, but he had been at a loss of how to prove it. He was certain that Susan had not killed the man either.

"I am grateful for your confidence in me," said Susan, but as she burst into tears, her gratitude was difficult to discern.

Tom passed her a handkerchief, then looked away as Susan dabbed her eyes and attempted to regain self-control. "I came out here to cheer you up, but obviously I am making a poor go of it."

She tried to apologize, but her murmurs were unintelligible.

Tom returned to the most important subject. "It is difficult enough to imagine my late aunt Norris hitting anyone on the head. But to imagine *you* kneeling by a man and then carving his throat! – no, no, my fancy, like a stubborn horse, refuses to jump that gate."

Susan thanked him again. A little calmer, she said: "I know that I did not go to the stables that night. But how do I prove it?"

Tom assured her that they would manage to establish Susan's innocence somehow, and somehow convince Lord Dexthorpe as well. "The baron stopped ranting long enough for my father to persuade him to be more cautious in his assumptions and his accusations, and I pointed out that if my aunt Norris could hit George Yates on the head and poison Rushworth and try to poison Crawford, she would have no scruples writing falsehoods about you."

Tom's words lifted Susan's spirits a little. But only a little, for other vexing thoughts assailed her. She realized that Tom, if he had spoken with his uncle, must have seen the letter that she had written to Fanny and had not sent.

Tom admitted that he had indeed, seen Susan's letter. "My father showed it to me. By G—, that Yates! If I had known how he treated you, I might have taken a knife to his throat myself."

His anger on her behalf warmed Susan, and almost smiling, she was able to warn her cousin that it might be wise to keep silent about *that* particular impulse. Then she asked: "And the rest? Did you read that?"

"Yes, I saw that you were uncomfortable by what Mrs. Norris said about you and me. I did not enjoy her speeches either, Sue. Think no more of it, and come inside before you miss tea altogether."

Susan consented, letting her cousin help her to her feet. They first went to the kitchen gardens to collect Elissa, who was watching a gardener dig up a potato plant. Elissa informed them that potatoes grew in the ground, and that you had to wash them before you could eat them. She showed them the beds of cabbages and parsnips with such delight and wonder that Susan could not help smiling. By the time they reached the house she was sufficiently composed to enter.

"Will you venture into the drawing-room?" asked her cousin. "Or do you want your tea upstairs?"

Susan said she would face her relations. Tom gave his daughter over to the care of a housemaid and then the two of them entered the drawing-room, although Susan was tempted to run away when she saw Lord Dexthorpe.

Lady Bertram addressed her niece at once. "Susan, could you fetch me another cup of tea? And explain to me why my sister declared you to be a murderer? I am quite confused; I do not understand it at all."

The two requests were of such differing import that Susan found it difficult to move or speak. Sir Thomas intervened, asking Maria to bring Lady Bertram her second cup of tea and inviting his niece to sit down. Mrs. Rushworth poured tea for both her mother and her cousin.

Susan took a deep breath and explained, in what she hoped were reasonable tones, that she had not murdered Mr. Yates, that after encountering him and Mrs. Norris on the stairs she had gone upstairs to her room where she had remained the entire night.

"So, what happened in the stables?" demanded the baron.

Susan explained again that, as she had not gone to the stables that night, she did not know.

Lady Bertram wanted to know why Mrs. Norris had written that Susan had gone to the stables that night, and Susan said that she could not answer why Mrs. Norris had written such a thing, as it was not true. Susan's answer seemed to confuse Lady Bertram even more, so Maria suggested that perhaps Mrs. Norris had been mistaken, while Julia suggested that Mrs. Norris might have been writing an untruth, because sometimes people told untruths, even for very good reasons. "Or for very bad reasons," added Tom.

The myriad explanations seemed to puzzle her ladyship even more, or at least give her a great deal to contemplate, for she fell silent.

The baron repeated that he wanted to know what had happened in the stables, and Sir Thomas, to forestall this useless inquiry, or perhaps to keep Lord Dexthorpe from haranguing his niece, asked Susan to recount what had happened that night.

Susan was not happy with having to review those embarrassing moments, but in comparison with being suspected of murder, the vexation was minor. She related how she had been ascending the stairs to her room, how she had encountered Mr. George Yates on the stairs – he had been examining some object, which he had then slipped into his pocket – and how he had taken her hand and had talked about how he could take her to London and how he had leered at her and had refused to release her hand. She had been mortified by his words and his behavior, mortification growing into alarm. When Mrs. Norris appeared, and had accused her of being forward, Susan had actually been relieved, for her aunt's interference had permitted her to escape and go to her room. She had found Mr. Yates's manner so unsettling that she had put a stool and a chair before her door, and had actually pulled out her silver knife, although she thought it would make a poor weapon. And, unable to sleep, and wishing to confide in someone but unsure of whom she could tell, she had then added those words to the letter that she had been writing to her sister but had never sent.

Sir Thomas asked if Susan had remained in her room the rest of the night; she affirmed that she had.

Lord Dexthorpe asked about the other exchanges that Miss Price had had with Mr. George Yates during his visit.

Susan considered before answering. Susan had met him when he arrived, and had been with him at meals and in the drawing-room, but besides the initial introduction and when she had gone with everyone to the stables to admire the black horse, they had exchanged very few words.

The baron noted that Susan *had* been in the stables with Mr. George Yates, but as that had been in the company of many, and during the day, and everyone agreed that Miss Price had neither taken a shovel to the back of his head nor placed a knife to his throat, even his lordship found it difficult to declare that this was proof of Miss Price's murdering his son during the middle of the night.

Tom inquired again about the encounter on the stairs. Had Miss Price seen what Mr. Yates had been holding in his hand, the item that he had slipped into his pocket? By any chance had it been Sir Thomas's snuffbox, the one made from the hoof of a famous warhorse?

Susan shook her head. The object had been too small to be her uncle's snuffbox; Mr. Yates had been able to conceal it completely in his hand. "Besides, it glittered as if it were made of gold"—then Susan stopped speaking, for she realized what the object was, but she could not comprehend why Mr. Yates should have been holding *that* particular object. Her expression and her hesitation revealed to all – except Lady Bertram – that she had remembered something.

"Susan, what did you see?" asked Sir Thomas.

"Perhaps a watch?" suggested Maria.

"George's watch was broken," said Mr. John Yates. "He left it with a jeweler in London for repair."

"I – I am not sure."

"Miss Price, what was in my late son's hand?" demanded the baron.

"It was not a watch," said Susan. "It was – I think it was – Mrs. Rushworth's sapphire necklace."

CHAPTER TWENTY-NINE

All eyes turned towards Maria, who in shame turned her face away. Sir Thomas asked if Susan meant the necklace currently adorning his daughter's throat; Susan confirmed that she did. Sir Thomas then asked his eldest daughter if this were true, and Maria, although she attempted to deny it, could not; the guilt, which she wished to conceal, was plain on her face and confirmed when she burst into tears. Several interviews were necessary before Maria shared all of what she knew, but one thing she avowed as soon as she could speak: *she* had not killed Mr. Yates, and she did not know who the murderer was.

Eventually her story was told. Maria had met Mr. George Yates in London a few times when she was there with Mr. Rushworth, and after her divorce she encountered Mr. George Yates in Ireland. "He was gallant, extremely gallant," said Maria, and her cheeks turned bright red. "I was not in love with him, as I had been with" — and she paused, unable to utter the name Mr. Crawford — "but he promised that he would marry me. I believed him, because, as my sister was married to his brother, I did not anticipate poor treatment."

But Maria had been wrong; Mr. Yates had not wished for an engagement or a wife but a dupe with means to extort. She had written him indiscreet letters – Susan was comforted to learn that she was not the only woman in the family to confide inappropriate musings to paper, and she could flatter herself that she had never posted hers – and he had threatened to show them to her father if she did not give him money. So, when she had met him again at Mansfield Park, she had given him her necklace to buy his silence.

Susan suspected that Maria had been seduced by Mr. Yates, another matter that could elicit harsh judgment on the part of her father – but at the moment everyone was more interested in murder and not seduction.

Mrs. Norris had learnt what had passed, in Ireland and in Northamptonshire, and had been angry on her niece's behalf. After Susan left Mrs. Norris and Mr. Yates on the stairs, he had taken the sapphire necklace out of his pocket and taunted her with it. Mrs. Norris had gone straight to Maria, who confessed that she had given Mr. Yates her necklace, and that she believed that Mr. Yates was planning to leave Mansfield Park that very night. Mrs. Norris ordered Maria to follow Mr. Yates to the stables and to demand the return of the sapphire necklace, or else she would tell Sir Thomas about the indiscretion herself.

Maria had not wished to go, but Mrs. Norris was adamant, so Maria put on a cloak and ventured outside. When she arrived at the stables Mr. Yates was saddling his horse. Maria recounted what happened: "I asked him to give back the necklace, telling him that he had procured it under the cruelest circumstances. Mr. Yates laughed. He – he called me names, and attacked me. When we were struggling, my aunt arrived and hit him on the back of the head with a shovel. He collapsed to the ground, but I did not know whether he was alive or dead. My aunt told me to carry his bag back to the house, while she remained behind in order to search his pockets, in case my necklace should be in one of them." Maria added that she believed that she was the young woman who had been seen by the coachman that night.

"You mean to say that Mrs. Norris then slit my son's throat? And then covered his body with hay?" These were the points that concerned the baron.

"Hitting him with a shovel was not sufficient?" inquired Tom.

Maria said that she did not know. Distressed by what had happened, she had not remained in the stables, but had returned with Mr. Yates's traveling bag to the house. After looking for, and quickly finding, her sapphire necklace – she had been hasty and had overlooked the snuffbox – she had placed the bag in Mr. Yates's room. Therefore, Maria had not witnessed Mrs. Norris's behavior after her own departure from the stables. But she could confirm that Mrs. Norris had not taken very long to come to her own room, and that Maria had not detected any blood or hay on her aunt's clothing, only a little dirt on her skirts, not surprising if she had knelt on the ground in order to search Mr. Yates's pockets. Maria added: "The next morning, my aunt was genuinely surprised to learn what had happened. She was convinced that he had recovered from his injuries and departed on his horse, and after his body was discovered, she seemed to believe that the murderer was a horse thief."

Sir Thomas asked if Mrs. Rushworth could say where exactly Mr. Yates had fallen in the stables, and if it had been near the corner with the hay. Maria explained that the incident had taken place closer to the center of the room, several yards distant from the hay.

Lady Bertram asked why this mattered, and Sir Thomas explained that if Mr. Yates had fallen near the corner with the hay, then Mrs. Norris would not have had to move him, not more than a few inches, and then could have covered him where he lay.

The baron said that this was proof that someone else killed his son. "Miss Price is not in the clear."

"Nor am I," said Tom.

"But Mrs. Norris blamed Miss Price in her letter."

Susan was distressed to discover that the baron persisted in his presumption of her guilt.

But assistance, surprisingly, came from Maria. "My lord, no one is in the clear, but I think we should not be so ready to blame Miss Price. My aunt Norris resented Miss Price. She was angry because she did not think that she and I should be in cold, wet Ireland, at such a distance from our friends, while my cousin sat comfortably in Mansfield Park, usurping the affections of my father and my mother. I believe that was why my aunt Norris blamed my cousin in her letter to my father, and was rude to Miss Price beforehand." Mrs. Rushworth then conceded that she should have explained all of this earlier, especially when Lord Dexthorpe was charging Susan for the murder of his son. "Cousin Susan, I apologize for not speaking earlier," and admitted she had been both ashamed and uncertain what to say.

Although the hours during which Susan had been under suspicion had seemed very long while they occurred, she was grateful to Maria and pointed out that Maria had taken less than a day to come forward. Maria's male relatives were less forgiving. Sir Thomas said that Maria should have spoken to him weeks ago; her information was necessary for his investigation, while Tom was angry because the suspicion on him had lasted for days. Sir Thomas then asked why Mrs. Norris had committed such heinous acts.

Mrs. Rushworth colored but continued to explain. Mrs. Norris had been extremely angry with these men – Mr. Rushworth, Mr. Crawford, and Mr. Yates – whom she believed had taken advantage of her favorite niece and who deserved punishment for their actions. It had been grossly unfair for the men to go about enjoying large incomes and unsullied reputations, when their guilt had been greater than Maria's. "I do not defend myself," said Maria hastily, "especially not with respect to Mr. Rushworth. I simply explain my aunt's motives."

Susan asked how Mrs. Norris had procured the poison, and wished to know if their aunt had truly been ill. Maria said that Mrs. Norris had indeed had a little heart trouble, and had learned to make an infusion from foxglove. She had spoken with neighbors and discovered that the cherry laurel tree in the garden should not be confused with a bay laurel tree, as the cherry laurel tree's leaves were toxic.

Lady Bertram remarked that her sister had often treated the Mansfield Park servants for their ailments. "She was so clever!"

No one else in the room was prepared to praise Mrs. Norris's memory, and Lord Dexthorpe was anxious to return to his preferred topic. The baron reminded them that the identity of his son's murderer was still unknown. If Mrs. Rushworth's account was to be believed, the murderer was more likely to have been a man, because a woman would have lacked the strength to move Mr. Yates from the center of the barn to the area with the hay.

"Which means I am still your favorite suspect," said Tom.

Mr. John Yates had another idea: what if George had awoken and had moved himself, crawling perhaps, and fainting again from his injuries? Then anyone could have done it, and he proceeded to name every person at Mansfield Park, from the scullery maids and the stable hands to Sir Thomas himself. "Even I should be included, although Julia can aver that I was with her during the night."

Julia, who so far had listened much but said little, asked *why* the murderer had hidden Mr. Yates's body. "It is not as if the body could remain hidden for long."

This point was discussed. The only reason to hide the body would be to keep it from being discovered – presumably so that the murderer could get further away, an idea that, as it acquitted everyone at Mansfield Park, pleased everyone save Lord Dexthorpe, who wished for a guilty party to punish. He argued that although the murderer might have hidden Mr. Yates in order to increase his time for escape, that was not the only possible explanation for concealment. Perhaps he had planned to return to the body and move it later.

The conversation continued quite a while, through dinner and afterwards in the drawing-room. Sir Thomas did not linger over his wine, but asked Susan to join him in his office, where he dictated letters to be sent to Thornton Lacey and to Sotherton as soon as the sun rose. Susan felt happier when she went to bed, remembering how her cousin Tom had come looking for her, and how kind he had been – and how she was no longer a murder suspect – and then she felt anxious, for they still did not know if Mansfield Park housed a knife-wielding killer. Before she retired, Susan pushed a chair before her door.

CHAPTER THIRTY

No one attempted to enter Susan's room during that night or the next, and she rose early enough to move everything to keep from inconveniencing any of the housemaids.

On both days, a steady rain fell, and tempers were subdued. Susan assisted with much of the necessary correspondence, while Maria, in an effort to prove herself useful and to keep away from everyone else, looked after little Elissa.

On the second morning after her body was discovered, Mrs. Norris was buried beside her husband in the parish cemetery. As women rarely went to funerals, all the ladies declined to attend, but sat with Lady Bertram while the sad event took place. Mr. Edmund Bertram rode over for the occasion, and stood with his male relatives. Afterwards, Dr. and Mrs. Grant and Miss Crawford called at Mansfield Park. Dr. Grant, who had been no friend to Mrs. Norris, composed himself sufficiently to speak with gentleness to Lady Bertram on the loss of her sister. Mrs. Grant and Miss Crawford offered their condolences as well, but Miss Crawford managed a private moment with Miss Price, and uttered what Susan believed was Miss Crawford's true opinion. Mrs. Norris had been an unpleasant individual, who had murdered Mr. Rushworth and Lady Bertram's dog, and who had attempted to murder Mr. Yates and Mr. Crawford. "You comprehend why my brother did not come today; he could hardly honor someone who attempted to do him such ill." Susan replied that she understood. Then Miss Crawford – somehow, the inhabitants of the Parsonage were as familiar with the details of recent events as the inhabitants of the Park – attempted to elicit information from her. What would happen with Mrs. Rushworth? Susan answered that she did not know; that much still needed to be decided. Miss Crawford had to content herself with that, and with a civil exchange with Mr. Edmund Bertram. Susan noticed that Miss Crawford looked at Edmund when he was conversing with others, but other than a blush, Miss Crawford behaved with delicacy. Susan pitied her.

Dr. Grant informed the Bertrams of another death, the long-awaited demise of the mother of Mr. Hawk. At the moment, Mr. Hawk had to remain where he was in order to take care of business, but he expected to return in a fortnight, at which point the Grants would leave the country and go back to London. With the sun coming out, the Grants and Miss Crawford readied themselves for the walk to the Parsonage. "To everything there is a season," said Miss Crawford, and although she was quoting the

Bible, she could be speaking of the change in the weather, describing the mortality of recent weeks, or simply referring to the festivities of the next winter in London.

After the departure of the Grants and Miss Crawford, Sir Thomas met with his sons to discuss the disposition of Maria. Until they were free of Lord Dexthorpe's threats, no final decision could be taken, but possibilities could be explored, and the baronet wished to hear the opinions of his sons. Tom said that, given Elissa, his guilt was as great as his sister's and he suggested leniency and forgiveness. Edmund said that Maria's involvement with Mr. George Yates proved that she had not reformed, and that her character was just as weak as it had been when she had deserted her husband to elope with Mr. Crawford. In addition, Mrs. Norris had attempted to murder three different men in order to improve Mrs. Rushworth's position. Edmund did not believe that Maria had been involved *directly* in these crimes – at least he hoped she had not – but the association with guilt and scandal were undeniable.

Sir Thomas listened to both, weighing their arguments against his affection for his daughter. He inclined towards the opinion of Edmund, especially as any leniency towards his daughter might offend the baron who was still threatening his ruin. The baronet comforted himself with the fact that Maria had never been particularly happy at Mansfield Park. But where could he send her?

It might seem strange that these conversations took place without Maria, but the men were accustomed to making decisions for the women, and Sir Thomas intended to consult her eventually. Besides, nothing could be acted upon until he could persuade Lord Dexthorpe not to ruin him.

Lord Dexthorpe was miserable, for not only did he still not know the identity of his son's murderer, he had learned most terrible things about that son. First, that son had been a thief, a cheat, a blackmailer and even a seducer of women. The baron could have dismissed the complaint of one woman, or the complaints of two or three, but there seemed to be many, confirmed by words from John Yates, Julia Yates, and even Mr. Crawford. Lord Dexthorpe had called upon Mr. Crawford at the Parsonage, and in the privacy of a tête-à-tête, had heard such a myriad of dreadful details that when he returned he would not speak for two full hours. "At least George was alive," said the baron, when he terminated his self-imposed silence, repeating the only thought that consoled him. "More alive than any of the rest of us." Mr. John Yates did everyone else a service by taking his father into the billiards room quite often.

"It has been three weeks!" exclaimed the father, with as much drama as could be found in the rants of his second son. "And it feels longer!"

Everyone agreed with his lordship that it felt longer. They all hoped that something, such as the start of the hunting season that was still several weeks distant, would persuade the baron to return to his estate, because the chance of finding the murderer seemed small. Many were suspected, but with so many motives, no one could be deemed guilty beyond a reasonable doubt unless new information was discovered.

"There seems to be no exit from this crisis," Susan remarked to her uncle.

Sir Thomas was more sanguine. "I do not know that we will ever discover the murderer. Perhaps Mrs. Norris was the guilty party and did not confess." But he had hopes with respect to Lord Dexthorpe, whose mood was subdued and who had been making fewer threats. "He is grieving for his son, and we should be patient with him."

The other situation requiring resolution was little Elissa: should she remain at Mansfield Park or not? She was innocent of any wrongdoing, but not only was she illegitimate, the color of her skin reminded everyone of that fact. One solution would be to house her in a cottage full of children. However, Tom did not want her sent away, and even Lady Bertram had grown attached to her. Another solution would be to hire someone to take care of her, but the nursery maids they had interviewed had not been satisfactory. For the time being Elissa was cared for mostly by Susan, Maria and the housemaid Ann Jones, with occasional supervision from Lady Bertram and her maid Chapman.

Then one morning, soon after breakfast, Chapman reported to her mistress that Ann Jones was ill, information that had been relayed to her by the little girl.

Lady Bertram was sitting with her niece and daughters when this information was brought to them. "The housemaid has not been poisoned, has she?" asked Julia.

The possibility struck them all with alarm, including her ladyship. "Dear me," remarked Lady Bertram. "I hope it is nothing serious. Susan, my dear, please go and see what is the matter."

Susan hastened to the nursery, hoping that the housemaid was still alive. She was, but as Chapman and Elissa had reported, she was sick as she knelt over a basin.

"What is the matter?" asked Susan. "Have you taken poison?"

The housemaid shook her head.

"Did you drink too much?" asked Elissa, from her corner. "Some men, when they drink too much rum, are sick like that."

"No," said Ann Jones, and tears were on her face. "I did not drink any rum."

Chapman, who had walked up the stairs – unlike Susan, who had run – finally appeared in the threshold. She insisted that Ann Jones tell everything, that Ann Jones was with child.

"Oh!" exclaimed Susan, for many things began to fall into place. "Is Stephen Jackson the father?" *That* would explain why Ann and Stephen had quarreled.

No, she declared, Stephen Jackson was not the father.

The father was Mr. George Yates.

CHAPTER THIRTY-ONE

The tale of guilt and misery emerged. During his first night at Mansfield Park, Mr. Yates had forced his attentions on Ann Jones, and now she was with child.

Lord Dexthorpe tried to hold the housemaid responsible for all that had passed, but this proved impossible, even for him. Everyone informed him that Ann Jones had always been scrupulously respectable. Everyone confirmed how agitated and unhappy Ann Jones had been ever since the night of her encounter with Mr. George Yates. Lord Dexthorpe had already heard how Mr. Yates had seduced Mrs. Rushworth, had attempted to force himself on Susan, and had been informed by Mr. Crawford of many reports concerning other women. And when the baron finally interviewed the housemaid, her modesty and her distress prevented him from blaming her for the encounter between herself and his son.

Had she killed him? That was Lord Dexthorpe's next suspicion. It was difficult to imagine the delicate young woman committing such an act, but as Mr. George Yates had been unconscious, murder would not have been beyond her strength.

This idea swept through Mansfield Park with the rapidity of galloping horses, and Susan, so recently the target of suspicion herself, pitied the young housemaid. However, the notion did not last long. Stephen Jackson, eyes wild from lack of sleep, came forward to confess.

Jackson had learnt of Mr. Yates's outrage on the young woman he hoped to marry from Jones herself, whom he had discovered in tears. Afterwards Jackson and Jones had argued, because he wanted to tell Sir Thomas what had happened. Ann Jones had been reluctant, because she did not expect to be believed, not when she was a housemaid and Mr. Yates the eldest son of a baron. She was afraid of being sent away from Mansfield Park with a ruined character. They had quarreled, increasing poor Ann Jones's distress even further.

The next morning, Jackson had been the first in the stables, arriving in the gray light before dawn. He had had his knife out to treat the horse's hoofs, when to his surprise he had discovered Mr. Yates, lying in the dirt in the stables. No, Mr. Yates had not been dead, but had been barely conscious. Jackson had not known what to do, but had accused the baron's son of violating his intended. Mr. Yates, despite his aching head, had not denied it, but had laughed. Actually laughed!

Mr. Yates's scornful mirth infuriated the groom, and Stephen Jackson attacked Yates with the knife in his hand. Afterwards, horrified by what he had done, he dragged the heavy body to the corner of the stable and covered it with hay. He had hoped to move it later, but no opportunity presented itself. He released Mr. Yates's horse – confirming Maria's statement that it had already been saddled, presumably by Mr. Yates – to make it look as if Mr. Yates himself were gone.

Sir Thomas, to whom this confession was made, in the company of Tom and Mr. John Yates, sighed. The baron did not see how, despite the extenuating circumstances, Jackson could avoid being hanged. When he informed Jackson of this, Jackson, pale but resolute, said that he understood. He could not risk Ann Jones's suffering that fate. He just hoped they would treat Ann Jones fairly, would realize the cruelty that had been inflicted on her. She had done nothing wrong.

The men conducted an additional interview with Ann Jones, who confirmed portions of Stephen Jackson's account. She had guessed what had happened and had begged him to run away. He had refused, out of his concern for her; besides, if he did as she asked, everyone would realize he had killed the baron's son.

Sir Thomas arranged for Stephen Jackson to be jailed by the local constabulary until a formal sentencing could be accomplished. After these interviews – Susan assisted at those with Ann Jones – the results were communicated to Lord Dexthorpe and the rest of those living at Mansfield Park, who were shocked and saddened and who pitied Stephen Jackson. Sir Thomas was concerned that he had lost his next coachman; Wilcox's rheumatism was such that he needed to retire, and Cooper, he feared, was not up to the work.

The baron could no longer complain that the murderer of his son had not been apprehended. Some of his anger disappeared, while the grief that he had been suppressing all this time swelled to the surface. But that grief was soured with deep regret, regret that his son's legacy was so terrible. George had seemed so charming, so capable, and so handsome, that the baron had liked thinking of his title and his lands passing on to that son. Now everything would eventually go to John, who was tolerable but could hardly be expected to bring glory to the barony.

Some of these feelings were conveyed to Sir Thomas as the patriarchs sat. The baronet had never experienced the death of a child, but he was familiar with bitter disappointment in the characters of his offspring. He counseled patience, and suggested that Lord Dexthorpe work at familiarizing Mr. John Yates with the running of the estate in

Lincolnshire. Sir Thomas felt some misgivings at this recommendation, for Julia rather disliked her father-in-law, but as Julia's husband now expected to inherit, living at her father's estate was a rational solution. It would reduce the living expenses, too, of Mr. and Mrs. John Yates, and ease Sir Thomas's sense of responsibility with respect to his younger daughter.

The baron said he would consider this, and then the baron, the baronet and Tom met with Ann Jones. The housemaid requested that Miss Price and Mrs. Rushworth also assist at this interview. The baron agreed, and so Susan took notes, while Maria occasionally made suggestions on what could or should be done. Not every woman who was expecting survived her lying-in, but Lord Dexthorpe assured Ann Jones that he would provide for her and the child if it lived, including a small house and a public education if it were a boy.

Lord Dexthorpe made his proposals, but before the housemaid would agree, Jones asked about the fate of Stephen Jackson. Lord Dexthorpe said that he wanted his son's murderer to hang. Tom said that this execution might not be the best means of gaining the good will of the mother of his son's child. "A fair point," said Sir Thomas. Lord Dexthorpe was adamant; he could not have Jackson at liberty, potentially raising the son of the man that he had killed. Susan suggested that Stephen Jackson be sent far away, perhaps to Antigua.

The compromise made no one particularly happy. Lord Dexthorpe wanted revenge, but there were mitigating circumstances in his son's death, and he needed to be on speaking terms with his grandchild's mother. Stephen Jackson and Ann Jones would never be together, but Stephen Jackson would live. The most satisfied was Sir Thomas, who thought the young man would prove useful on his estate in the West Indies. Furthermore, the baronet employed several of Stephen Jackson's brothers and cousins, and their loyalty would be greatly improved if the young man were sentenced to transportation instead of execution.

"So that can be arranged?" asked Ann Jones.

The baron and the baronet had influence. They conferred and dictated letters, which Susan wrote carefully, that would serve to secure Stephen Jackson's release and passage. The baron would not consent to Ann Jones meeting with Stephen Jackson, but agreed to her sending him an epistolary message. Mrs. Rushworth offered to help Ann create this letter of adieu to Jackson; the two young women sat at a table in the library to write. Poor Ann Jones was much affected as she composed this farewell, and as her tears fell, Susan detected how even Lord Dexthorpe was made uneasy by her unhappiness. Susan also noticed, with some surprise, the patient kindness that Maria showed Ann Jones. Was Mrs. Rushworth charitable towards Ann Jones because Maria, given her own difficulties, had sympathy with the housemaid's situation? Or was this improvement in

Maria's personality due to the removal of Mrs. Norris's malevolent influence?

Ann Jones's farewell letter to Stephen Jackson was soon finished, and she and Maria were excused, while Tom and Susan remained to assist the baron and the baronet with the remaining business. While the men discussed shipping and sugar, Susan wondered what the future held for the star-crossed lovers. Would Jackson thrive in Antigua, or would he succumb to some local disease? Would Ann Jones survive her lying-in? Were they destined to be apart for the rest of their natural lives, or would fate somehow relent and bring them back together? The housemaid's artless tears had made Susan sentimental, and she was glad when the business was finished, the letters franked, and they could repair to the drawing-room for tea.

Sir Thomas also hoped the business was truly finished. Less than a month had passed since the murder of Mr. George Yates, and so the investigation had not taken that long to complete, but during those weeks there had been uncertainty, suspicion, and additional deaths, and the threat of Lord Dexthorpe on Sir Thomas's business interests, so the days had dragged. Now that his son's killer was caught, and his punishment decided upon, Sir Thomas's greatest wish was for the baron to leave Mansfield Park sooner rather than later. Sir Thomas, disgusted by what the baron's late son had done to the baronet's daughter, niece, and servant, was uncharitable in his opinion of the dead. Mr. George Yates had been a complete scoundrel; the world was a better place without him in it. Sir Thomas reproached himself mentally for having such a thought while in the company of the still-grieving father, and aloud reminded him that a happy occasion was expected: a grandchild.

Lord Dexthorpe frowned, and muttered that a natural grandchild from a servant was not exactly a cause for celebration. Elissa, seated next to her grandmother on the sofa, prevented him from saying more on the subject. Sir Thomas reminded the baron that several natural children had made great impacts on history. The baron agreed, mentioning William the Conqueror, while Mr. John Yates named Leonardo da Vinci and Tom Bertram gave the example of Alexander Hamilton, who, although American, had certainly made a difference in the world.

Susan reflected that all had been rebellious men in their way, but perhaps that was what was needed for a man to make a difference in the world. Perhaps illegitimacy bestowed a kind of freedom on some men, as the illegitimate had fewer expectations restraining them. If you had no reputation to safeguard, you could do more of what you wished.

Lady Bertram observed that it was very pleasant to have a grandchild, and said that she had been instructing Elissa in saying "please" and "thank you" when she wanted a biscuit.

Lord Dexthorpe supposed that a grandchild would be pleasant, especially as George, for all his faults, had been so vital. It was a pity he had never produced a legitimate heir. These words, uttered before Mr. John Yates, now his heir, seemed rather cruel – but the baron was so despondent that no one reproached him for them.

Consolation came from Lady Bertram. She said that she supposed the baron's words were true, but that it was time for Julia to relate her own news. She beamed at her younger daughter, who sat on another sofa between Mr. John Yates and Maria.

Everyone turned to look at Julia, who blushed but admitted that she was expecting a child. Exclamations followed and congratulations were uttered by many in the room, except for Lord Dexthorpe, who for once was speechless.

After some discussion on this topic, during which Susan wondered how she could have failed to perceive Julia's condition, but supposed she had been distracted by the murders and everything else, her aunt spoke again. Lady Bertram confirmed that she had known Julia was expecting for some time, as her symptoms were exactly what she had experienced. Lady Bertram was aware, however, that Julia had suffered several disappointments during the last two years so had not wished to mention it until she was further along. Mr. John Yates, also aware of his wife's situation, confirmed that Julia had sworn him to silence.

Rarely could Lady Bertram claim expertise in anything, but on this subject no one could contradict her. Lady Bertram had recognized the cause of Julia's excessive fatigue, and said she was perfectly aware that Julia had been stealing bread from the kitchens in order to calm her unhappy system. Lady Bertram had actually pretended to be the bread thief herself in order to protect her daughter's secret. Susan was rather surprised at the extent of her aunt's initiative; generally Lady Bertram roused herself so little.

"You will have to inform Cook," said Susan, "and set her mind at ease."

Lady Bertram promised to restore tranquility in the kitchens, then enquired minutely of her younger daughter regarding her health, a conversation which rather embarrassed the men, but the women persisted.

"My dear, I remember when I was carrying Tom, that I felt exactly the same way." Lady Bertram informed Lord Dexthorpe that in five or six months he could expect to have a grandson. And a few months after that, another grandchild could be expected from Ann Jones.

"Life continues," said Sir Thomas, also pleased by the prospect of a legitimate grandchild, especially as it – if a boy, as Lady Bertram predicted – could one day expect to be a baron himself.

Lord Dexthorpe was unsettled by this joyous news. He had intended to remain cross, but in these circumstances he could not. Unable to speak happily, as that would be at odds with his personality, he glanced out the window and determined that the rain had stopped. He decided to take a walk to relieve his feelings, and he asked his remaining son to come along with him.

Julia, finally speaking unreservedly of her condition, asked her mother if she could recommend anything to stop from feeling so wretched.

Lady Bertram knew there was something, but could not remember. "Something my sister recommended," she said. Fortunately, Sir Thomas's ability to recollect those times was better than his wife's, and he reminded her that fennel had shown the most utility.

"Oh, yes, fennel!" exclaimed Lady Bertram. "You will soon feel better. Come, Julia, my dear, let us go to the kitchens. We can explain to Cook at the same time."

For Lady Bertram to exert herself sufficiently to go to the kitchens was a grand occasion indeed, but announcing the news had given her strength, while Julia was eager to seek any remedy that could give her relief. Susan wondered how many years it had been since Lady Bertram had visited the Mansfield Park kitchens, and if her aunt even knew where they were. Of course, Julia, who had been purloining bread from them, was aware of their location. Elissa wanted to see the kitchens as well and so the three generations left together.

"A happy day, indeed," said Sir Thomas.

Susan and Tom congratulated Sir Thomas, and after a moment Maria, who had been silent while the others rejoiced, composed herself sufficiently to do so as well. Poor Maria! thought Susan. A few years ago, Maria's future had shone brightly, with a rich husband and an estate in the neighborhood. Now her younger sister was ascendant, with a title and a fortune in her future, while Maria could only look forward to more years of disgrace. Would Sir Thomas allow her to remain at Mansfield Park or would he send her away? Maria's former companion, Mrs. Norris, was dead, so with whom would she share her banishment?

Tom, standing by the window, reported on the progress of Lord Dexthorpe and Mr. John Yates. Tom could not hear them, but he could see them, and he described their many gestures. "Dexthorpe is pointing at something – now he is patting Yates on the back in a friendly manner – now Dexthorpe is smiling and shaking his son's hand. It appears that Yates has been able to lift his father's spirits."

Susan felt more amiable towards Mr. John Yates than she ever had before. She would have been content for Lord Dexthorpe and Mr. Yates to remain in the rose garden, but Tom then announced that several large raindrops had hit the window, and that an afternoon squall would certainly force the baron and his son back inside.

Tom was right; the baron came back inside. Lord Dexthorpe announced he would leave for Lincolnshire the next day. "If the weather is fine, that is."

Everyone in the room hoped fervently for fine weather on the morrow, then they all went to dress for dinner. With the fear of poisoning gone and Cook informed about the actual bread thief, the meal was better than it had been in days. After dinner, Sir Thomas invited Lord Dexthorpe to his rooms for brandy and conversation – the baronet, confident now that the baron would be departing soon, found it easy to be civil; Tom and Mr. John Yates went to the billiard room, and the ladies spent their time in the drawing-room. Maria read aloud to the other women; Lady Bertram held a pillow where her dog used to sit; Julia sipped an infusion of fennel and looked happier than she had for the last month, and Susan applied herself to the long-neglected poor basket.

CHAPTER THIRTY-TWO

The next day, the weather was good enough for Lord Dexthorpe to depart; Mr. and Mrs. John Yates followed the baron to Lincolnshire several days later. After learning that the Grants were about to leave for London, Tom invited Susan to accompany him to the Parsonage to bid its occupants farewell. Tom thanked Mr. Crawford for making the journey to Northamptonshire, as the information that he had brought had helped clear him of the suspicion of murder, while Susan, after exchanging pleasantries with Dr. and Mrs. Grant, was escorted into the Parsonage shrubbery by Miss Crawford, who had much to say. Most of the discussion centered on the events of the summer, with Miss Price answering many questions and satisfying Miss Crawford's curiosity.

"With so many gone, will it be too quiet for you?" inquired Miss Crawford.

Susan did not think so; she had plenty to keep her occupied. She had been assisting her uncle with his correspondence, which, due to the summer's events, had fallen behind. Also, as Sir Thomas had disliked being threatened by Lord Dexthorpe and Tom had hated the cruelty of the sugar plantation, they were working on finding alternative sources of income.

"You do not find that dreadfully dull?" inquired Miss Crawford.

On the contrary, after being suspected of murder, Susan found it relaxing. "I prefer to keep busy."

"And I suppose you find shipping contracts of more interest than this season's sleeves. Well, Miss Price, I admire you. And do not take me wrong, but in one respect you resemble your late aunt: you are active and strong." Before Susan could protest the comparison or the compliment, Miss Crawford changed the topic. "I do not know if I will ever return, therefore I have a request to make. Will you correspond with me? My letter-writing habits are not much better than my brother's, but I hope not to be excluded entirely from news of Mansfield Park. I have a great interest in all of you."

Susan said she was happy to do so. She appreciated what Miss Crawford had done for her, and she was also aware that having a friend in the Crawford family could be advantageous for the Price family. Miss Crawford's uncle was an admiral with influence, and not just William, but several of Susan's brothers, were in the navy.

Mr. Bertram appeared with the Grants and Mr. Crawford; the visit had been long; they were certainly wanted at home. Susan made her farewells and she joined her cousin for the walk back to the Park. Tom remarked on the number of departures.

Susan said she was looking forward to some tranquility. "I used to wish for more company at Mansfield Park, but no longer."

Tom laughed and agreed, but when they arrived at the house they discovered that the family party had increased for the day, as Mr. and Mrs. Edmund Bertram had come over from Thornton Lacey. Fanny had brought a gift for her mother-in-law.

"I have a great favor to ask of you, Aunt," began Mrs. Bertram.

Lady Bertram was not accustomed to granting favors, so she listened with some surprise.

"With my duties as the wife of a clergyman, I am too busy to give this puppy enough attention. Would you be so kind as to care for him?"

Lady Bertram hesitated, as if no other animal could replace her dear Pug, but then Fanny placed the dog on the sofa beside her aunt. The dog licked her hand and then Elissa, on her grandmother's other side, begged to be allowed to pet him. "What is his name?" asked the little girl.

Fanny said she would allow her aunt to choose the dog's name, but Lady Bertram had little imagination and could only think of "Pug." Finally, Maria suggested "Norris." Susan did not know if they should honor a murderess – the woman who had poisoned Lady Bertram's last pet – but the name pleased her aunt. And was it such an honor, for a namesake to be a dog?

Eventually the men withdrew; Elissa and Lady Bertram settled down for naps; and Maria was summoned by Sir Thomas for a discussion about her future. Fanny and Susan went into the garden for a tête-à-tête. Each had much to tell: Fanny, about all the calls she had received and all the calls she was making, as she became acquainted with the members of her husband's parish, and Susan, about the many difficulties of the last month. Susan explained that she had agreed to correspond with Miss Crawford, something that surprised and did not entirely please Fanny.

"How could I refuse?" asked Susan. "Besides, Admiral Crawford may be of assistance to our brothers."

Fanny acknowledged the sense in her sister's approach. "You were always more practical than I."

"Perhaps," said Susan.

"Certainly, you are stronger."

"That, I doubt," Susan said. She explained that Mrs. Norris had been especially unkind, and she had not understood how Fanny had endured her cruelty for so many years. Susan could not regret her death, just as she could not regret the death of Mr. George Yates. The only deaths that touched her were Pug and poor Mr. Rushworth.

Fanny did not upbraid Susan for her lack of Christian charity; she only counseled Susan to do her best to put the unhappy memories of Mr. Yates and Mrs. Norris behind her. "They both stand before their Maker now, and He will decide their reward or punishment. You need not concern yourself."

Susan found the words comforting and told Fanny she made Edmund an excellent helpmate. "I hope so," said Fanny, and then the sisters returned indoors, where they were wanted by Lady Bertram. They learned that decisions for Maria and Ann Jones had been reached; the women would live together in a small house owned by Lord Dexthorpe. The funds for the residence would come from the baron, in order to support his natural grandchild and to make amends for some of the trouble his son had caused. Mrs. Rushworth said she was satisfied with the arrangement. The house was near the boundary of the counties of Lincolnshire and Northamptonshire, so she would not be as distant from her relations as she had been while in Ireland. She could hope for eventual readmission into her families; if not from the current baron and baronet, from their successors, as Julia, the future Lady Dexthorpe, and Tom, the future baronet, were not so harsh in their judgments. And the money she had been given by Mrs. Norris gave Mrs. Rushworth some independence that she had not had before.

"I must be wiser in the future," Maria admitted, and entertained her relations by playing the pianoforte. Afterwards, Susan organized a quiet game to amuse them, and the evening passed serenely. Edmund spoke the most, describing a new lamp that had been invented for going into mines, a topic that intrigued them all as they sat in candlelight. Tom, who was always interested in new objects, mentioned a project that had been started by a Frenchman to capture permanently the image made with a camera obscura. Susan and Lady Bertram both expressed an interest in seeing how a camera obscura worked, and as the principle was simple, Tom and

Edmund had some deal board brought in and constructed a rudimentary version of the apparatus.

Mr. and Mrs. Edmund Bertram, alas, had to return to Thornton Lacey the next day. As Edmund made his adieus to other members of his family, Susan had a moment alone with Fanny. "I know you are happy where you are now, but I miss you," said Susan.

"You care for him, do you not?" asked Fanny.

Susan blushed. She did not need to ask who the *him* was.

Fanny added, "I think you would be good for him. Edmund thinks so as well."

Although Susan had been reluctant to broach the topic, now that it had been opened, she was eager for its continuance, and wanted to hear why Edmund held that opinion, but it was too late. The carriage arrived. Susan noted that Dick Jackson, a nephew of Stephen's, was sitting with Wilcox, and was being trained to replace his recently departed uncle. Sir Thomas warned them to be careful, and Mr. and Mrs. Edmund Bertram climbed into the carriage, which then drove away.

CHAPTER THIRTY-THREE

During the next fortnight, after learning that the house was ready for them, Maria and Ann Jones departed from Mansfield Park as well. After such an eventful summer, the Park seemed very quiet, and everyone had to resume more ordinary tasks. Lady Bertram stocked up on baby linen, Elissa played with Norris and progressed in the alphabet, and Susan was busier than ever, writing letters for her aunt and her uncle. Tom had a friend visit for a few days, and the men went hunting nearly every day. No longer an estate with a curse, Mansfield Park received calls from neighbors. The new, good-humored Mrs. Charles Maddox was not nearly as old as everyone had expected, and her husband was devoted to her. Mr. Hawk, resuming his position in the pulpit, saddened by his loss, preached quietly. They met Mr. Walter Rushworth, who seemed to hold no grudge for Mrs. Norris's murder of his cousin.

Fanny had said that Edmund approved, but Edmund and Fanny could not speak for Tom. Susan wondered if she had misinterpreted her sister's hint. Susan and Tom spent hours together nearly every day, laughing, working, discussing plans for Elissa, but she detected no passionate romance on his part. She was not certain if Tom felt anything more than a comfortable fondness for his young cousin and did her best to repress her own feelings. Still, when he entered a room she smiled.

Mrs. Yates sent a letter, in which she wrote that she and John had taken up residence in a large apartment in her father-in-law's estate. All was well; Lord Dexthorpe's spirits were much improved, and the hunting season offered the men plenty of exercise. Her own health, she assured them, was good, and she expected to be a mother in the coming January.

Julia's letter was passed around, along with a happy account from Fanny. Tom, whose friend had left Mansfield Park that morning, remarked to Susan that the younger Bertrams were faring better than the elder Bertrams.

"What do you mean?"

"I mean that Julia and Edmund are more successful than Maria and me. I suppose it is understandable: parents are inexperienced when they raise their older children, but with their younger children they know what they are doing."

"I cannot dispute your comparison regarding your sisters, but how can you consider your position inferior to Edmund's?"

"Because Edmund has found happiness. Edmund is a credit to his position."

"And why do you think that you will not find happiness? That you will not be a credit to your position?"

They were excellent questions, but at that moment Tom did not answer them. Lady Bertram wished to be amused, and Susan suggested a game that she had heard about from Miss Crawford and had recently acquired: "The Panorama of Europe." Sir Thomas joined them, and by spinning a teetotum they raced from Portugal, with Lady Bertram winning by being the first to reach London.

"I have not been to London in years," remarked Lady Bertram. Sir Thomas asked his wife if she had any desire to go, but she did not. "This is much more pleasant." Her ladyship pulled Norris to her lap and Sir Thomas picked up a recent newspaper and read its contents aloud for all.

After a while, her ladyship dozed and Sir Thomas read silently. The cousins found themselves again in conversation. Susan, still very aware of what they had been discussing earlier, chose a different topic. "Do you miss her very much?" Susan asked.

"Miss who?" Tom inquired.

"Elissa's mother."

"Oh! I did at first, when my father first sent me away from Antigua. He disapproved so strongly."

Reminding Tom of his previous mistress stopped the conversation; finally, he found a transition. "But my father has given me my blessing for"—

Again, he stopped, and Susan had to offer encouragement. "Blessing for what?"

"For the woman I wish to be my wife."

"Congratulations." And Susan's heart rose – surely he meant her? – then fell – what if he meant someone else? – and finally settled into a fluttering state.

"Do not congratulate me yet, I have not yet asked her."

"What is stopping you?"

"Courage. Or rather, cowardice. I am a coward."

Even when one is offered one's heart's desire, it rarely arrives in the manner one expects. Tom accused himself of being a coward, and perhaps he was. Nevertheless, he managed to propose, and to ask Susan to be his wife – all done in low tones, while Sir Thomas read by the fireplace and Lady Bertram slumbered on her sofa.

"My uncle approves?" inquired Susan. "Even though I bring no fortune? No connection?"

Tom assured her that the baronet approved, more than approved. Susan's abilities more than compensated for her lack of wealth; she would help keep Mansfield Park respectable and responsible; she would make sure that Elissa was treated well. And, if Tom married Susan, he guaranteed the happiness of the current Lady Bertram – her ladyship depended on Susan – and the next Lady Bertram would make sure the next Sir Thomas shone.

"And this is something that *you* want to do?" Susan asked. "You are not simply pleasing your parents?"

Tom smiled, and said that this was his own decision; he was not simply pleasing his parents. His only reluctance to speak had been due to her youth; she had just reached eighteen – and the fact that she *was* so indispensable at Mansfield Park. What if Susan refused him? Everyone would be so uncomfortable, and she might choose to leave, which was something that neither his parents, his daughter, nor he could bear. He assured her that his affection was genuine. The love inside him had started small, like a mustard seed, but had grown so great that he, too, could not imagine a future without her.

Susan was aware of her cousin's faults, but she had seen far worse in many other men. Accepting his offer would allow her to remain in Northamptonshire; she would never be banished. Moreover, she was genuinely fond of Tom. He was handsome, he was intelligent, and he was good humored. He had shown her great kindness over the past few weeks, supporting her when she had been suspected of terrible crimes. She was happier in his company than she was in the company of any other. Was that not love?

"Then, Tom, nothing would please me more than to become your wife."

With his parents in the room, only a mild display of affection was possible, but Tom took Susan's hand. And Sir Thomas, who had only been pretending to read, congratulated them, then roused his wife so that she could partake in the excellent news.

Lady Bertram needed a moment to comprehend, and then she smiled at the young woman who would be the next Lady Bertram.

"I knew everything would end happily."

AUTHOR'S NOTE

The following includes some background on the story, as well as some spoilers. You have been warned!

Some readers may be aware that I have been writing a series of mysteries based on Jane Austen's novels, in which I reunite the main characters a year or two after Austen's story ends. Applying this pattern to *Mansfield Park* presented some challenges, as most of its main characters – Edmund Bertram, Fanny Price, Henry Crawford and Mary Crawford – had little reason to be at Mansfield Park after the novel's close. In fact, the Crawfords, especially Henry Crawford, would not have been at all welcome. Furthermore, timid Fanny – whether you love her or hate her – struck me as a poor choice as a heroine in a mystery novel. Hence, I settled on Susan Price, Fanny's younger sister, who was described by Austen as speaking to her mother in a fearless tone. I found reasons for the characters who had the largest romantic roles in *Mansfield Park* to appear in *The Mansfield Park Murders,* but I found more story in the other characters. For example, Maria Rushworth: would she have been banished permanently? And why had Tom left Antigua early?

To answer the latter question, I turned to the history of William Murray, the first Earl of Mansfield, also an influential Lord Chief Justice of the King's Bench from 1756 to 1788. Some of his decisions paved the way for ending the British involvement with slavery. One notable fact in the Earl of Mansfield's life is that he and his wife raised two of his great-nieces: Lady Elizabeth Murray and Dido Elizabeth Belle. The latter was the natural daughter of a nephew (Captain Sir John Lindsay) with a slave woman, Maria Bell. Dido's story was dramatized (with a few liberties) in the movie *Belle,* and there is plenty of evidence that the first Earl of Mansfield relied heavily on this great-niece in many ways.

Austen was certainly aware of the Earl of Mansfield and had even met Lady Elizabeth Murray (apparently she never met Dido, who died in 1804). The choice of "Mansfield" as the name of the estate was a nod to him – as was the choice of the name "Norris" – the last name of a notorious slave trader. I have imitated Austen by choosing the name "Elissa" for Tom's natural daughter. "Dido" was the name of the queen of Carthage in Virgil's *Aeneid,* but Queen Dido was also known by "Elissa."

Animal lovers may resent my killing poor Pug, Lady Bertram's dog. Also, readers of *Mansfield Park* may wonder that I made the dog female, for at one point in the text, Lady Bertram refers to her dog as male when she was trying to keep him out of the flower beds (Chapter 7). However, later in the story, Lady Bertram offers Fanny – if she accepts Mr.

Crawford's offer of marriage – a pup from Pug's next litter (Chapter 33). The latter is only possible if the dog is female. I chose the gender most convenient to my own story.

I have done research into coroners and the justice of the period, but have taken liberties in order to create a satisfying story. Then, as now, influence often prevailed.

I must thank Patricia Walton, for offering encouragement as well as alerting me to many typos and other issues in *The Mansfield Park Murders*. Any typos and problems that remain are completely my own.

Thanks so much for reading!

Victoria Grossack
Tucson & Troistorrents

Made in United States
North Haven, CT
07 January 2024

47153175R00096